* * *

"I'd like to come by later and check on you," Detective Gray Evans said. He tried to grin and I tried harder to resist him.

"How about I call you?" I lied.

He nodded. He knew I was lying.

I walked him through the house to the front door, opened it and stood just inside the hallway while he said goodbye. The farther away from me he was, the less chance there was of me giving in. I forced a smile, thanked him again and closed the door.

However, deep down inside, I was thinking a fish might not need a bicycle, but it sure would enjoy a ride every now and then.

Dear Reader,

You're about to read a Silhouette Bombshell novel, one of the most engaging, exciting and riveting books on the shelves today. We're pleased to bring you fast-paced, compelling reads featuring strong, admirable women who will speak to the Bombshell in you!

In *Sophie's Last Stand* by Nancy Bartholomew, Sophie Mazaratti's trying to start over after her marriage ends *very* badly—but it seems her slimy ex has left her in a sticky situation involving the mob, the Feds and one darned attractive detective....

Get ready for a thrilling twenty-four hours as military author Cindy Dees continues the powerful Athena Force continuity series with *Target*, featuring an army intelligence agent on a mission to save the President-elect from being assassinated. To gain his trust, she'll give the villain someone new to chase—herself....

It's a jungle out there when a determined virologist races into the Amazon to stop a deadly outbreak—a danger that authorities seem determined to cover up, even at the cost of Dr. Jane Miller's life. Don't miss *The Amazon Strain* by Katherine Garbera!

And a protected witness must come out of hiding after her sister mysteriously disappears, in Kate Donovan's adventure *Parallel Lies*. It's up to Sabrina Sullivan to determine which of two charismatic men is lying—or if they both are—to save her sister's life.

The stakes are high and the pressure is on! Please send me your comments c/o Silhouette Books, 233 Broadway, Suite 1001, New York, NY 10279

Sincerely,

Natashya Wilson

Natashya Wilson
Associate Senior Editor, Silhouette Bombshell

Please address questions and book requests to:
Silhouette Reader Service
U.S.: 3010 Walden Ave., P.O. Box 1325, Buffalo, NY 14269
Canadian: P.O. Box 609, Fort Erie, Ont. L2A 5X3

SOPHIE'S LAST STAND

NANCY BARTHOLOMEW

Silhouette®

BOMBSHELL™

Published by Silhouette Books

America's Publisher of Contemporary Romance

SILHOUETTE BOOKS

ISBN 0-373-51355-0

SOPHIE'S LAST STAND

Books by Nancy Bartholomew

Silhouette Bombshell

Stella, Get Your Gun #13
Stella, Get Your Man #25
Sophie's Last Stand #41

NANCY BARTHOLOMEW

didn't seem like the Bombshell type at first. Sure, she grew up in Philadelphia, but she was a gentle minister's daughter. Sometimes, though, true wildness simmers just below the surface. Nancy started singing country music in biker bars before she graduated from high school. And, yes, Dad was there, sitting in the front row, watching over his little girl!

Nancy graduated from college with a degree in psychology and promptly moved into the inner city where she found work dragging addicted inner-city teenagers into drug and alcohol rehabilitation. She then moved south to Atlanta, and worked as the director of a substance-abuse treatment program for court-ordered offenders. Her patients were bikers and strippers and they taught her well...lock picking, exotic dancing, gunplay for beginners and hot-wiring cars.

When the criminal life became less of a challenge, Nancy turned to the final frontier...parenthood. This drove Nancy to writing. While her boys were toddlers, Nancy spent their nap-times creating alternate realities. Nancy lives in North Carolina, rides with the police on a regular basis, raises two hooligan teenage boys and tries to keep up with her writing, her psychotherapy practice and her garden. She thanks you from the bottom of her heart for reading this book!

For Becky,
the wonderful sister
who provided the inspiration and the motivation,
and didn't disown me for writing it all down!
Thank you!

Chapter 1

The first time I spotted him, I figured I was just a little bit paranoid.

Being followed by strangers was my daily ritual in Philadelphia, but I was in North Carolina now. I couldn't imagine that anybody from up there would take the time and energy to follow me all the way to New Bern just to ruin my vacation.

Besides, my sister was already doing a fine job of that. In fact, just moments before I saw him, obviously out of place in his dark suit and wraparound glasses, I was plotting Darlene's impending demise. My sister just has that effect on me. She pushes me to the brink of homicidal frustration, all the while acting like she's just a well-intentioned love child with the best interest of her sister at heart. It drives me crazy. Now as I stood on the sidewalk, with Darlene not three feet away from me, I was thinking about how I could give her a little shove into oncoming traffic and have it be all over with. But the minute I saw the guy I stopped thinking about Darlene.

He was trying to be noticed. At least, he had gotten my attention in that getup.

Darlene was oblivious. She stood with her back to him, her long brown hair flying out and tangling with the ribbons from her fake flower wreath. In her singsong little girl voice, she said, "I know just what you need." Without waiting for me to ask what, she rushed on. "You need to marry an architect."

I felt my eyebrows shoot up as I looked away from my pursuer and gave Darlene the briefest once-over.

"Why in the world would I need to marry an architect?"

Darlene smiled, triumphant in the knowledge that she'd hooked me. She spun in a little circle of ecstasy, her hands outstretched to encompass the historic homes that surrounded us, and said, "Because *this* is your true world. You love these old houses. You want to fix one up into a cozy little nest and live happily ever after. You can't afford to do that, so you should marry a guy who likes old houses and can take care of you. An architect would be perfect!" She spun around again. "I *so* know you!"

I scowled at Darlene. "Have you lost your mind? My divorce has been final for less than a year. Do you think I want to ever, *ever* go through that living hell again? I'm taking care of myself just fine, Darlene. So, if I want an architect, I'll hire one!"

I glanced over Darlene's shoulder and realized the guy who'd been following us for three blocks was gone. I scoured the street and saw no sign of him. It was paranoia, pure and simple, that kept me on guard and expecting trouble. If this had been South Philly, I really would have a guy tailing me. Lately it seemed I was always being followed, hounded and harassed by someone looking for Nick, or worse, someone wronged by Nick. I figured a change of scenery would erase the Nick factor from my day-to-day life, and maybe it had. I mean, why would someone follow me all the way to North Carolina just to harass me about my ex-husband?

Darlene was hugging her arms to her ample chest, rubbing them, as if she were cold. "I just had an insight! Maybe you were here before. You know, like in a past life? That's why you love the old houses. It's your destiny to walk among your ancestors. Sophie, you should not mess with your destiny."

"Then I should marry a sea captain, not an architect. New Bern's a port, Darlene. My dead ancestors would be sailors. Besides, why would I want to get married again? Like Gloria Steinem said, a woman needs a man like a fish needs a bicycle, Darlene."

"Yeah, well Gloria probably said it when she broke up with some jerk, but now even she's happily married! Sophie, it's been two years since Nick got arrested and you broke up. Aren't you lonely?"

Lonely maybe, but not foolish enough to think that a relationship was the magical cure for whatever ailed me.

"Actually I'm relieved, Darlene. Now I can have a life without sitting around and waiting for some Prince Charming wanna-be to ride up on a white mule and make an ass out of both of us. I think you've been down South too long, honey. It's starting to warp you."

But it wasn't just the South that affected Darlene's mind. Darlene had been playing Snow White and Cinderella for years, long before her three marriages, subsequent divorces and move to New Bern. Darlene was just like that, a dreamer on a quest for the ultimate, idyllic, Happily Ever After. Not that I had much room to talk. Ten years I was married to a man who turned out to be a mirage—a meek, stereotypical accountant with an underbelly of pure slime.

"Nick the Dick" they called him. You couldn't pick up the

Philadelphia Inquirer last fall and not see that name plastered all over the articles about his trial. Nick the Dick, the King of Voyeur Porn; Nick, the quiet accountant, who snuck up to all our neighbors' windows with night vision goggles and a video camera. Nick, selling pictures of naked housewives on his Web site, hiring prostitutes, making illicit movies, and then posting it all on the Internet. Oh yeah, I needed a man, all right…just not in this lifetime.

Darlene stood in front of me wearing that smug, patronizing look she gets. She reached out and patted my shoulder, which further pissed me off.

"One day you'll want someone," she said, her voice soft and mushy with idealism. "You feel bitter now, betrayed, but this will pass. You're a Leo. You need a water sign to provide balance in your life. I know these things, Sophie." She straightened her shoulders and tossed her head defiantly. "After all," she said, "I am a trained, professional therapist."

"Darlene, you're a physical therapist, not a psychiatrist."

"Whatever!" She was insulted now. "I know people—that's all I'm saying. And you need a soothing water sign. There's too much fire in your personality."

Once again I began contemplating putting Darlene out of her unenlightened misery.

"I don't need a husband, Darlene."

She ignored me, waited for the light to turn and began crossing the street toward the Tryon Palace Visitors Center. She reminded me of a cruise ship leaving port. She charged off ahead of me, streamers gaily flying out behind her, blending their cheerful colors with those of her brightly patterned broomstick skirt. Life was just a pleasure cruise for Darlene and the rest of us were left to wallow in her wake.

"Where are you going?" I called after her.

Darlene consulted her tour handbook. "Number 23. The Beale House."

"Go on ahead. I'll meet you at 24. I need to make a pit stop."

Darlene looked back over her shoulder, smiled that self-satisfied, I'm-right-and-you know-it smirk and took off, because she knew if she so much as slowed up, I might've wiped that look right off her face, thereby recreating every childhood encounter we'd ever had.

When she turned right, I made a beeline for the darkened interior of the air-conditioned welcome center. Marry an architect indeed! I stayed inside the building a full five minutes, cooling off, before allowing myself to head back out after my errant sister.

Number 24, the tiny Episcopal chapel, was one short block away. I could see the blue-and-white sign shimmering in the midafternoon heat as I made my way toward it. I walked slowly, taking my time and looking at everything—the Tryon Palace grounds, the other tourists, the flowers and gardens. I was soaking it all in but I was also looking for the suit. He was nearby. I could feel him. Damn.

New Bern was old, but not in the dirty, dingy way Philly sometimes seemed. New Bern had a fresh-scrubbed, healthy glow to its old buildings. It felt as if someone, many someones in fact, cared about this old town, cared for every brick and windowpane, cared enough not to let it decay with grime and misuse. It breathed in color, while Philadelphia stayed sepia-toned and dull.

I stepped inside the darkened chapel, inhaled the scent of lemon cleaner, stepped forward and ran smack into the proverbial bicycle—the most incredibly handsome man I'd ever seen in my life.

"Oh, God," I said, and then realized I was in church, and crossed myself hastily. "I'm so sorry. I didn't see you."

He was making the same apologies and backing up a step, his gray-blue eyes the first thing I could see clearly because they were so intense and bright in the gloomy church.

"Don't apologize," he said, and then flashed me a smile that seemed to light up the dark interior of the ancient building. "I should know better than to stand right in front of the door. This is the third time today I've done this."

As my eyes adjusted, I could see what he meant. He stood in front of a card table that was covered with tiny paper cups and plastic pitchers of lemonade. Behind the table stood two prepubescent Boy Scouts, both grinning and looking at Mr. Wonderful like he was the funniest thing going.

"Here," he said, holding a cup out toward me, "at least have some lemonade."

"He spilled it on the last lady," one of the Scouts volunteered.

"Yeah, I'd take it quick," the other added.

The guy laughed and shot them a look that said they were all pals, anyway, despite the boys' comments. And for a moment I was completely and totally charmed. I stood there watching him, frozen to the spot like a deer staring into a set of oncoming headlights.

"Is it all right? It's a new batch but it shouldn't be too…" He paused.

"Oh no," I said, breaking out of my stupor. I took a huge gulp, choked and sputtered. "It's great, really!"

And then I ran, darting across the room, where I stood examining the baked goods like my life depended on it, and wondering where in the hell Darlene was. I shot a glance over at *him* and found he was watching me, the same hundred-watt smile stuck on his face.

He was handsome, all right. Tall, maybe six foot two inches. I put him a few years older than me, perhaps in his early forties, with a salt-and-pepper, supershort haircut and faint lines that crinkled around his eyes when he smiled. I realized with a start he was still smiling at me and that I was still, and most obviously, staring at him.

I flipped back around, pretending to study a display that covered the history of the tiny chapel. This was too ridiculous. What was I doing? I was no better than Darlene, getting myself all hot and bothered over the very gender I'd just sworn to avoid like the black plague. Men were a disease. They crawled under your skin and poisoned you into believing that this time it would be different.

"Fool me once, shame on you," I muttered. "Fool me twice, shame on me."

I took a deep breath, ignored the pull of infatuation at first sight and forced myself to walk right past him, outside into the brilliant sunlight. Darlene was probably lost in the ozone of her past lives and had wandered into another house, forgetting all about her sister in the process. She'd turn up, but when or where was anybody's guess.

I walked slowly, turning down the side street where I'd seen Darlene last, looked for her and imagined what my life would be like if I lived here and not in crowded South Philly. I tried to see myself in every perfect garden, watering flowers with an ancient metal watering can, or sitting on a white wooden swing and rocking slowly in the moonlight. I tried not to worry about my sister. After all, this was New Bern and not Philadelphia. If someone was looking for me, he wouldn't bother my airhead sister. Still, I felt the shiver of apprehension and suddenly wished like hell I could catch a glimpse of colorful ribbons up ahead in the crowd of tourists.

When I didn't see her on the street in front of me, I turned again, wandering down a block shaded by ancient oaks. The sidewalk was bumpy brick, rippled with tree roots and narrowed by the paving of what had to have once been a cobblestone street. Darlene stood outside a house at the far end, talking to an elderly woman and gesturing wildly with her hands. I heaved a deep sigh of relief. Now that I knew she was all right, I really was going to kill her.

I started toward her, walked maybe fifty feet and stopped. Behind a battered picket fence, behind a gigantic magnolia tree, behind overgrown bushes and weeds, sat my dream house, a battered brown-and-white cottage with a sagging porch and a rusted tin roof. In bad shape now, but, oh, what potential!

A For Sale sign, faded but firmly planted just inside the front yard, and brochures in a box beside the sign called to me. I grabbed a paper and stood looking up at the little house. I could see it all as it would be with a little attention, with a little hard work and, of course, a little money. I looked at Darlene, caught her eye and pointed toward the house. She waved, but made no move to join me.

I examined the house as I walked up the tiny driveway. It would take a chainsaw working overtime to actually make it possible to enter the house, but if it was structurally sound... Well, the possibilities were all there, waiting for the right person. I made my way down the length of the house, trying to look in through the grime-covered windows. The faint scent of the nearby waterfront mingled with the smells of honeysuckle and wild roses, and I found myself falling deeper and deeper into the trance of possibility.

The man I'd seen earlier suddenly reappeared, trying to take me as I pushed open the back gate. He lunged for me, springing out of the shadows that framed the back porch and rushing me. In his hand, he held an ugly black knife. I whirled, dropping my purse as I turned, and stepping into his move, hitting him low and inside with my body as I turned to grip his knife arm with both hands.

I yelled, guttural and hoarse, and brought his arm down across my thigh, heard the welcome snap of the bone breaking, and saw the knife skitter away into the bushes. His scream got caught short by the brick wall as I slammed him into it, bringing the useless arm up behind his back and working the weight and momentum of his big frame against him.

"Tell whoever sent you that Nick worked alone. I don't have his money. I don't have any of his nasty pictures and I sure don't have whatever else it is you want. Tell him to leave me alone. You got that?"

When the man didn't answer, I jerked his arm higher. His answering cry cut through the blood pounding in my ears as adrenaline sent my overworked emergency alert system into overdrive. How much longer was this shit going to go on? When was everybody going to finally figure out that I'd been even more hoodwinked by Nick's betrayal than the rest of them?

In my world, Nick had been just a bad husband. Until the police had come through my front door with a search warrant and a squadron of uniformed officers, I'd only known about Nick's day job as an accountant. So how could I possibly know anything about missing money?

I pushed the big man tight against the wall and stretched up on tiptoe to say my piece. He moaned, the fight gone out of his huge frame, and I thanked God for Vinny and Krav Maga. A year ago, I would've been this moron's prey, but now I could take care of myself. In the two years since Nick's arrest and our separation I'd grown up. In the past year I'd gotten divorced, watched as my ex-husband got convicted and sent to prison, and learned to kill a man ten different ways. Not bad for a kindergarten teacher.

I sighed and watched as my attacker ran away. I now understood the concept of, "use it or lose it." I just didn't like it. There was something wrong with having to defend myself against hairy ogres, irate husbands and loudmouthed police officers. I hadn't done anything wrong. Well, I'd married Nick ten years ago, but aside from that, nothing. So why did everyone think I knew more than I did? Why did people keep coming up to me on the street, yelling about how their lives had been ruined by my husband? Hadn't my life been ruined? How would I ever pick up the pieces?

My heart was pounding and my hands shook as the shock and reality of my recent attack set in and overwhelmed my body. It wasn't the first time a confrontation had turned physical, but it was the first surprise attack and by far the worst. I closed my eyes for a second, seeing it all over again in my mind's eye. The guy had meant business. He wasn't another irate husband, or one of Nick's former business associates accusing Nick of embezzling money, and he was most certainly not a cop. No, this guy had been hired help. Why had he gone to the trouble of following me on vacation? Did they think I had a suitcase full of stolen money and was coming to tiny New Bern to spend it?

People just kept turning up, out of nowhere, all saying Nick owed them money, or wanting revenge. Who were all of these people and when would it all end?

"Sophie! I've been looking everywhere for you!" Darlene had snuck up on me and now stood on the sidewalk swatting at imaginary mosquitoes and looking annoyed.

I stared at my sister for a moment, wondering if she noticed that I looked a little the worse for wear, and realizing that she of course didn't. It was actually better that Darlene not know about my encounter. She'd only run straight back to our parents and tell all, and then I'd have *that* to deal with.

"You were looking for me?" I sputtered. "Where were you?"

I saw her catch her breath and get ready to start in on the defense, and short-circuited her.

"Never mind. Would you look at this place?" I said, hoping she wouldn't notice I was sweating bullets and slightly out of breath. I stared down at the brochure I held in my hands and started spouting off information, hoping to distract Darlene with facts. "It was built in 1886. It's perfect."

Darlene's expression changed to one of wary concern. "Perfect for what? It's falling apart."

"Darlene, look. It's got good bones. It might need updating, some paint and a new roof, but the brochure says that most of the structural renovations have been completed. It's mainly cosmetic work now. Best of all, it's only sixty-eight thousand.

"Dollars?"

I gave her a look that said her sarcasm wasn't wasted on me. I knew what she was saying. "Darlene, it's a steal. Do you realize what one of these would cost in Philly? In Society Hill? This is unbelievable."

"Unbelievable is right," she said. "It's probably just a shell. And you see those brick apartments back there? Those are the Projects. Sophie, this is not a good neighborhood."

I looked where she was pointing, almost exactly behind the house, maybe a block away. Then I turned and looked across the street in the other direction, at the little cottages that had already been renovated, sweet with flower boxes and periwinkle shutters, rich with fresh paint and gingerbread trim. Suddenly the decision was an easy one.

"It's a steal, Darlene."

"They'll rob you blind, Sophie."

"I could make money on resale."

"You could be killed in your bed one night."

"I love it," I said, but I was thinking, *I'll be killed for sure if I stay in Philly. It's only a matter of time. Besides, what school administrator in Philadelphia would renew the con-*

tract of a kindergarten teacher who'd been married to Nick the Dick?

"You live in Grandma's old house," she attempted to remind me. "You complain about it constantly."

"I rent the place," I said. "Uncle Butch owns it and I bitch because he won't fix a damn thing. And if you want to talk about crime, look at my neighborhood. How many homicides do you think South Philly has a year? Probably more in a week than New Bern has in a year. Since Nick's been in jail I've been mugged twice and had the house broken into three times!"

"Yeah, but there's cops up there, lots of them."

"Darlene, there are cops everywhere."

"Sophie, think about it. This is a small town. You're single. You really want to leave Philly for this?"

I stared at her. She was in the same boat as I was and suddenly she didn't think New Bern was such a great town? What was this all about?

Like a mind reader, Darlene honed in on me. "Look," she said, "I moved down here because Ma and Pa retired here. They put on the pressure, the guilt. 'We're old,' they said. 'Who will take care of us?' So I came. Why not? I was single. But finding a man here is like winning the lottery. It just doesn't happen."

Mr. Wonderful flashed across my mind but I shoved him out. "Good, I'm not looking for a man. Ma and Pa have been after me to move down here, too. Why not? What do I have to lose?"

Maybe I could start over.

Darlene was looking even more anxious. "You don't have a job," she said.

"I teach school, Darlene. I can work anywhere. I've got all summer to find something, and besides, I've got the money Aunt

Viv left me when she died. With what this place costs I could buy it and fix it up and still have a little money in the bank."

Darlene didn't look convinced.

"Look, Joey moved down with Angela and the kids. That didn't turn out so bad, did it?"

"That's different," she said, pouting.

I got to the heart of the matter then. "Darlene, Nick's not gonna be in prison much longer. You think I don't know he's carrying a grudge? You think he won't haunt me, trying to make my life a living hell? You think I want to walk down the street every day waiting for the time I round a corner and there he is? Do you think I don't see the looks on the faces of the people we know? They're thinking, There's Sophie, the pervert's ex-wife. You think I don't know this and feel it every time I walk out my front door? Darlene, the man took pictures of me naked in the shower. He videotaped us making love and sold copies on the internet for $14.95. It's not the sort of thing you live down easily."

I couldn't bring myself to tell her how they didn't just look, they yelled, hurling insults and obscenities at me. I didn't want her to pity me, or worse, to be afraid for me. I was Darlene's big sister, not a victim to feel sorry for and take care of. Not me.

But Darlene looked sad anyway, like she saw through me, like she was feeling my life and it hurt. Something inside me snapped then, and before I could stop myself, the words tumbled out.

"Even if I wanted to meet somebody, even if I actually met a man up in Philly," I said, "what are the chances he's seen those pictures of me? Even if he hasn't, what chance is there he won't know who I am? Everybody knows what Nick did, Darlene. I see it in their eyes. I feel dirty even when I've just bathed. Can't you see what I'm telling you, honey?"

Darlene's eyes filled with unshed tears and she nodded slowly.

"I want something new. Something fresh, where I don't have to feel ashamed just walking around in my own neighborhood. I don't want to live in the subdivision with you guys. I don't want to bust up what you've got going with Ma and Pa. I just want to be somewhere where people love me."

Darlene was crying now. She looked up at the broken-down house and back to me. "Okay," she said, her voice soft with tears. "I get it. If this is what you want, at least have it inspected. Bring Joey and Pa over—let them check it out, too. And no matter what," she said, straightening up and becoming her know-it-all self, "don't pay the asking price. This dump has probably been on the market forever. Lowball 'em."

I threw my arms around her chunky shoulders and hugged her. "Thanks, honey. Don't worry. It'll work out fine, you'll see."

We turned away then, walking back toward the car and jabbering away about shutters and paint colors. I was so lost in my new house trance that I almost missed it, the little prickle of awareness that made me look up and stare out ahead of us.

Mr. Wonderful from the chapel stood in the middle of the sidewalk, the folded up card table in one strong hand and two Scouts by his other side. His smile seemed to reach out and cover me. His presence felt like an electrical current that arced from his body into mine. I had the foolish urge to run to him and say, "Hey, guess what? I'm going to buy that old house around the corner." But of course, that would be crazy. So instead I looked away, kept on babbling to Darlene and walked right past him.

"Okay," she said, when we were a half a block away, "what in the hell was that?"

"What?"

"Don't do that," she said. "You know what. That guy. What was with you and that guy? How do you know him?"

"I don't."

"Sophie, that look, that energy between you two. You know him."

"No, really, I don't. I just bumped into him, that's all."

Darlene sighed. "That was fate," she said. "He is your destiny and you walked right past him."

"Like a fish needs a bicycle, Darlene," I said.

"Start peddling," Darlene said. "'Cause, honey, that was some powerful karma, if you ask me."

"I didn't. It wasn't. And I don't want any complications in my life."

Darlene was muttering to herself. It sounded like she was saying, "We'll see. We'll just see about that."

I looked down at the brochure from the dream house and forced my attention onto the things I could control in my life. I could make this dream happen. I could turn a pile of wood and weeds into a home. But turning a smile into a relationship, now that was just plain foolish. At least the house was a sure deal. A house doesn't vanish like a puff of smoke. A house is real. You can reach out and stroke the wood, feel the walls solid and sure. A house is what it is; it doesn't lie. A house doesn't write letters from prison saying you've ruined its life. A house doesn't threaten to hunt you down and kill you.

Chapter 2

My brother, Joey, is a poet. I don't know if Pa will ever recover from this. If Joey didn't look and act so normal on the outside, I think Pa might've disowned him. As it is, Pa, the retired ironworker, just ignores the poetry part and tries to believe that Joey's simply an English teacher, a college professor. Each year, when Joey's newest book comes out, Ma carefully lines it up with the others on the top row of the bookshelf, and there it stays, never read by Pa and misunderstood by Ma.

Joey, for his part, doesn't spout off rhymes or stare into space all misty-eyed like Darlene. Joey plays rugby on Saturday afternoons. He roughhouses with his kids, is openly affectionate with his wife and can fix anything. Pa holds this out as incontrovertible evidence that Joey is somehow just passing through a phase with his writing.

"Poetry, schmoetry," Pa says. "He don't mean nothing by it."

Ma's kind of flattered. It appeals to the well-hidden, romantic side of her personality. "He's writing about growing up," she says, like this is a tribute.

I've read Joey's stuff, the stuff he doesn't show our parents. Believe me, it is not a tribute. He talks about all the things we good Italians don't mention, like the brutality of growing up Catholic, or the pain of living poor when the layoffs happen and the jobs don't come.

Joey feels everything. He cried when Angela stood holding her father's arm in the back of the church, right before she walked down the aisle and became his wife. He sobbed when his first baby, Emily, was born and he held her in his arms. He cried when the second baby, Joseph Jr., arrived two years later and cried yet again when the third baby, Alfonse, completed the trio. He laughs hard, he plays hard and he loves his family, all of us, more than we can ever truly know. I watch Joey so I see all of this, but my parents, they miss out sometimes when they don't allow themselves to see the real Joe.

It was Joey who saw the dream in my old house. Joey who convinced Pa that this would be okay, that we would all pitch in and it would actually be fun, a family thing. He showed up for the inspection with Pa in the car, the two of them ready to find fault with my future acquisition. Instead, Joey wound up rubbing his hand lovingly along the old banister, kneeling down to show Pa the strength in the ancient heart pine floors, and crawling up under the rafters in the attic to feel the "bones" of my new home. It was Joey who won Pa over, and Joey who cheered me on when I had doubts.

"Soph, look," he said, his fingers tracing the pattern in an etched glass window, "you can't find detail like this anymore. It's art. Oh, kid, you have scored here. What a deal!"

Joey didn't let me back down on my dream, not for one minute. "You're a Mazaratti, Soph," he said. "Look at you—

you divorced that piece of crap husband, you took your name back, you remembered where you come from and now you'll be where you belong—with family, starting over."

He drove the rental truck up to Philly with me that very week, loaded my belongings and waved goodbye to the old neighborhood as we pulled up onto I-95 heading south.

"Don't look back," he said. "I never have. I don't miss it and I didn't leave half the baggage you're dumping. I say good riddance to bad rubbish, Soph. Step out there, make yourself a life and don't worry about Philly 'cause Philly ain't gonna worry about you."

It was also Joe who convinced Ma that the reason I didn't move into the planned community with them and Darlene was because I had a mission to teach inner city kids and needed to be close to my future students. Now this was all bullshit, but Ma bought it on account of it was Joey doing the sales pitch.

So it made sense then that it was Joey I called when I got into trouble—big trouble. I called him at his community college office, before I called Pa and before I could control my emotions. I called him not because I didn't know what to do and he did, I called him because he would know what to say. He would know how to put the picture back in focus without shattering the lens.

"Joey," I said, when he came to the phone, "you gotta get over here, quick."

"What's wrong?" Joey's voice was strong and deep and, most of all, calm.

"I was…I was working in the backyard…." I clutched the cell phone, pressing it to my ear. I kept gulping, swallowing, standing there in the weeds, staring at the ground and trying not to lose control. "You know, hacking at those vines so I could get to the trash pile and haul it out to the bin."

"Yeah?" Joey didn't get impatient like Pa would've done; he let me tell the story in my own time and manner.

"I hit something, Joe, with the machete, and when I did…"
I swallowed very hard, looked at the long, thin blade stuck
where it had landed, and tried to continue. "It, like, sank into
something—you know, something soft?"

"Sophie," Joe said, "tell me about it."

"Joey, there's someone dead in my backyard. I was just
chopping weeds and I hit her. Joey, I think I might've killed
somebody."

I heard him exhale. "I'm coming," he said, and hung up.

I stood there as if the gravity of the universe was pinning
me to the planet, and stared at the body in front of me. If I'd
really thought about it, I would've realized that she was probably dead before I hit her. How else could she have come to
my backyard, rolled up in dark green plastic and positioned herself beneath bushes and weeds, waiting for my impending discovery? Who alive or conscious would wait for death like that?

Besides, there was no blood when I hit her. I mean, I knew,
instantly, that I'd hit something that was flesh and blood. I
shuddered because I could still feel the initial hit and then the
sinking in of the blade. I'd knelt down, tugged at the plastic
and fell backward as it gave in my hand, revealing the slim
arm of a woman, the side of her body exposed to the bright
morning sunlight.

That's when I'd called Joe. Now I looked back at her and
realized how I'd known she was dead. It was the paleness of
her skin, an ashy-gray tone that live bodies just don't have.
The machete blade stuck upright from the middle of her chest,
but there was no blood. I reached down nonetheless and
touched her forearm. It was cool, even on a hot summer's
morning. She was definitely dead.

I lifted the cell phone once again and punched in 9-1-1. I
drew in my breath and forced myself to say the words slowly
and clearly. "My name is Sophie Mazaratti, I live at 618 West

Lyndon Street and I have just found a dead woman in my backyard."

It didn't take much beyond that to get the ball rolling. The police station is only two blocks away. I live in the highest crime area in town. Three cruisers were in my driveway before I could hang up. The officers found me still rooted to the spot, the cell phone clutched in my hand and the body sprawled out in front of me.

"Jesus," the first one said.

I crossed myself and turned around to face him. He looked like a kid, like he wasn't old enough to shave. His eyes were huge when he saw the body, and he stopped just as I had, frozen, his ruddy complexion paling as the reality of what he was seeing hit him.

I could see his fingers twitch and he seemed to want to unsnap his gun even though a gun would be no protection against a dead body. He looked at me. I didn't look like a threat—at least, I hoped not. I could see my reflection mirrored in the window of his squad car. I looked like the Blessed Virgin only with dark, curly hair and blue eyes. I can't help that I look like a kindergarten teacher, and at this moment I was actually thankful. With a dead body in the backyard and my fingerprints on the machete, innocent and harmless were just the qualities I needed to portray to this trigger-happy first responder.

The young cop's partner arrived, paired up with two other cops from the two other cars. Everybody was young and anxious and clearly experiencing something out of the ordinary. Hell, a machete sticking out of a body, that's not ordinary in almost anyone's experience. The three other cops stopped short in a clump of dark uniforms and aviator sunglasses. Two were women. One of the women was tall and big-boned, but the other one, a blonde, was about my size. I found myself ridiculously thinking, I could take her. What is it about cops that make people start feeling claustrophobic?

"Did you call us?" the blonde asked.

I looked back at the body. I sort of figured that part would be obvious. Who else was gonna call, the victim? "Yeah. I'm Sophie Mazaratti and that, there, is a dead body."

One of the men snickered softly, then spoke into the microphone clipped to the front of his uniform. In the distance a siren wail started, then stopped. Dead. No need to rush—time was no longer a concern.

"Ma'am," the big woman said, "why don't you come with me and I'll take your statement." She looked at the first officer, the young redheaded boy. "LaSalle, secure the scene." She looked past him, over the fence, into the neighboring backyard and on toward the projects. She was formulating an opinion.

Joey arrived right after she asked, "Was the machete already in her chest or did you do that?" I didn't like her tone.

Joey reached my side just as I was answering her. "Yeah, well, I figured since she was already dead I might as well chop her up so's she'd fit in the trash can better."

"Soph," Joe cautioned. "Let it rest."

I turned around and went to him, right into the strong arms of my brother. "Joe, she's a fucking idiot who's trying to get wise," I muttered in his ear. "I was just letting her know I don't play."

"Enough," he whispered. "Let me talk to her."

He turned away from me, loosening his grip and taking a step to offer his hand to the cop. "I'm Joe Mazaratti, Sophie's brother. Listen, she's a little upset. I mean, it's a dead body. I guess I don't have to tell you we're not used to this sort of situation."

The officer shook Joe's hand. She wasn't charmed yet, but she was on the slippery slope headed downhill to him. Women couldn't resist Joe. I don't know what it is. He's good-looking enough, but he's going bald. Personally, I think it's his eyes. He's got the Mazaratti eyes—intense, warm—and when he finally smiles at you, it's like winning a prize. Of course, it could just be that Joe's a nice guy and it's genuine with him. If he likes you, you know it.

Joe was reading her nameplate. "Officer Melton?" He sounded the name out slowly and smiled. "How can we be of further assistance? You want Sophie here to come down to the station? You want something to drink, water? Move our cars? What?"

Melton, given too many options, hesitated briefly. "No, Mr. Mazaratti, if y'all could just wait on the front porch, or inside the house, that's all we need right now. They'll send out a couple of detectives and they'll probably want to talk to Ms. Mazaratti, ask her a few questions."

She didn't even look at me now. It was all Joe. But that was fine by me. I was watching the cops string yellow crime scene tape across my backyard and feeling like everything was happening at the other end of a tunnel.

Joe took me by the arm and walked around the side of the house, up to the front porch steps. We climbed them and slowly sank down onto the top riser. Joey waited until Officer Melton joined the others in the backyard before he asked for the full story. He made me tell him twice, asking questions until at last I could see he was satisfied and had an accurate picture in his head of the events leading up to my finding the body.

"You don't know who it is or anything, do you?"

I frowned at him. "Joey, I don't know hardly anybody in this town but you guys. Besides, all I saw was an arm. It's kind of hard to identify somebody by their arm, although she did have a kind of unusual arm."

Joey was on it. "What do you mean unusual?"

"Well, she had this kind of tattoo on her knuckles," I said. "Letters, you know, spelling out a word."

"What word?"

"*Hate*. And then there was a, like, dragon symbol above that, on the back of her hand, but kind of small, toward her thumb."

"You're right," Joe said. "That's weird for here, but up North, you know that would be considered normal." He laughed then and I had to laugh with him. It was eerie, laughing in the presence of a dead body, but it was like laughing in church—you know you shouldn't, and that just makes it all the funnier.

The detectives pulling up in their unmarked, but totally obvious, sedan must've thought we were crazy. I saw the driver look up with a puzzled expression, check something on a piece of paper and then look back at the house. He was probably thinking he had the wrong address, what with us laughing like that, but the cop cars in the driveway confirmed it. They were on the scene with lunatics.

The crime scene van pulled right up in front of them and two technicians piled out and scurried up the driveway. If Joey's stifled laughter and my giggles seemed odd, they weren't stopping to mull it over. They had business in the backyard and time was wasting.

The detectives, though, were cooler. Detectives don't rush. Rushing means you're not in control, and I knew from Philly that detectives were always in control. The doors to the sedan slowly swung open and the two men got out of the car, the driver for a moment obscuring my view of the second detective.

The driver, a reed-thin older man, moved and started walking up the walkway. The second detective followed, head down and face partially obscured as he spoke into his cell phone. But even from a distance, even with his head down, I felt the shock of recognition. Mr. Wonderful was about to walk back into my life and this time I couldn't run away.

He saw Joe first. I stayed on the porch, half-hidden by the overgrown magnolia tree, half hiding behind the porch pillar, watching. It had been almost six weeks since that first meeting in the tiny chapel, since the day I'd passed him on the sidewalk like there wasn't a thing to it but two strangers smiling politely. Now here he was, poised on the edge of my life, about to change everything. But it was Joe he recognized.

I watched the detective snap the cell phone shut and follow his partner toward Joe, who stood in the driveway. Mr. Wonderful wore dark, well-tailored trousers, a white starched shirt and a subdued red tie. It picked up the intense gray color of his eyes, deepening them. His skin was darker, more tanned, as if he'd spent even more time outdoors since I'd first seen him. He moved like an athlete, graceful but with a coiled energy that seemed ready to spring forth at any opportunity.

I saw the detective's eyes light on my brother, and the broad smile that had first drawn me to him appeared, unchecked, as if he had forgotten that this was a homicide scene and not just a chance meeting between two friends on the street.

Joe had the same sort of smile on his face, easy and warm. As I watched, he clasped Mr. Wonderful's hand, then drew him in and hugged him, the way we do family or close friends up North.

Italians don't love casually. We take hostages. You are either all the way in with us or a stranger. There is no phony Southern "Y'all come back now, hear?" If we don't want to see you again, we don't invite you back. I could tell just by watching that Joe knew this guy, knew him well and liked him. My heart flipped over and I rubbed my palms across my thighs, smoothing the fabric of my faded overalls.

"It's a mess," I heard Joe say. "My sister Sophie just moved down from Philly...gonna live in her dream house...now this. *Marone.*"

Mr. Wonderful was looking at the scene, over Joe's shoulder, not seeing me there on the porch. He shook his head, agreeing with my brother.

"You know the district," Mr. Wonderful said. "It's transitional. These things happen sometimes...probably a hooker who got dumped after a bad deal." He shook his head again, but his eyes darkened and his expression was grim. His good humor was gone and he was all business.

Mr. Wonderful looked at my brother and the smile flashed back for a second. "Joe, you got a sister? Why didn't you tell me? She doesn't take after you, does she?" Now he was grinning, trying to lighten up the situation for my brother.

Joe touched the top of his scalp and grinned. "No, Gray, she's got hair."

His name was Gray. It was perfect for him. It matched his eyes. Oh God, I was drooling like an idiot.

But Joe didn't waste time. "Sophie," he called, turning and revealing my hiding place on the steps. "Come here. I want to introduce you to someone."

I stood, my hand touching the porch rail so I wouldn't trip walking down the steps because the way I felt, I couldn't trust my body not to betray me. I saw him do a double take, as if he couldn't believe this was happening, either. I saw the easy smile flash, then grow tentative as I suppose he remembered me passing him on the street like a stranger.

I smiled back because I couldn't stop myself. I was suddenly so very glad to see him. My brain wasn't working right. My inhibitions, the stuff that would normally put on the brakes and stop me from looking foolish and desperate, were gone.

Instead it was just me, smiling up like he was someone I already knew well, someone I wanted to keep close to me.

"She don't always look this good," Joe said, picking up on something, but uncertain of what it was. "She's down here, what, two weeks? Already she's with the overalls and the work boots."

That stopped me. I suddenly saw myself as Gray must be seeing me. I was covered in dirt and yard grime, sweaty, probably smelly, too. I was wearing one of Pa's old V-necked undershirts, worn overalls from the thrift shop and a red bandanna around my hair. I lifted my hand to touch the bandanna and the unruly curls my grandma Mazaratti once said would trap birds. This was wonderful. Dirty, no makeup and standing right in front of what Darlene called my destiny. *Marone a mia.*

"Like a fish needs a bicycle," I muttered under my breath.

"What's that, Sophie?" Joe asked.

"I said hello." I started to extend my hand toward Gray, then realized it was probably filthy and that I had touched a dead body with it. When I moved to withdraw it, Joey's friend was too quick. He read my hesitation, reached for my hand and took it, anyway, and then held it, like he was trying to reassure me, his grip warm and firm.

"Sophie," Joe said, "this guy here is a friend of mine, Gray Evans. We play rugby together—only he's good at it. Just so happens he's a police detective and got himself assigned to this case. Our lucky day, right?"

I smiled, opened my mouth, and for the first time in my life, words failed me. "Uh."

"She's eloquent, my sister is," Joe said.

Gray's eyes held mine. "Hell of a morning, huh?" he asked softly.

I could only nod. The big cop came walking toward us and

Gray dropped my hand and turned to her, then looked back at Joe.

"Excuse me a minute. I gotta go do this," he said. Then he looked at me. "I'll probably have a few questions I'll need to ask you in a little while. Can you stick around?"

I think the last question was directed at both of us; at least Joe seemed to take it that way. "We're not going anywhere," he said. "Come inside when you're ready."

With that, Mr. Wonderful vanished and Detective Gray Evans went to work.

"He's a friend of yours?" I asked Joey, trying to keep my tone casual.

Joey looked away from the crime scene, glancing sharply at my face, then back to the crowd of police officers. "Yeah, I like the guy, but we travel in different circles. He's single, I'm married and got kids, so we mainly see each other at practice or a game. Nice guy, though. Even read my books. Go figure that, huh? A cop reading poetry?"

I shrugged, watching Gray talk to the uniformed officers. I liked the way the sunlight glinted off his hair, tinting the gray into a brilliant silvery white and somehow managing to make him look even younger.

"What? You're saying a cop can't be sensitive?"

Joey barely seemed to hear me and I was surprised when he answered. "You know any like that? Sensitive?"

Well, no, I didn't. In Philadelphia the streets hardened them, and even if they had felt an emotion, I never saw it. But then, I only knew the South Philly boys, the ones from the neighborhood. I can assure you, sentimentality was not their forte.

"He works with Boy Scouts. That's sensitive."

This grabbed Joey's attention. "I thought you didn't know the guy?"

I could feel the heat rising up into my cheeks, spreading

like a rosy wildfire across my face. I looked away, focusing on the activities of a slow crime scene technician who seemed to be gathering blades of grass from the ground around the victim's body.

"Oh, I ran into him at the Tour of Homes. He was helping them sell lemonade."

Joey's attention sharpened. "So you run into him at the tour and still remember him?" he asked.

"Well, I guess he sort of stuck out in my mind, that's all. You know, Joe, women are observant."

Joey snorted. "Tell me about it."

"So have you met his girlfriend?" I asked, fishing.

Joey had switched his attention back to the scene. "Met who?" he asked without turning.

"His girlfriend, Joey. He has one, doesn't he?"

This earned me another sharp glance. "What? No, I haven't met her. I don't know who guys bring to the game with them. I'm just there to play. I didn't notice anybody in particular. Lots of women come to the games, but so do guys."

Men were so unobservant. "So he brought a lot of different women to the games, huh? What is he, a player?"

Joey's attention was only marginally on my interrogation. He shrugged. "Whatever. Yeah, I'd say he's a good player."

I looked back at the detective. He radiated charisma; of course he was a player. Why not? He was a man, wasn't he?

Like a homing pigeon, my sister Darlene arrived. How she knew something was going on at my house is a mystery, but then, that's Darlene, ruled by the cosmos, victim of supernatural wavelengths. Our grandmother always said Darlene had the gift—the Eye, as the family calls it. She said Darlene "saw" things and "knew" things, things that other people don't know…yet.

Darlene drives a beat-up Chevy Colt. It resembles an empty

soda can on wheels, half crushed up and dented by what would be normal wear and tear in a regular vehicle. Of course, Darlene drives the way she thinks, in a nonlinear fashion, weaving from one location to another, which probably accounts for the car's condition more than anything.

She parked, if you want to call it that, halfway down the block and then strolled back toward the house. She was wearing another one of her hippy outfits, a flowing chiffon dress and pink sandals. She didn't wear a floral wreath today, probably because she'd come from work, but two slender braids pulled her straight brown hair back into a post-sixties look. She appeared to be oblivious to the police cruisers parked in the driveway. As she drew closer, I realized she was humming.

Joey rolled his eyes. He has no patience with her because he says she's a disaster waiting to happen. I think actually she stresses him out because he feels he needs to protect her because she's divorced two husbands and buried one. He's worried because she doesn't seem in a hurry to find number four.

"Good morning," she said, her voice a singsong lilt. Then she stopped, seemed to take stock of her surroundings and said, "Oh, I guess it's afternoon, huh?" Still no acknowledgment of the police cars.

She wandered up to where we stood before the change came over her. "Oh, man, something feels weird here. There is, like, a total disturbance in the energy level." She actually shivered, wrapped her arms around herself and looked toward the backyard.

"Oh…it's cold here, even colder back there." She looked from me to Joe. "All right," she said, "who's dead?"

"Sweet Mother of God!" Joe gasped in mock astonishment. "What was it gave it away, the crime scene van or the three cop cars and the entire New Bern police force in the backyard?"

Darlene gave him her patronizing smile. "You should give up meat, Joe. It makes you mean." Then she looked back at the scene and saw Mr. Wonderful.

How the woman recognized him again, after only seeing him one time in passing, is beyond me, but she did. She broke out in a triumphant grin. "Aha!" she cried. "What did I tell you? It's your destiny! Fate cannot be denied!"

"Have you lost your fucking mind?" Joe cried.

"It's the meat, isn't it, Joe? You're probably constipated," she said, and dismissed him.

"He's a detective," I said. "Who knew?"

Darlene smiled. She knew. You could see she was thinking it. *I knew.*

At that moment, Gray Evans looked back at us and smiled. He knew, too, I thought. He knew all along.

"Let's go inside," I said. I couldn't take it, couldn't take everybody seeing my future, even me. I knew that it was all an unrealistic fantasy we were creating, not real life. In real life people simply do not fall in love at first sight or cement their relationship over a dead body. It just didn't happen and the sooner we all got that, the sooner I could get on with my life.

We stood in the kitchen, or what would be the kitchen, and stared out the back window into the yard where Gray Evans and his squad of officers toiled. It was a close-up view of things we probably shouldn't have seen.

A technician nodded to a question asked by Gray's partner, the tall older man with a permanent look of sorrow on his well-worn face. With a quick nod to Gray, the senior detective leaned forward, pinched the edge of the plastic between two latex covered fingers and slowly tugged the wrapping away from her body.

Joe and I crossed ourselves, with him saying the Rosary softly and Darlene on my other side murmuring an incantation that sounded like "Now I lay me down to sleep." As the police officers moved and the technicians snapped pictures, we had a pretty good view of the victim. She was young and had worked hard to disguise any natural beauty that might have been evident. Her hair was black, cut into a scalp-hugging cap of short, shaggy layers.

Joe whistled softly, cutting off his prayer at the sight of this poor dead thing. She was wearing a black leather halter top, complete with bright chrome studs, cutoff jeans and heavy black boots. Her skin, pasty in death, was covered with a number of intricate tattoos.

I watched the police officers exchange glances, a couple of them seeming to snicker. I looked back at the dead girl. She looked more like she was sleeping than dead. Her eyes were closed and her body wasn't contorted into any of the anguished positions I'd expected of a violent death.

Darlene studied her. "Would you look at her boobs?" she said finally. "You think those are real?"

"Darlene!" Joe and I both yelled at her. "Have a little respect for the dead," Joe added.

"I am respectful," Darlene said. "I don't have tits like that. I mean look at them. They have to be a triple D cup. Do you think they're real?"

Joe was rolling his eyes, but I looked at the dead woman again. Darlene did have a point. Whatever she'd packed into that halter top, real or otherwise, was a pretty full load.

Darlene was entranced for another minute, and then she sighed and turned to look at me. "Bet she had back problems."

"You think?"

Darlene, not sensing the sarcasm, nodded wisely. "I am a trained therapist, you know. I should be in a position here to judge." Then, as if having another thought, she stopped, looked back at the victim and said, "You think she got shot there? I don't see any blood, but then if the bullet hit a saline bag and it ruptured—"

"Darlene!" The image was too gruesome to imagine.

Darlene held up her hands and backed up a step. "Professional curiosity, that's all. I mean, do they deflate if you hit one? You know, if they're implants? It would answer a lot of questions if we knew that."

"Darlene." Joe's tone was ominous. "Enough."

I had no idea what kinds of questions would be answered for Darlene if she knew that, and I didn't want to know, either. Somehow, though, I was sure we hadn't heard the end of it from her. As soon as Gray Evans hit the doorstep, Darlene would be on him, relentless with her need to know. Let her tell Gray she was a professional therapist and see what that got her. I was betting he'd brush her off like a speck of dust.

Joe didn't want to see any more. He started wandering around the kitchen, inspecting the wiring, looking at the pipes that were poking out of the subflooring, waiting for their sink.

"What's the plan here?" he asked, indicating the entire room and all the details.

I sighed and pulled myself away from the window, turning my back on Gray Evans and the dead girl.

My dream house was a shamble of renovations and unchecked deterioration. What had been advertised as "partially renovated" was actually the equivalent of saying "We've stopped the bleeding, now you can try and put the pieces back together." The major systems, the heat and air, the electrical wiring, had been replaced, but the lathe in some rooms lay naked and exposed, while a few others had new Sheetrock, unprimed and unpainted, waiting like empty canvases.

I'd moved in anyway. I'd made the offer, closed quickly and hauled my belongings from Philly to New Bern before I could have regrets, before I could change my mind. Did it matter that the kitchen was basically a gutted shell? No. That's why God made microwaves.

Did I care that my bedroom was the intended dining room, while the master bedroom was yet to be reclaimed from years of neglect and trash? Absolutely not—it beat living with Ma and Pa and knowing that no matter what I did, it wouldn't be right by their standards. Parenting to Ma is like redoing an old house; you don't ever declare it done because there is always room for improvement.

"The plan is to finish the walls first," I told Joe. I was attempting to go along with his distraction, but the scene in the backyard tugged at me and I found myself looking over my shoulder. "I can't afford plaster. Besides, the owners who started the work were using Sheetrock anyway, so that'll come next, then the floors. I'm going to refinish what I can and try to match up the rest with new wood."

Joe nodded. "Wood everywhere then?" he asked, but his eyes followed my gaze into the backyard.

"Yeah. I want to keep the house as close to original as possible. Maybe not the fixtures so much, maybe reproductions there, but you know, an old-timey feel."

"Here he comes," said Darlene, and no one had to ask who.

Joe walked to the back door and pulled it open. Darlene looked over at me and smirked, as if this was a social call and not a death scene investigation. I was once again frozen, standing rooted to the middle of my kitchen floor like a big dummy.

Gray was peeling off his gloves as he stepped onto the enclosed porch, stuffing them in his pockets and talking to Joe in a low voice. When they entered the kitchen, Joe looked at Darlene and said, "Come on."

"But I want to—"

"Come on, Darlene." Joe wasn't giving her an option. As she approached the two men, he reached out, grabbed her arm and pulled her out the door. Darlene let out a high-pitched squawk and was gone without further ado. That left me alone with Detective Evans.

"Wish I had that lemonade now," he said, his voice soft and easy.

"I've got bottled water," I said, flying into a fluster of activity, opening cabinet doors, overlooking the cooler on the counter and finally realizing it was right in front of me.

Gray Evans moved across the room, took the cooler lid from my hand and set it down on the counter. Then he took the dripping water bottle that I handed him and put that down, too. He was inches away from me, so close I could feel the heat that radiated from his body, and smell the scent of musk.

"You know, it's all right," he said. The words brushed against me like a quiet breeze. "It's all right to be scared and upset. Just try to relax a little bit, okay?"

I nodded and swallowed hard.

"Nothing like this has ever happened to me before," I said.

That brought a smile. "Me, either."

"You never found a dead body?"

He shook his head. "Nope. I get called in after the body's been found. I know what to expect. It's not a shock when I show up—not like it was for you."

I looked away and turned my attention to fitting the lid onto the cooler.

"I…it was so…she was… When that blade hit her and I looked down and saw her arm, I thought, my God, she was sleeping here and I killed her."

Gray was watching me, the water bottle unopened in his hand. "She was probably dead maybe six hours before you found her," he said. He twisted the cap off the bottle and took a long drink.

"How did she die?"

Gray shook his head. "We won't be certain until the medical examiner finishes, and it might take the autopsy to tell for sure. I'm pretty certain she's got a head trauma, though."

"Was it accidental or do you think she was murdered?"

"Almost certainly foul play," he answered.

Right outside my window, just behind my house, a woman had been killed and then dumped. I hadn't heard a thing. I'd slept through someone's violent death and never even imagined it. I'd stood in my kitchen, drinking my morning coffee and looking out at the backyard, without any awareness at all.

"Do you know who she is yet?" I asked.

He shook his head. "Probably a crack whore, at least from the way she's dressed, but with that hair, I don't know."

"Hey, maybe she worked a particular kind of clientele," I said. "You know, the whips and chains, 'I've been a bad, bad boy' set."

That made him smile. "You're Joe's sister, all right."

"What makes you say that?"

"He's quick, always got a comeback or the last word on a situation. And you look like him." He hesitated, and then added, "Not the hair part. It's your eyes. You've got eyes like his."

"So, if Joe had hair, we'd be twins? Because I think what you're really trying to say is I've got a mouth."

He was looking at me, at first laughing a little, and then studying me. "Not really, not the twins part. But yeah," he said, his voice thickening, "that's some mouth you got there." The way he said it, he could've been kissing me and I wouldn't have felt the connection any stronger.

I backed up and changed the subject. Gray Evans scared me. He didn't seem to know about women needing men like fish needed bicycles. I had the feeling that if I'd told him, he wouldn't have cared, either. The guy was a player and spreading chemistry like fertilizer. Oh, this was one to stay away from, all right. But that wouldn't be my problem for long. Right now he still didn't know about me, about Nick. Later, his attitude would change and it would be a whole new ball game. He wasn't going to ever be my problem.

"Okay," he said, as if reading me. "Here's what will happen next. The forensics people will finish processing the scene, and we'll get the body out of here. When it's all done, the yard will be yours again and you won't have to worry about having any restrictions on working back there."

"What if there's another body?"

"We checked. There's not. What probably happened is that she was killed nearby and your yard was convenient because of the overgrowth and the low fence. It was easy, that's all."

"I'll finish clearing it out tomorrow," I said. "I don't like the idea of this happening again. I don't like this at all."

"Hey, the chances of it happening again are incredibly small. We don't have that many homicides here, maybe four a year. This was a fluke. Relax." He looked out the window into the backyard, inspecting it carefully. "Are you doing all that by yourself? Nobody's helping you? What's with that sorry brother of yours?"

I smiled despite my stomach flipping over and my heart racing, despite the warmth that seemed to be spreading throughout my body in a long-ago remembered way. Oh man, this guy was trouble.

"Joe helps when he can," I said, "but he's got a family and work…."

"And you don't?" Gray asked. His eyes were fastened on my face as if everything hung on my answer.

"No. I'm a teacher," I said, and ignored the other part of his question. "I don't have a job yet and besides, it's summer. Teachers have the summer off." I looked around the kitchen, away from his face, letting him follow my gaze. "So, I'm doing what I can. I've got most of the major work contracted out, but I need to keep the costs down."

I looked up and caught him watching me.

"I'm not afraid of hard work. That's why I was out there cutting back the undergrowth...." But as I remembered how the morning ended, I felt myself slow to a stop. We all knew how the morning's work had ended.

"So you wouldn't mind a little free labor?" he said, slipped it right in on me without me seeing it coming.

"Free labor?"

"Yeah, I can cut down bushes with the best of them, and I have something else I bet you don't have."

Now he had me. "What?"

He smiled mysteriously, his eyes sparkled and one thick eyebrow arched. "A chainsaw." He gestured toward the back-yard and grinned. "You ain't seen nothing until you see what short work a chainsaw will make of your jungle. Hide and watch."

For the first time since we'd met, I heard the faint twang of a Southern accent. Gray Evans was a country boy at heart.

"You better with a chainsaw than you are at pouring lemonade?" I asked. "Or should I tell EMS to stand by?"

He laughed and was about to answer me, but of course, Darlene with her Extrasensory Perception picked this moment to escape Joe and reclaim the kitchen. She sailed in through the dining room, a froth of pink chiffon and ladylike smiles, and focused one hundred percent of her attention on Mr. Wonderful.

"So," she said, apropos of nothing at all, "were they her real breasts or not?"

Chapter 3

The next morning my car exploded. I use the term "morning" loosely. It was 4:23 a.m., according to the clock on my makeshift nightstand, but the room lit up like a Roman candle as my Honda went up in flames.

I reached for the phone, hit 9-1-1 as my feet touched the smooth wood floor of my makeshift bedroom, and ran toward the kitchen.

"It's Sophie Mazaratti, 618 West Lyndon Street. My car just exploded and it's on fire."

"Hold on," the female voice said. In the background, I heard her say, "Start trucks one and two to 618 West Lyndon. Unit 2314, go ahead. Unit 2316, why don't you start as well." Then she was back with me. "We'll be there in a few minutes," she said. "Stay away from the vehicle."

That's what I like about police communicators. You could tell them you'd murdered your sister, then hacked off her head so you could fit her in a trunk, and they'd stay just as cool as a cucumber.

I hung up, grabbed my slippers and a sweater, and ran out onto the front porch. The neighborhood was on full alert. All the lights were on in the surrounding cottages, as one by one the residents came out into the street and stood staring at the burning car in my driveway. The wail of sirens woke anyone who might've slept through the explosion.

Most of my neighbors had missed the prior morning's excitement, returning home from work to hear about the discovery of a dead body in my backyard on the local news. Now they clustered in a group, talking and watching my car turn into a blackened shell.

"You okay, Sophie?" one of them called.

I nodded, but there was no safe way to approach them. The burning car blocked my path and the overgrown front yard made walking that way impossible. I stood on the porch instead, watching and shivering. It was a warm night, made warmer by the fire, but I felt cold and very alone. I could dismiss the dead woman in my backyard as a happenstance occurrence, but my car, now that was a different matter.

I looked back at the neighbors. Did someone not want me here? I knew this was a paranoid way to view the situation, but the car had to have been destroyed intentionally. Was it kids? Vandals? Who else would want to torch my car? I thought about Nick and dismissed him. He hated me enough to do this, but he was in prison. The worst he'd been able to do so far was send threatening letters. He wasn't due out for months. As mad as he was about me turning him in, he wouldn't know where I was now, and if he did, I doubted he'd spring for a torch job. In the first place, New Bern wasn't Philly. He'd have to import talent and pay for their trip down here. Nick was way too cheap for that.

I looked up and down the street, saw the fire trucks rolling toward my house, and wondered who else could've bombed my car. Someone connected with the body in the backyard? Someone who thought maybe I knew something or needed a warning?

"Don't be ridiculous," I told myself. "This is not Hollywood. You're imagining things. Maybe it was just a freak accident. Things like that happen, don't they? Gas vapors could ignite on a hot summer night, couldn't they? It could happen, right?"

The firemen were pulling out hoses, rushing around to keep the fire from spreading, but my car was gone. A policeman edged around the smoldering hunk of metal and made his way up the driveway. He was using his flashlight, looking at the ground, searching for clues, I supposed. When he reached me, he glanced up and said, "Ms. Mazaratti? You all right?"

"Relatively speaking," I answered.

"Wasn't there a call here earlier today?"

"Yeah, there was a dead body in my backyard."

It was another young cop. He kept staring down at his clipboard, like it was going to tell him what to do, and then looking back up at me. "Okay," he said at last, "tell me what happened."

"At 4:23 a.m., my car blew up. I was asleep, and when it exploded I woke up. End of story. You think it was an accident?"

"Well, ma'am, I don't know. The arson investigator's looking it over. He's with the fire department, so he'll tell us when he's through. You didn't see or hear anything of a suspicious nature before the car blew?"

I shook my head. "Like I said, I was sleeping."

A familiar form was making its way up my driveway. Gray Evans, dressed in a T-shirt and shorts, had arrived, a worried look on his face.

"You all right?" he asked me. I nodded and he turned to the young officer. "What you got?" The boy handed him the clipboard, Gray scanned it and then nodded. "All right. Go rope it off. We'll get forensics over here."

When we were alone, Gray looked back at me, his lips twitching with a suppressed smile. It took only a moment to figure out why he'd see this as funny. Long enough for me to realize that I was wearing bright green-and-pink pajamas covered in dazzling red cherries and fuzzy pink bunny slippers that Joe's daughter, Emily, had given me.

"I was sleeping," I said.

"And the slippers?"

"My niece gave them to me. She would be hurt if she found out I didn't wear them."

He looked over his shoulder as if searching for her in the crowd.

"Well, they're comfortable. You wanna try them?"

He shook his head and smiled. "Your niece might not like that," he said. "Besides, I'll bet they're way too small for me."

I looked at his feet, remembered the things people said about the correlation between foot size and, well, you know, and started turning red. Gray noticed immediately and smiled even more.

"Y-you probably have your own," I stammered.

"Bunny slippers? No." He had no intention of making it easier on me. The young cop helped me out by calling Gray away.

I looked down at my feet and wiggled my toes. The pink bunnies tossed their ears and danced. They *were* cute. I looked back at Gray and saw that he was now talking on his cell phone, his back to me. My car was a sodden mass of ashes and debris. Men poked at the wreckage, examining it, taking samples of charred material and bagging them in small paper bags. The neighbors were disbanding, returning to their homes in ones and twos. Soon the sun would begin brightening the horizon.

I watched for another minute and then decided to make coffee. I figured that was useful. We could all use coffee. It gave me something to do. It made me feel like I had control over something, if only my coffeepot.

When Gray returned, he found me sitting on the front porch steps holding a thick mug in my hands. I'd pulled on jeans and a sweatshirt, replaced the bunny slippers with sneakers and tried to tame my hair.

"Coffee?"

"Yeah, that would be nice," he said, but he seemed distracted and distant. The smile was gone.

I led him through the house and into the kitchen, poured his coffee and motioned him to the table, where the milk and sugar sat waiting. He pulled out one of the heavy wooden chairs and gestured me into another.

"We need to talk," he said.

"Okay." The air in the kitchen felt heavy. I knew he had something unpleasant to say.

"So, somebody blew up my car and it wasn't a freak accident." I thought if I said it first it might make it easier for him, but that didn't seem to help.

"Sophie," he said, "earlier today, as part of our investigation, we ran routine checks on all the cars parked in the area. We do this in case one of the cars belongs to the victim. You know, if it gets left behind then we know maybe it was hers, or if it clearly doesn't belong to someone in the neighborhood we can begin to narrow the field a little."

I nodded, feeling impatient.

"We identified a white, 1996 Mercedes convertible, registered to Nicolas Komassi, 532 Hartford Street, Philadelphia."

Gray looked at me, his eyes smoky and somber. "Your ex-husband, right?"

I felt my hands begin to tremble, and the sudden urge to cry tightened my throat. I nodded, took a deep breath and said, "Nick's in prison. He won't be out for another eight months. And that address you have, it's not his anymore—it was mine."

Gray just stared at me. "Sophie, Nick got out of prison a week ago. I talked to his parole officer. He got an early release for good behavior. They tried to notify you, but you didn't leave them a forwarding address."

I slapped my hand down on the table. Coffee sloshed out of my cup and stained the napkin beneath it. "I didn't want him to find me! I thought it would be better if no one knew how to reach me. I didn't even leave a forwarding address with the post office. I just went in the house with Joey, packed my things and drove away."

Gray covered my hand with one of his. "Okay, Soph. It's okay. But somehow I'm thinking he found you."

"No! He couldn't. He wouldn't do that!"

"It's his car."

That much was irrefutable. Nick's car didn't drive itself down to New Bern. Nick was in town, in my new town, in my safe haven, and now bad things were starting to happen, just like he'd promised.

Gray was watching me and I knew there had to be more. "What else?" I asked.

"His parole officer can't find him. He's been missing for three days."

My stomach clutched into a knot. For a year, since Nick had been sent to prison and the divorce finalized, I'd felt relatively safe, but now this. I looked at Gray briefly and felt my future slip away, contaminated by the past. Even if I were interested, who wants a relationship with the ex-wife of a sicko-pervert convict? He'd look at me and think of Nick. He'd wonder what kind of a woman lets herself get taken in by such a twisted man. And Gray Evans didn't know the half of it.

Gray hadn't seen that Web site, hadn't seen the pictures and videos Nick took of me without my knowledge. Gray didn't know how I felt, what it was like to feel scummy and dirty every day, no matter how many showers I took or how long Nick spent in prison. Like a fish needs a bicycle, I reminded myself, and squared my shoulders. No one would ever use me that way again. I would never let myself be that vulnerable.

I shivered involuntarily. "Okay, so he followed me down here. I'll handle it."

Gray frowned slightly. "What do you mean?"

I tossed my head and ran my fingers through my hair like I do when I'm thinking or upset. "I mean I'll get a restraining order."

Gray looked over his shoulder, toward the front of the house, still frowning. "If that's Nick's work out front, I don't think a restraining order will cover it."

"I said I'll handle it and I will. I can take care of myself." I stood up, shoving my chair back so hard it screeched on the plywood subflooring. I knew I sounded harsh and defensive.

Gray ignored it. "I know you can handle yourself, Sophie. All I'm saying is you don't have to do it all alone. I'll have the officers in this zone make extra patrols. If you want I can check your doors and windows and help you put more secure locks on. You're not alone, Soph. Let us help you."

Don't you see? I don't want your help! I screamed silently. I wanted a fresh start, clean, without the film of scum that covered my life in Philadelphia. Now it felt hopeless. I had let myself dare to think everything would be fine, and now this.

"I'm tired," I said. "I think I just want to go back to sleep."

He pushed his cup aside and stood up. I looked at him and felt numb, almost. He couldn't possibly understand, and it showed in his kind, concerned eyes and worried expression. He wanted to help and couldn't understand why I was pushing him away. Gray Evans was never going to be anything to me because I couldn't take the pain of coming to love someone and then losing him. Nick would ruin it. Nick ruined everything. Ruining my life had become his passion.

"I'll come back later and help you clean up out there," he said.

"No, that's all right. I have good insurance. I'll call the company and they'll send people out to take care of it." I wasn't half believing this story, but it sounded good. "Thanks for your help. Please let me know if there's anything I can do or any information I can give you that will help with the investigation."

Gray was looking at me like I had two heads, like I'd changed and, of course, I had. What he was seeing now was the survivor, the Sophie that got cornered and came out swinging. I could take care of the car, the ex-husband and my life just fine, without anybody's pity and without any help. I was going to figure out what was going on and why people thought I had something to do with Nick's dirty business or else I would never, ever be truly free to have my own life. I couldn't wait for cops to figure it all out. A fairy godmother wasn't going to appear and set things straight. No, this was my battle and I could handle it.

"Still," Gray said, not getting it yet, "I'd like to come by later and check on you. I could bring my chainsaw…." He tried to grin and I tried harder to resist him. If he stayed much longer, I'd cry, and that was unacceptable.

"How about I call you?" I lied. "It may be a day or two before I'm ready to tackle the backyard."

He nodded. He knew I was lying, but what could he do? He wrote his home phone number on his business card and handed it to me.

I walked him through the house to the front door, opened it and stood just inside the hallway while he said goodbye from the other side. The farther away from me he was, the less chance there was of me giving in.

"Sophie," he said, "I know you're upset. Try to go back to sleep and see if things don't look a little brighter later."

Right. Brighter. Gray Evans was an anomaly, an optimistic cop, or maybe he thought I was as naive as I looked. I forced a smile, thanked him again and closed the door. Goodbye, Gray Evans. I've got work to do and a life to live and I will be just fine without you. However, deep down inside where I keep my secrets, I was thinking fish might not need bicycles, but they sure would enjoy a ride every now and then.

Chapter 4

Darlene couldn't wait to tell on me. It was payback for not letting her ask Gray twenty questions about the dead body. She rushed right back to Neuse Harbor and proceeded to tell my parents every single gory detail. Then, when she rode past my house on her way to work and saw the charred Honda, she hit the speed dial on her cell phone and told my parents I was most probably dead, but not to worry because she was investigating.

While Ma was becoming hysterical and Pa was asking questions, she hung up. Later, when I pinned her down, and I do mean that literally, she tried to say she'd hit a bad cell and the phone had dropped the call. Upon further interrogation and perhaps even a little physical intimidation, Darlene admitted she had "accidentally" hung up on them.

This is why, at 8:19 a.m., I was roused from a deep and dreamless sleep to find Darlene and my parents standing at the foot of my bed. Ma was crying. She stood there, barely coming up to Darlene's shoulder, clutching her old black purse, her gray hair a wire-brush double of my own. She wore thick, sensible shoes and a black dress with tiny white flowers all over it, her standard, Italian mother uniform. Darlene, dressed in an outlandish, bright purple silk dress and wearing a fake orchid in her hair, stood patting Ma's shoulder and beaming. This is just how she likes it, a crisis with her in the middle, coordinating the fireworks. Pa shifted from one foot to the other, looking like an embarrassed, older version of my brother.

"What's wrong?" I asked. "Is somebody dead? Is it Joey?" I sat up, my heart pounding into overdrive, trying to read the expressions on my parents' faces.

"I'll make coffee," Darlene said, vanishing like the night.

"Darlene," Ma sputtered. "She said you was probably dead! Why you didn't call? What happened to your car?" Then Ma lapsed into Italian, saying something about how she just knew the evil eye was on me and that my new house was filled with malice.

Pa was still standing there, looking from her to me and waiting for the initial storm to subside. Instead, Ma turned on him. "What?" With lightning quick speed her hand moved, slapping Pa upside the head. "You gonna do something here? You let this happen! What, you no fix it now?" She slapped him again, a rough head shot that Pa was used to because this is how Ma punctuates all her comments.

"You look all right," Pa said to me.

"I am," I said, raising myself higher in bed and trying to look calmer than I felt.

Ma shrieked. "How can you say that at a time like this? A dead woman in the garden?" Here Ma crossed herself. "Your car burned to cinders? What? All right, you say? You're all right? *Stunade!*"

Darlene appeared in the doorway behind us. "Ma, coffee's ready. Come have some."

I shot Darlene a look that promised retribution. Ma, still slapping at Pa, allowed herself to be led into the kitchen, leaving me to hop out of bed and trail along after them.

Darlene, all sweetness and light, made a big fuss, handing us coffee, spooning three teaspoons of sugar into Ma's cup and stirring it for her, then clucking like a satisfied hen over her brood of chaotic family members. It was disgusting. I sat there for thirty minutes and answered questions, at least half of them about how a daughter could disrespect her family by not coming to them personally and presenting the information firsthand, preferably as the events were actually occurring.

The phone rang three times while I was under interrogation, and each time when I picked it up and said "Hello?" the person on the other end hung up.

"Probably someone else's old number," I explained, but of course, I didn't believe that for a second. If Nick could find me in New Bern, he could get my unlisted, private number, too.

Darlene had to throw gasoline on the fire. "Tell them about the cute cop," she said. Of course, Darlene had already given them her version, probably leaving it that we were "fated" to become man and wife.

I looked at Ma. "The detective in charge is very efficient," I said.

"*Stunade!*" Ma barked. "Darlene says you *know* him."

Darlene was going to die. I was going to enjoy killing her. It would be a long, slow death, accompanied by many pleas for mercy on her part.

"No, Darlene imagines that I know him," I said. "I have only seen him one other time, from a distance, and that was a thirty-second encounter." I was shooting daggers at Darlene with my eyes, daring her to dispute this.

"What? You would lie to your mother?" Whap! The hand was upside *my* head.

"Ma, don't do that! I'm telling you the God's honest truth."

The sound of the back porch door opening saved me from further mayhem. Joe stepped into the kitchen, looked at us all sitting there, and said, "I brought coffee cake."

"What?" Ma said, "Did you buy that? How much did you pay for it? I got that at home. I make that better. Why you buy that?"

Joe was unflappable. "Ma, Angela made it."

Ma's expression said it all. Despite her name, Angela was not Italian. Ma shrugged, resigned to eating inferior food, and gestured to the center of the table. Then she slapped my hand when I reached for it. "What is wrong with you? Get the plates!"

My entire morning continued this way. I excused myself, took a shower and returned, but they were still at it. The conversation now turned to what they should do to protect me, and this without me even mentioning Nick. I drank another cup of strong coffee, rolled my eyes at Joe and went to check the mailbox.

The note was folded up and stuffed into a plain white envelope, typed on computer paper, and generic in all respects except for what was written on it. *"She didn't cooperate, but you will, won't you? You have what we want. We'll be in touch."*

Joe came up behind me, took the note from my hand and read. "It's probably just some local crackpot looking to scare you," he said. "I'll call Gray."

"No. I'll call him later, when they're gone. That's all I need, Ma whacking Gray upside the head because he didn't prevent this, or Darlene batting her eyes at him and asking stupid questions."

"I'll handle it," Joe said.

"No, Joe, let me do this."

Joey looked into my face, into my eyes, and then pulled me to him, holding me tight against his shoulder. "You know, Soph, I've known you all your life. You won't call him." He reached up and stroked my hair. "You won't call on account of you're embarrassed. You don't want to be any trouble. Worst of all, you don't want to make this real."

I pushed back and looked up at him. "Joe, Nick's out. He got early release."

Joe sucked his breath in through his teeth. In the background I could hear Darlene chattering on about nothing with Ma and Pa. "I thought they were supposed to let you know?" Joe said. "I thought you got a say in that?"

"I didn't leave a forwarding address when I left," I said. "I didn't think."

Joe tried to smile. "Well, good then. He can't find you."

But I was already shaking my head. "He already has, Joe. The police found his Mercedes around the corner yesterday. They were checking plates, thinking they might find out about the girl in the backyard."

"I'll kill the son of a bitch," Joe said, his voice pitched low so Ma and Pa wouldn't hear him.

"No, Joe. Look, Nick is a twisted little man who thinks he can frighten me. He's mad because he ruined his life and he wants to make that my fault. He'll get over it." I looked at Joe like I believed my own propaganda. "After all, what's a sawed-off little accountant going to do to me? I'll cut his balls off and hand them back to him before he knows what hit him."

Joe was shaking his head again. "Look, I don't doubt your intentions, but I don't think we should underestimate Nick, either. He blew up your car. Hell, he probably killed that woman and put her in your backyard to scare you. He's a nutcase, Sophie, but that doesn't mean he isn't dangerous. I'm calling Gray."

He brushed past me, stepping out onto the front porch and flipping open his cell phone.

"And I moved here to take control of my life," I muttered.

"You cannot twist fate to suit your needs," Darlene said. I jumped, wondering how long she'd been listening to Joe and me.

"Put a sock in it, Darlene," I said, and pushed past her back into the house.

Ma was talking to Pa in Italian, so fast and low that I had trouble following anything she said, but she made it easy on me by switching to English as I entered the room.

"You are coming home with us," she said. Her arms were folded across her chubby middle and her expression said that the matter was not open for discussion.

"Ma, I am fine. I'm not leaving. The insurance company is sending out someone today and I need to be here. Joe'll take me to get a rental car later and I'll be good to go."

"You are living in the presence of death," Ma said.

"No, they carted the body off yesterday. Death has departed." I gave the look right back to her, strong, like I wasn't moving an inch.

"I'll check in on her," Pa said, but only because he hadn't heard about Nick yet. They'd be on me once that piece of news leaked out.

"Joe's gonna check on me, too, Ma." I wasn't going to lie and tell them the car thing was due to spontaneous combustion, but I wasn't going to tell the entire story, either. This might be called a sin of omission, but better that than moving in with my parents.

Joe walked in, saying, "That's true, I'll be right here. Besides, I'm only five minutes away if I do go home. Don't worry." He put his hand on Ma's shoulder. "Ain't nothin' gonna happen to Sophie. *Capishe?*"

He was looking over the top of Ma's head at me, then toward the front door, nodding his head imperceptibly in that direction.

"Ma, you guys should go back home and Darlene should go on to work. Sophie's a big girl. She's fine. I'm looking out for her. Ma, why don't you make the braciola, eh? I'm coming for dinner. I'll bring Angela and the kids. Sophie, you're coming, too, right?"

I took the hint. "Yeah, yeah. Ma, there's no decent food here. Look, all I have is a microwave. The stove isn't even hooked up yet. What kind of life is that?"

Ma sniffed. "That is why a good daughter stays in her parents' home."

"Ma, I did that already. Then I got married. I moved out on my own ten years ago. It's too late for moving home again."

The hand, quicker than the eye, whacked me hard. "*Stunade!* It is never too late to respect your mother," she said.

"Dinner, Ma. I'll be there for dinner."

"Good morning!"

We all turned. Gray Evans stood in the doorway. He was giving Ma the smile, the one that had melted my heart just yesterday, the smile I was trying to avoid thinking about.

"Hey, y'all," he said, his voice like molten chocolate. "I knocked, but I figured you didn't hear me and wouldn't mind…."

"What? Get the man a cup of coffee and some cake! Where are your manners?" Ma cried. She was struggling to stand and do it herself, but Joe's hand was still clamped firmly on her shoulder. Gray moved into the room and over to the table to meet my mother and father.

"I'm sorry," he said, "I didn't introduce myself. I'm Gray Evans." He didn't add that he was the investigator working on the murder case.

"The detective," Darlene said with a sigh. "You know," she added, looking at Ma, "*the* detective."

Gray didn't seem to hear her. He was shaking Pa's hand and pulling up a chair, flirting with my mother and making it seem totally genuine, like he didn't have a care in the world and this was a social call.

I watched him, taking in every detail about his appearance. This was the first time I'd noticed the gold shield clipped to his waist, or seen the holster and the thick, black gun protruding from his side. He wore another white shirt, but the pants were a charcoal-gray and the tie today was navy. When I handed him his coffee, his fingers touched mine. A current of electricity seemed to jump from his hand and I willed myself not to feel it. He radiated heat and musk, and it was all I could do not to reach out and lay my palm on his shoulder.

"So," Ma was saying, "you know who burned my daughter's car?"

Gray shook his head. "Not yet."

"Vandals, eh?" Pa was asking.

Gray looked him in the eye, a look Ma couldn't see because Gray was turned to face Pa, but I saw it. It was the look between men when they wish to keep their secrets for later.

"Maybe," Gray stated, and that was enough for Pa.

"You think she should move home?" Pa asked.

"Hey, what did I say?" I interrupted before Gray could answer and possibly ruin my life by accident. "I'm fine. I'm staying here. There's no danger."

But Pa was watching Gray. The detective's eyes never wavered. "I'll make sure she's safe," he said. "If I think she isn't, I'll bring her to you."

Marone a mia, you'd think I didn't exist. You'd think this was the old country. Here they were, two men, discussing my whereabouts and living arrangements like I wasn't even in the room, like I didn't count.

Gray took it a step further and saved himself from certain death at my hands. "Sophie's a smart woman," he said. "She took care of herself up North and didn't seem to fare too poorly. I'm thinking a little town like New Bern won't be too much of a challenge. She'll be all right. And, like I said, I'll be around."

He looked at me then, as if it was a statement of fact, as if I hadn't ever said, "Don't call me, I'll call you."

Gray stood, smiled and said, "I do need to ask Sophie a few more questions, just nitpicky details and the like for our records."

"Sure," I said. "Let's go sit out on the front porch."

"No need for that, honey," Pa said, standing up and assuming control of the family. "Your mother and me have to go." He gave Darlene The Look. "You'd better get to work."

Ma, utterly charmed by Gray, didn't whisper a murmur of protest. "Mr. Detective," she said, "you eat real Italian ever?"

Gray gave her everything he had—the smile, the eyes, the works. "Home-cooked Italian? No, ma'am, I can't say as I ever have."

Ma looked scandalized, turned to me and said, "Tonight you bring your detective home for supper, eh?" She didn't wait for an answer. In Ma's world, she commanded and we obeyed.

"Well, Ma, maybe he's got plans."

"No, I don't have any plans," Gray answered. "I mean, I wouldn't want to impose…."

"Good. It's settled then," Ma said, smug in her superiority over my paltry attempt to head off what had to be certain disaster.

Tonight I would be taking Gray Evans to my parents' house for dinner, alone with him in a car, forced to sit next to him, to feel the energy between us, doomed, as Darlene would say, by destiny and my mother.

I shook off the thought of sitting inches away from Gray Evans. "Like a fish needs a bicycle," I muttered under my breath. Hearing him chuckle, I realized I'd spoken too loudly.

Pa got everybody moving. Joe personally escorted Darlene to her car, while Gray hung back, carrying mugs and plates to the sink.

"Don't," I said. "I'll get them later."

Gray kept on working. "I don't mind."

But I do, I thought. *I mind.*

Order was restored in the kitchen in only a few minutes. Gray poured himself another cup of coffee, easy and relaxed in my home, and then sat down across from me.

"Joe gave me the note. There probably won't be any prints on it. It's been handled, anyway, so that's not going to give us too much."

"I guess I touched it before I realized what it was," I said.

"Who looks in their mailbox expecting threats?" he answered. But he peered at me like this was more of a question, as if he were wondering if there'd been others before this one.

"Nick blames going to prison on me. I know," I said. I spread my hands, as if warding off Gray's protest. "It was his own fault, he broke the law, but because I testified, he blames me."

"That's crazy," Gray said.

"No, that's just Nick. He has his own little reality where he never accepts the blame for his actions. In Nick's world, he was right and I was wrong." I looked at Gray and thought, what the hell, give him the whole picture. What did I have left to lose? Any chance of a relationship was long gone in my mind. Besides, I reminded myself, this man was taken, even if he didn't act like it.

"Nick had a secret life. I thought he was an accountant. He left for work every morning and didn't come home again until dinnertime. He ate supper and he went back to the office—at least, that's what he always told me, and I had no reason to doubt him. He had no other life, no friends, no hobbies, no other interests really, other than work. The only socializing we did was with my friends or my family. So it was a total shock to me when the federal agents came to our home with a search warrant."

I glanced down into my coffee cup and tried to pretend I was someone else, the woman telling the story and not the story itself.

"I'm sure the local FBI office already told you this yesterday."

Gray nodded, his expression so kind I had to look away. "I've heard what they have to say—now I want to hear how you saw it."

"The agents in Philly showed me what he was doing. They showed me the Web site and the pictures. They showed me the things they found in our home, the cameras, the microphones hidden in the walls." I could hear my voice starting to crack, to shake with the same uncontrollable tremors that happened every time I tried to talk about it.

Gray's warm hand covered mine, but I pulled back. I didn't want to look up and see pity on his face or hear the words that everyone always said but couldn't ever really mean.

"I'm all right," I said, and made myself go on. "There were pictures of me on the site—video clips, too. I was asleep, naked, and he snuck in and took pictures of me. He had hidden cameras in our bedroom, in our bathroom—" I broke off, choking on the words because I knew Gray could see in his mind's eye what those pictures had shown, my most intimate, private moments, my life detailed for the world to watch, my ignorance earning Nick money and ultimately destroying my false sense of security.

"That bastard," Gray swore.

"Whatever," I said, shrugging. "It doesn't change the fact that he blames me. I lose my world and he blames me." I gestured to the note. "And now this." I tried to laugh, but it rang hollow. "Guess it just goes to show, 'No matter where you go, there you are.'"

Gray reached out, touching the tip of my chin with his fingers, forcing me to look up at him.

"Sophie, I'm not going to let him hurt you anymore," he said. "You are strong and kind and good. You're a survivor, not a victim. This is your new life, whatever you choose to make of it. No one has a right to take that away from you. I won't stand by and let a scumbag like Nick Komassi destroy that."

I looked at him and felt my eyes welling up with tears. Deep inside I felt a flicker of hope ignite and catch, but the rest of me was thinking, *It's too late already.*

"Nick's already ruined my life," I said. "He started using drugs. He embezzled money from his clients at his accounting firm. It wasn't enough that people kept coming up to me on the street and yelling at me, thinking I was in on it with him. It wasn't enough that his partners in the firm think Nick stashed money away somewhere and that I know where it is. No, he's somehow followed me down here and will make my life a living hell before it's all over."

Gray had said this was my new life, whatever I chose to make of it, but he never put himself in the picture with me, and I couldn't see how he would, even if we knew each other better. He would always know my life was other people's pornography. What if we became a couple and one day ran into a friend of his who suddenly realized I looked just like the woman in the dirty movie he had stashed away at home?

"Now," Gray said, getting to his feet, "I'm going to take this note to the lab, file the report and start looking for Nick. In the meantime, lock the doors. If you go outside, make sure it's where you can be seen. I'll have the patrols increased around here, but keep your cell phone in your pocket, program my numbers into it and call me if you even feel funny. Don't wait for trouble, don't wait to be certain, call me if the breeze in your backyard so much as shifts direction. Okay?"

I nodded and sighed. It all felt so hopeless.

"Sophie, this is going to go away. I'm going to take care of it," he said.

"What makes you think you'll have any success when the feds and the Philadelphia police haven't been able to keep Nick contained?"

Gray smiled. "Ah, but I have a motivation they didn't have."

"And what would that be?"

"I'm a gonna eat a real Italian food, made by a little Italian mama. I can't let her little girl be troubled by goombahs, eh?"

The Italian accent was terrible but it made me smile, and that's what he seemed to want. "That's better. You light up the room when you smile, Sophie Mazaratti."

"Yeah, and I light up the driveway when my ex blows up my car, and where does that get me?" I smiled, trying to deliver the wisecrack like I didn't care, but hearing it fall flat as I spoke.

"Hey," he said, the Italian accent even worse, "count your blessings. That fire burned off half of the bushes along the driveway. That's bushes you don't have to pull now, right?"

"Go!" I said, and felt my heart lift like a hot air balloon.

Chapter 5

I will be the first to admit that I know basically nothing about renovating a house. It didn't look that hard, not when the real estate agent showed me the "before" pictures, and then contrasted those with the house as it appeared today. It looked like a walk in the park, like all I had to do was pick out paint and wallpaper. Well, almost...

This honeymoon lasted exactly one week, and then I sought professional help. I opened the phone book and let my blistered fingers do the walking. I knew enough to get several bids for each project. I knew to ask for references and proof of insurance. My downfall was that while I knew to ask for these things, I sometimes hired people just because I thought they were interesting. Not necessarily "nice" interesting, sometimes it was just that I felt sorry for them. However, "nice" did enter into it now and again.

I hired my carpenter because he looked like Santa Claus.

He twinkled and laughed. He even drove a red truck. But I hired him without so much as asking if he could drive a nail. I was lucky with him.

I was not so lucky with my house painter. I hired him because he looked like James Dean, only shrunken, wizened with age and cigarettes. He could paint, all right, but not without complaining and whining every step of the way. Every morning I found myself meeting him at the door with a hot cup of coffee and a smile, just so I could entice him into working a full day. It never helped. He started after 10:00 a.m. and knocked off at 2:00 p.m., every single day.

I found my newest employee while I was standing in the driveway inspecting the burned-out frame of my former car. A tall blonde with stringy hair and a tight sleeveless T-shirt was making her way slowly down the street, stopping at every house to stuff a flyer into each mailbox. I tried not to watch her, but it was impossible. She couldn't walk in a straight line, and not because she was impaired, but because of her sidekick, a gray-black-and-white furball of a dog.

The little dog pranced, leaping from the sidewalk into the street, darting past the blonde, crossing back across the bricks and into someone's yard. The leash would become tangled around the blonde's legs, drawing the entire procession to a halt as the girl slowly disengaged herself and tried to continue.

"Durrell," I heard her say, her voice impatient, "walk right, will ya? This ain't no parade."

On they came, closer and closer, until finally they were even with the burned out car.

"Dang," the blonde said. "I thought I had it rough, but this sure beats my luck all to hell."

"Guess that's why there's insurance," I said.

The girl's gaze shifted from the car to me and then up to the house and yard. "Here," she said, "you might need this."

I took the flyer she offered and began reading. "Durrell's Handy Work," it read, hand done in barely legible block printing. "No job too big. Housework, repairs, yard work. Try us, you'll like us."

I looked from the flyer to where she stood waiting. "Who's 'us'?" I asked.

The girl smiled. "Me and Durrell, here. Honest. We've got lots and lots of experience. I can even get you references. Durrell's my helper. He goes wherever I go. He's no trouble and he's right good at fetching stuff for me."

She looked down at the little dog. He turned his head and stared up at me. He had huge brown eyes, but that wasn't what I noticed most about him. The odd thing about Durrell was he appeared to be grinning. His pink tongue lolled out of the side of his mouth, and his lips stretched back from his teeth into what can only be described as a huge doggy smile.

"Durrell, fetch!" The girl balled up one of the fliers and threw it across the driveway.

The dog watched the paper arc in the air and land with a soft bounce on the other side of the car. He looked back at his mistress, yawned and lay down at my feet, his furry head resting on my sneaker.

"Durrell!" She looked up at me. "I don't know what's eatin' him," she said, clearly disgusted.

"Performance anxiety, maybe," I said. "It happens." Durrell looked anything but anxious. Bored maybe, but not anxious.

She threw her hands up in exasperation and turned instead to inspect my property again. "Looks like you got somebody doin' the paintin'," she said, nodding to the ladder that stood against the side of the house. Her tone was wistful, as if work had been hard to come by and my house was yet another missed opportunity.

Durrell sighed, as if echoing her sentiments, and that was all it took.

"Can you pull vines and clear out brush?" I asked.

Her face lit with a slow smile, as if she couldn't quite trust that her luck was turning. "Why, it is one of my specialties. Like we say, 'No Job Too Large.'"

"Can you start today?" I asked.

She looked a little surprised, but said, "Now is good." She looked down at the dog. "Is now good for you, varmint?"

Durrell moaned.

"That means yes," she said. "Now is very good. My name is Della. We charge ten dollars an hour, cash only. So, what you need done?"

I looked at the backyard, trying to choose between it and the front. "I guess we could start out back and work our way forward," I said.

Della's eyes narrowed. "I'd start there, too, if I was you," she said. "Way it's overgrown, you could hide an army of outlaws back there and no one'd be the wiser."

"Exactly."

"All right," she said. "Are the tools in your garage?" I nodded. "Then me and Durrell will get started. Don't worry about showing us what to do, we know. 'Sides, you got company." I followed her gaze and found Darlene sailing up the sidewalk, pink chiffon billowing behind her.

"Looks like it's the Happy Neighbor lady or the Avon girl, one," Della said.

Durrell jumped to his feet, his stumpy tail wagging hard enough to knock him sideways, and ran to greet Darlene like a long lost relative.

"Get off me, you mangy hound!" Darlene cried.

"Darlene, don't talk to Durrell like that! He has issues," I said. Darlene hates dogs, always has, ever since we were kids and Mr. Frangini's cocker spaniel used to chase her home from school. I was going to enjoy this.

I looked down at Durrell, who hid behind my legs, grinning out at Darlene. "Good boy!" I murmured. "Terrorize the nice lady."

Della called Durrell in a tone that brooked no options, and the two of them walked up the driveway and into the one-car garage.

"Who is that?" Darlene asked.

"My landscaper," I said. "Why aren't you at work?"

"Late lunch and two cancellations." She was fanning herself with one of the flyers Della had left lying on the hood of my used-to-be car. "Wanna go shopping?"

She looked so hopeful. I felt sorry for her. "Okay. I need to look for curtains at Target, anyway. Let me run in and get my purse and we'll go."

Darlene watched Della reemerge from the garage carrying a pair of hedge clippers. "Bad karma," she said.

"You just don't like dogs."

Darlene shook her head. "Look at the way she holds those clippers. She doesn't know a thing about cutting hedges."

I scowled at Darlene. "Oh, and like you do? Give the kid a chance." I didn't wait to hear the next criticism. Darlene had probably heard Della say she looked like an Avon lady and would now proceed to hold a grudge against her forever. Karma, my ass, it was wounded pride and nothing more than that.

I left Darlene stewing and went inside to find my purse. I walked through the kitchen and stole a glance through the window at Della. She was hard at work, chopping ivy that covered a pin oak's trunk. I stopped by the bathroom, applied a little makeup and ran a comb through my hair. I looked terrible. There were dark circles under my eyes, my skin was too pale and I had wild witch hair. "Yeah, but who's going to see me?" I asked my reflection.

As it was, my attention to detail didn't matter. Darlene wasn't going shopping, at least not for curtains and not with me. When I stepped out onto the porch I found her at the foot of the driveway, apparently waltzing with Gray's partner.

There was no mistake about it; they were dancing. The detective, tall and lanky, seemed to float with Darlene in his arms, down the driveway and out into the middle of my quiet street. They stopped there and held a soft-spoken conversation. The man's arms dropped to his side as Darlene talked. He was listening attentively and nodding, as if Darlene were imparting some great secret of the universe.

Without warning, he pulled her to him again, their heads swiveled right as they extended two arms before them in a perfect tango position. The thin man started forward, winced and then stopped, grasping his lower back.

Darlene turned, followed his fingers with her own and gently prodded at the spot the man indicated. She nodded, put one firm hand on his left shoulder, and then pulled him into her with a sharp tug of her right hand. He gasped, loud enough for me to hear from my spot on the porch, and then smiled.

"That's it," he said. "That's the spot." He straightened and beamed down at my sister. "How'd you know?"

I muttered the words under my breath as Darlene said, "Well, after all, I am a professional therapist."

"Can it be fixed?" he asked her.

Darlene drew herself up to her full five feet ten inches, and smiled. "But of course," she said.

I moaned and didn't think the sound would carry, but it did. Their heads turned, focusing on the porch, and Darlene motioned me toward them.

"Hey," she commanded. "Come here." I slowly walked

down the steps and along the driveway to the sidewalk as Darlene and her new friend, the detective, stepped out of the street.

"Sophie, this is Wendell Arrow, Gray's partner. He's got sciatica and it just plays hell with his ballroom dancing. He competes, you know." She grinned up at him, clearly taken with the man.

"Pleased to meet you," I said, and extended my hand. He took it, clasped it firmly and looked deep into my eyes. "Sorry about all the trouble 'round here."

I shrugged. "Thanks, but it's not your fault. I guess these things just happen sometimes."

Darlene regarded us both with a somber expression. It was like watching an accident about to happen. You know something bad is coming and you are absolutely powerless to stop it.

"It's her destiny," Darlene said. "Why, if this hadn't happened, Sophie wouldn't have met up with Gray again." She looked at Wendell Arrow. "They're fated, you know."

"Darlene, will you stop that!"

Darlene, intoxicated with herself, turned to Wendell and continued. "Well, all's I'm saying is that I wouldn't have met you, either. And then what would've happened to your poor back?"

Wendell melted. It was pitiful to watch. He just turned into a little pile of putty in Darlene's hands. His sad eyes turned worshipful and I wondered if the backyard would be finished in time for a fall wedding. It was only a matter of time once Darlene made up her mind, and if the goofy way she was acting was any indication, what little mind she still had was already made up.

Darlene rooted around in her oversize straw bag and pulled out a black appointment book. She touched Wendell's arm gently. "Let's get you a time to come see me." She blushed, almost simpering. "I mean, professionally. The sooner we get that sciatica under control, the sooner you'll be back on the floor competing."

While Wendell pulled out his own appointment book, I studied them. He wasn't as old as I had at first thought, maybe only in his early forties. The fine lines around his eyes deepened whenever he smiled, and Darlene seemed to make him smile constantly. The hangdog look had vanished. A shock of prematurely gray hair fell across his forehead, accentuating his blue eyes. But it was his clothing that really gave him away.

Wendell Arrow lacked a woman's touch in his life. A button was sewn on to the cuff of his white dress shirt, but Wendell had used bright red thread. The shirt itself was worn and too short, exposing his bony wrists and making his long hands seem even larger. The navy-blue suit was too large, as if Wendell had long ago lost weight and never bothered to buy clothes that fit.

Darlene would not notice these things about him. She would see the way his face became handsome every time he smiled at her. She would notice that she fit into his body perfectly as they danced. She would see deep inside the man and find all the special little surprises about him that might often go unnoticed by anyone other than my sister. She would delight in him, and that is why he would love her. I could just see it happening as their heads bent together over their appointment books.

For the first time in recorded history, I felt envious. Love came so easily to Darlene. Men seemed to fall at her feet. She'd been married three times. Of course, Darlene sometimes lost interest. With Husband One and Husband Two, she'd wandered off when faced with their absorption in the material world. But Husband Three was a true love match. Still, even love is not enough when faced with an out of control uptown bus that jumps the curb. Husband Three was flattened like a pancake and Darlene had been so heartbroken.

I sighed silently. Darlene was due. It was her turn. She needed true love much more than I did, because she believed in happy endings. She painted watercolors of fairies, danced by herself at the edge of the pond behind her condominium and saw magic in the crystalline frost that appeared on late fall mornings. Who better to find true love than Darlene?

As if she'd read my mind, she turned and smiled at me. She looked delighted. "What do you think, Sophie?" she said, "Wendell's never had home-cooked Italian, either!"

Go figure. One more place at the Mazaratti table. For Ma, it would be perfection, one more lost soul brought to salvation, transported from the earthly world of preservatives and fake Parmesan cheese into the nirvana of Ma's *vitello tonnato*. What more could one ask?

"Detective, did you come here for a reason?" I asked.

"Oh, yeah." The big man's face reddened. "I'm meeting Detective Evans here." Wendell's voice took on a professional edge that made my blood run cold. I turned slowly and walked halfway back down the sidewalk toward the waiting detective.

"But he was just here. Did something happen?" I asked softly.

Wendell Arrow shook his head. "No, um, Gray, er, Detective Evans just wanted me to tell you that he's on his way back over here. He's coming with some field agents from the local Bureau office. Seems they've got a search warrant."

"What?"

It was as if I'd suddenly lost the ability to understand the English language.

Detective Arrow swallowed hard, awkward in his cheap suit and lanky body. "We don't usually give people a heads-up, but he wanted you to know and I said I'd stay so you—" The detective broke off, not finishing his sentence.

"So I don't try to hide anything?" I answered.

The detective's face flushed scarlet and Darlene was now regarding him with a raised eyebrow. He was saved from further disgrace by the arrival of no fewer than six unmarked black sedans and one beige Chevy Tahoe.

I closed my eyes. "Oh, God," I whispered. "Not again."

Gray and the lead FBI agent reached me at the same time. The agent, a young woman in a black suit and sensible, low-heeled pumps, pulled out a warrant and flashed it at me with a cool, practiced air.

"We'll need you to stay out of the house while we search," she said. "One of my agents will remain with you while the rest—"

"I'll stay with her," Gray interrupted, his tone sending the clear message that he was unhappy with the search and even less pleased with the young go-getter.

The agent turned slightly, acknowledging him only with a short nod, and stalked off, barking orders to her people as she moved relentlessly toward my front door.

"What are they looking for?" Darlene asked. It was the first time I'd ever heard her sound so short and angry.

Gray looked at me when he answered. "I don't know, really I don't. Apparently your ex-husband had something they want and they didn't find it in his office in Philadelphia or in the evidence they removed from your home before the trial. They're not talking, which is unusual. Normally, we have a pretty decent relationship, but not on this one. I'm sorry."

I looked at him, studying his face as if I could actually read him and know he was telling the truth. He looked genuine, but then, Nick had always looked sincere, too.

Darlene hovered just behind us, a worried frown on her face. For once she had nothing to say. When the front door opened and the FBI agent reemerged, Darlene came to stand beside me, shoulder to shoulder, in a move that could only be seen for what it was—my sister's way of following the old school-ground rule, "You mess with my sister, you mess with me."

Our eyes met and I smiled at her, letting her know that I hadn't missed the gesture. When the chips are down, the Mazarattis kick serious ass. I looked back at the approaching agent and felt my smile harden. We were iron. We were bigger than the FBI or Nick or indeed any threat from outside the circle.

The agent walked down the front steps and made her way toward us without tripping on the broken bricks in the walkway. She never seemed to look down as she honed in on her target, me. She bore down on us with a single-minded determination that let me know there was more to her visit than a routine search for a missing item. I figured she thought I knew where Nick was, but I was wrong.

When she reached us, she extended her hand. "Ms. Mazarrati, I apologize for not introducing myself when we arrived, but these sorts of things must go according to a very strict procedure and, well, I suppose I'm a bit guilty of following the rules and regs out to the very last detail. I am Special Agent Cole, attached to the New Bern field office of the FBI and acting in cooperation with the Philadelphia office on this particular investigation."

Her smile exposed perfect white teeth, healthy pink gums and thin, tight lips that seemed unaccustomed to being stretched into such a wide and completely disingenuous grimace. I took the outstretched hand, felt the warm, firm grip, and looked up into ice-clear blue eyes. Agent Cole's eyes told me everything I needed to know about her. She was a machine, a highly trained, well-oiled piece of equipment that would do and say anything to further her progress in both her current case and her future career.

I felt Darlene shudder and knew she'd taken the same read on the thin woman standing before us.

"Ms. Mazaratti, I'm sure you're as invested in removing yourself from any involvement in your husband's criminal activities as we are in clearing you." The words spilled out of her mouth in a waterfall of smooth, slippery artifice, sounding as pleasant and affirming as the blessing uttered by the priest at the close of Mass.

"It's ex-husband, Ms. Cole," I said, "and I think we both know I have no involvement in my husband's activities, criminal or otherwise. I haven't seen him since I testified against him in court."

Agent Cole stiffened slightly and her smile narrowed into a thin, polite line. "Of course I believe you, but the Philadelphia office apparently has some questions."

Beside me, Darlene uttered a sound that hovered somewhere between squeak and growl. Gray Evans stood on the other side of Darlene, arms crossed, his eyes hidden by tinted dark glasses that mirrored the FBI agent's face. The only indication I had of how he felt was in the tiny jaw muscle that began to work as he clenched his teeth.

I raised one skeptical eyebrow and regarded my adversary with disdain. "Agent Cole, perhaps that bullshit works on the locals, but I didn't just fall off a turnip truck. Up until you arrived, no one in Pennsylvania questioned any involvement on my part in Nick's activities. So how about you stop trying to blow smoke up my ass. If you're looking for Nick, he's not here and your team just wasted an hour they could've spent looking elsewhere."

Gray was enjoying this. A quick smirk appeared on his face and vanished just as suddenly.

"Maybe I should update you, Ms. Mazaratti. In the past several weeks it has come to our attention that your husband—"

"Ex."

"Ex-husband has access to information that may help us

in the investigation of the murder of one of our agents. According to our sources, your *ex* left that information with you. And now he's vanished and his car is parked down the street from your house. What else are we to think here, Ms. Mazaratti?"

My heart jumped into my throat and I felt my face flushing with sudden heat. I wanted to lunge for the ice princess and teach her a few home truths in a very personal way, but I stopped myself, realizing it would only prolong my new agony.

"So, what information is it that I'm supposed to have?" I asked.

Agent Cole smiled again. "Let's not play games, all right? We couldn't find what we were looking for, but that doesn't mean you don't have it. It merely means we haven't located it yet. You aren't in the clear with the Bureau by any means. If Nick Komassi gave you information in the form of pictures, papers or anything pertaining to the death of one of our officers, I'd suggest you hand it over now before the case against you becomes too strong and we're unable to cut any deals."

"I have no idea what you're talking about."

Agent Cole nodded, as if this confirmed her suspicions. "Then it would behoove you to notify us immediately the next time he contacts you. Until then, I'm putting you on notice. You are a person of interest in the investigation of a homicide. If I find that you indeed do know of the whereabouts of any information leading to the identification of that agent's murderer or are concealing information as to Nick Komassi's whereabouts, you can and will be charged as an accessory in this case."

"What does that mean?" Darlene demanded.

"If I have anything to do with it," Agent Cole said, her eyes never leaving my face, "it means she'll pull time in a federal maximum security prison."

"That is completely ridiculous!" I said. "You can't possibly think I know anything about the murder of an FBI agent."

"And I'm just supposed to take your word for it, huh? The wife of a convicted pornographer who just happens to play a starring role in most of his X-rated videos and who—"

"That's enough, Cole!"

Gray's voice, harsh and strident, was the last thing I heard before I moved, reaching out to snatch the blond toothpick up by her silky, white blouse.

"Sophie, don't!" Darlene screamed, but it was too late.

While the Academy had taught the agent well, I was powered by conviction and rage. She went sprawling backward onto the hard surface of the concrete driveway, landing with a satisfying smack that I felt as I followed her to the ground. Strong hands grabbed me from behind, pulling me backward and off the stunned woman.

I attempted to keep swinging but couldn't move. It took two people to hold me back, Gray and my new yard girl, Della, who had somehow materialized out of nowhere and was hanging on to me with a surprisingly strong grip.

Wendell Arrow was likewise engaged, holding back a snarling Darlene, who had somehow lost complete touch with her Buddhist, nonviolent side and was attempting to hurl herself onto the disoriented FBI agent.

As I watched, Darlene suddenly shrieked and began kicking violently. "He's biting me! He's biting me! Get off me, you mangy hound!"

Della's dog, Durrell, apparently thinking Darlene posed a threat to his mistress, was hanging by the hem of Darlene's broomstick skirt, tugging for dear life and growling like a menacing guard dog.

Somehow the sight of Della's mutt earnestly attacking my

sister's skirt forced me back into a more sensible frame of mind. Both of us were engaging in a pointless battle and neither of us could do much to prevent the actions of our perceived enemies. If Agent Cole wanted to hunt me in her pursuit of Nick, well, there wasn't a damn thing I could do about it, except prove her wrong. And I could only prove her wrong by either finding Nick or finding his missing "information."

I watched as Agent Cole picked herself up off the ground without any help. She looked at me with a murderous glare and seemed about to make a move when Gray Evans spoke up.

"I'll handle this," he said. "Finish up and leave. We'll talk later."

"I want her charged," Agent Cole spat, her eyes glittering dangerously.

"Rethink that," Gray said. His voice was deceptively calm but it didn't match the determined look he gave the agent. "I'll get back to you."

She seemed disinclined to take an order from a local cop, but was interrupted before she could speak by an agent who'd stepped out of the house and onto my front porch.

"Cole," he called, holding up a cell phone. "It's Regional. Says it's urgent."

She scowled at Gray, turned and slowly walked up the brick pathway to the porch, snatched the phone from the agent's hand and disappeared inside the house.

Gray murmured, "You're lucky. She could lock you up for that."

"Let her!" I said, brushing his hands off my arms. "Let her try!"

Darlene mimicked my body language to Wendell. "Yeah," she said. "Let her try!"

Della had pulled Durrell away from Darlene's skirt and was

now watching me, waiting for an opportunity to speak where the others couldn't hear her. She walked Durrell around behind me and leaned close as she passed.

"You don't wanna mess with them people," she murmured. "They don't always play by the rules."

I rolled my eyes. "No shit."

Della shrugged apologetically. "I wouldn't have interfered otherwise," she said. "I just didn't want you guys getting the short end of the stick. I mean, you are my paycheck."

"That dog is a menace!" Darlene snapped.

"He was only doing what he thought was right," Della said.

Durrell growled, but when I looked at him he was grinning. The dog was toying with Darlene, who seemed to take him very seriously.

"Damn thing probably has rabies," she said. "I don't suppose he's had his shots, has he?"

Della hesitated. "Well, sure he has," she answered, but she didn't sound very convincing.

I glanced at Darlene's leg and saw that Durrell had only torn her skirt, not actually bitten my sister. "Just go on back to work, Della. My sister's fine." I gave Darlene a look and moved to block her view of Durrell and his owner. If Della lingered, Darlene would be asking for proof and that would only lead to disaster, as I was almost certain Durrell hadn't seen a vet in recent history.

Gray and his partner had moved away from us to stand on the sidewalk next to Gray's Tahoe. Gray held a cell phone to his ear and seemed to be having a heated conversation with the person on the other end. Wendell's attention seemed split between his partner and my front porch, where FBI agents were emerging from the house empty-handed. As the team began walking down the front steps, Wendell nudged Gray and motioned toward the agents.

Agent Cole led her people down the walkway, ignoring me and seeming to focus on the line of black sedans parked in front of the house. I had the ridiculous urge to jump out at her, just to see her reaction, but managed to stay where I was. How could these people think I had anything at all to do with concealing evidence in an FBI agent's murder? In any murder, for that matter?

"Hey," Darlene said suddenly, "I just thought of something. I bet I know why they're here. That girl in the backyard, she's the agent. That's why they searched the house. They think Nick whacked her and then hid the murder weapon in the house or something!"

I rolled my eyes, barely restraining myself from giving my sister a head whap.

"Darlene, that girl was no FBI agent."

She nodded, giving me her patronizing, know-it-all smile. "That's how they do it, Sophie. They disguise themselves so your regular John Q. Citizen doesn't have so much as an inkling of their true identity." My sister shook her head, closed her eyes and sighed. "The pain those people must go through, the attention to detail. You got to admire their dedication, Sophie."

"I'm telling you, Darlene, nobody goes to that much trouble to fit into a situation. The girl had tattoos on her hands. Tattoos are forever, Darlene."

My sister opened her eyes and smirked. "Temporary, Sophie. They do it all the time. And her haircut, just another indication of her attention to detail. No, that's not what impresses me. What gets me about her is she was willing to pump her tits up to a double D cup, all for the job. You know that's what they call it, don't you, 'The Job'?" Darlene sighed. "That surgery's painful, Soph. You gotta wrap them puppies up tight for two weeks. I should know…."

"Oh please, Darlene, don't tell me! You should know because you're a professional therapist, right?"

Darlene looked wounded. "No, Sophie. I know because Patrice Rodantini's boyfriend paid for her to have it done and she said there wasn't any man on earth worth enough to make her go through that kind of pain again, and she's had four kids! They split you in half when you have kids, Sophie, and still Patrice thought her D cups hurt worse!"

I considered kneeling down and banging my forehead against the concrete driveway.

My sister sniffed, her attention turning now toward Wendell Arrow as he and Gray slowly began walking toward us.

"Of course," she murmured, "there are some men who'll just drive you to do anything for them." She was smiling now, that stupid, simpering, on-the-market smile I call The Husband Catcher smile.

"They all have their little weaknesses, the poor dears," she said softly.

"Patrice tell you that one, too?" I asked.

Darlene flashed me her "go to hell!" look. "No, Sophie. That one I know from three marriages and because I am, above all else, a trained professional therapist!"

Chapter 6

Pa spent most of his life in the dark. He worked third shift at the naval shipyard, leaving home after we were all in bed and returning most mornings before dawn. He worked on the huge, gray ships, spending most of his time buried deep in their depths. The only colors in Pa's world back then were the sparks that flew between his welding iron and the red-hot metal before him. Was it any wonder that he dreamed of blue skies, water and sunshine?

The day after Pa retired, my parents moved to North Carolina. At first, none of us kids understood. How could our parents leave the only world we had ever known? How could they turn their backs on the house we grew up in and leave the relatives and friends from the old neighborhood? How could they leave us? We just couldn't figure it out, and then, one by one, we followed them, at first to visit and then to live. It was the magic of light and color that bewitched us.

Pa sits with Ma and eats his breakfast each morning on a sunporch overlooking the canal that leads out to the Neuse River and Pamlico Sound. He smiles and touches Ma's hand. "Look at that," he says to her, as if it were suddenly all new again. "Now this is what they mean when they talk about the American Dream," he says. "This is what life is supposed to be about, eh?"

Pa and his new cronies take to their powerboats and the river most mornings, motoring along in a loose convoy that will end with coffee, conversation and a doughnut at the marina. They gather, a pack of bandy-legged old men, to discuss the woes of the world and how it was all done so much better in their day.

"I'm going to see the old guys," Pa said to me when I first came to visit. "They need my help this morning." This was always followed by details. "Mort's wife is too sick to drive him to his colonoscopy." Or "Dave don't know how to switch out the motor mounts on his engine."

I would nod, thinking how nice it was they had such expertise. It only took a few days to realize that it was much more important that they had each other. "Old age ain't for sissies," Pa said, echoing the common sentiment. "We gotta hang tough."

When I told Gray about Pa, he smiled and nodded, as if this was the only way to approach aging. We left Della and the carpenter working in the afternoon sunshine and drove the seven miles out of town to my parents' development without ever discussing the events of the past twenty-four hours. The FBI search of the house, the body in the backyard and my torched Honda were put on a very temporary and tenuous hold as we went through the motions of having a normal family evening.

I needed to occupy myself with routine activity so that m·

unconscious mind could mull over the topic of Nick and what I would need to do to get rid of him and the problems that haunted me wherever I went. Gray seemed to pick up on this instinctively and was content to drive out to my parents' home without once asking any of the questions I knew would come later.

He pulled into my parents' driveway and nodded as he stepped out of his Tahoe, surveying my parents' house and yard, as if this were all as he expected.

When Pa came to the door, Gray shook his hand, saying, "Nice place you got here. Is that a Sportfish docked out back?"

Pa smiled. "After dinner," he said, "I'll show you."

Joey appeared in the doorway behind Pa, his face breaking into a wide smile as he saw us.

"What? You're not gonna let them in, Pa?"

Behind my brother I could hear the sounds of Joey's children laughing and calling to each other while their mother, Angela, tried to calm them, her voice a soft contrast to my brother's. There were other voices, Wendell, Darlene and Ma, and the smells of home—sweet tomato sauce, fresh sourdough bread, oregano and garlic.

I looked at Gray to see if I could read his reaction, wondering what it was like to be a newcomer among such chaos. But he was watching me. The blue-gray eyes sparkled and the tiny lines appeared at the sides of his mouth as he smiled.

"So this is you," he said, nodding toward the family room and past the children into the kitchen. "Yeah, it fits."

Joey broke the moment, pulling Gray into the center of his family and making the introductions. I poured a glass of Chianti and stood back, watching. I could still hear the reminder in a distant recess of my mind, whispering "like a fish needs a bicycle," but I was too far gone to pay much attention. I just wanted to keep the moment as it was, even if it only lasted this one night.

Joey walked up after a while and stood beside me, looking on as Gray noticed Angela setting the table and went to help.

"So," Joey said, "you like this guy, right?"

"Joey, I don't even know him."

My brother scoffed. "What's to know? He's a good guy. What, you gotta have his life history and résumé before you know if you like what you see?"

"Joey, come on."

Joey knew how I felt. I never had to say a word. He knew how I felt about Nick and he could read how I felt about Gray. Still, I wasn't ready to commit myself. There's something about saying the words out loud that dooms you to your admissions.

"He's a nice man treating me nice because he knows you," I finally said.

"Bullshit!" Joey said. "You like him, he likes you. This ain't no science project."

"What, Joey?" I said, turning away from the dining room to glare at him. "You following Darlene now? You think it's fate, my destiny to be with this man?"

Joey shrugged. "All's I'm saying is give him a chance. Don't write him off on account of you think you're a loser so you're quitting the game before they even draw up the teams."

"Mangiamo!" Ma cried, walking from the kitchen to the dining room with a steaming platter of braciola. "Everybody, come on!"

She set the platter of stuffed flank steak in front of Pa's place at the head of the long oak table, the table that had been in our family since the first Mazaratti stepped foot in America. Platter after fragrant platter emerged from Ma's sanctuary and was placed on the white lace tablecloth.

Darlene sat like a queen holding court in the middle of us, with a dazed but pleased-looking Wendell beside her. She attempted at least twice during the meal to pump Wendell and

Gray about the car bombing, the FBI and the murder. The first time, she said, "About that body," but Joey cut her off before she could go any further.

"*Marone a mia*, Darlene, have some respect, there are children here. This is dinner. What is wrong with you?"

Wendell smiled indulgently at my sister and Gray ignored her.

Darlene looked sufficiently chastised, a first for her in my opinion, but five minutes later she was at it again. "How exactly do you torch a car?" she asked, her voice pitched to sound innocent, but I knew my sister and innocence had nothing to do with each other.

"Darlene!" Pa said, warning her off the topic.

"Okay," she said, "be that way. I was just trying to make conversation. How about this—how do you become an FBI agent? Do you think they need any trained professional therapists?"

Joey looked at me and rolled his eyes. When I glanced at Gray, I noticed he hid a grin behind his white linen napkin. Ma grabbed a wooden spoon right out of the *pasta e cece* and attempted to reach Darlene, but she was safely out of range and the swat fell short, landing on Joey.

"Ma, would you watch with that?" he cried, nursing an imaginary bump on the top of his balding head. "I'm trying to grow hair here."

We all laughed, lulled by Chianti and too much good food. The daylight began to fade and as it did the candles on Ma's table bathed the room in a soft golden glow. Long after the children had excused themselves and wandered outside to play, we sat there listening to my parents tell stories from the old days.

When we all finally rose from the table and said our goodbyes, it was after ten o'clock. As Gray pulled out of the driveway and into the street, a satisfied sigh escaped his lips. "That was wonderful," he said. Even without looking over at him,

I could feel him smiling in the dark. "Does your mother always cook like that?"

I laughed. "You charmed her this morning," I said. "She lives to feed people, but for you, she went all out."

"I don't think I will ever forget that meal," he said, starting to slip into his bad Italian accent. "I think I can feel my blood turning Italian even as we speak. Look at me," he said. "I've got red sauce everywhere. I even look Italian now, don't I?"

I laughed at him and we drove on, crossing the span of bridges that looked like three spaghetti noodles swooping down on the twinkling lights that marked my new hometown. For a few hours I had lived in a dream world again, where people actually got fresh starts, where no one remembers you for your mistakes, and where good memories are the only ones that last.

When he pulled up in front of my house, Gray cut the engine and came around to open my door. In his right hand he held a long-handled, police-issue Maglite.

"You'd think there'd be streetlights out here," he said, shining the beam on the ground in front of us.

I pointed toward the post at the end of my driveway. "The heat from the fire must've popped the bulb." But I wasn't focused on the light. I was feeling the nearness of him and wondering what would happen when we reached my front door.

Gray took my hand, pulling me from the car and then guiding me onto the sidewalk. The contact made my head work overtime. Would he try to kiss me good-night? I imagined everything—the way he would take me in his arms and hold me, the strong reassurance of his chest as I leaned into him, the taste of his lips, the smell of him. I was driving myself crazy, and yet I couldn't stop.

I heard myself saying, "It's been a lovely evening. Good night." But the words never left my head. For some reason, I just couldn't let go of his hand, not just yet. I would make myself let go, really, I would. Because this was so wrong, for so many reasons.

We walked silently past my burned out car and up the steps to the front porch. My heart was banging against my chest and I was almost certain he could hear it. If not, then he could certainly feel the way my body trembled. Where had the self-possessed Sophie Mazaratti gone? And who was this silly girl that seemed to be left behind in Sophie's body?

It was totally dark. The humid air hung thick and damp over the neighborhood, making me long for air conditioning and a cold drink. In the distance, heat lightning flashed and a low rumble of thunder followed, then continued, growing louder as Gray and I approached the front door.

"What the hell?" he said, and moved his flashlight in the direction of the noise. Durrell the dog stood blinking and baring his teeth in the harsh glare.

"Durrell," I said softly, "what are you doing here?" I stooped down and held out my hand. The dog's tail began to thump on the wooden floor and he stood, attempting to walk toward me, but yelping as he moved.

"Gray, I think he's hurt," I said.

Gray knelt by my side and slowly stretched the back of his hand toward the snarling animal, offering him a sniff and talking in a low soothing tone.

"Hey, boy," he whispered. "It's all right. You hurt, buddy?"

Durrell whimpered and crept slowly forward, favoring his back left leg. "You think he's been hit by a car?" I asked.

Gray shrugged, inching up to pat Durrell's shaggy head, his fingers stroking the dog's back and then moving down to check the injured leg. "It doesn't feel broken," he said, "but that doesn't mean it isn't. Who does he belong to?"

I told him about Della and Durrell's Handy Work, "No Job

Too Large." As a welcome breath of air crossed the porch, a square of white paper wedged in the front door rustled. I stood up and pulled it down. Gray would've stopped me, I think, but he turned too late and the paper was already in my hand.

"'Your carpenter was working on the eaves and fell off the ladder. I'm taking him to the emergency room. He thinks his leg is broke,'" I read aloud. "'I'm leaving Durrell here. Be back later.'" If the scrawl was any indication, the note had been hastily written. Della hadn't even taken the time to sign her name.

"You hear that?" I asked Durrell. "Your mom will be back as soon as she can. In the meantime, how's about we try to make you a little more comfortable?" The little dog wagged his tail and took a few cautious steps toward the front door.

Durrell's eyes were sad, but his tail wagged furiously. He limped up to me, sat and placed a paw on my knee. I could've sworn he was trying to reassure me. "I bet you're hungry," I said.

I turned to Gray. "He and Della lead a rough life. If I hadn't hired them, they'd be eating Velveeta cheese and Minute Rice for supper. I think they live in a trailer somewhere out in the county. Of course there's no air-conditioning. Hell, they might not even have electricity."

"She tell you that, did she?" Gray asked, his expression clearly skeptical.

"Not exactly, but I imagine that's pretty close to how it is for them."

Gray studied Durrell for a moment, then looked back at me. "You sure are a sucker for a sob story," he said, but he smiled. "Durrell here says he walks twelve miles to obedience school, uphill each way, and when it snows, he skis."

Durrell's lips stretched back toward his ears in a huge dog grin. His long tongue hung out of his mouth and his white teeth gleamed.

"Okay," I said, looking down at the dog. "Point taken. Durrell, I'll feed you but I'm not cooking anything." Behind us, I heard Gray chuckle.

I unlocked the door, pushed it open and felt around for the light switch. Durrell began to growl again, this time louder than before. He wiggled his way through my legs and plunged into the darkened house. He was barking like a maniac.

"Durrell!" My fingers found the switch, but when I flipped it, nothing happened.

"Wait here," Gray said, passing me and moving through the darkened living room. He switched the flashlight to his left hand as he sought out the Beretta that sat nestled in its holster.

I ignored Gray's order and followed him, crossing the almost empty room and making a beeline for my bedroom.

Durrell stopped in the doorway, his bark becoming a menacing growl. Hackles slowly rose on his back as his entire body began to tremble. My heart pounded as my skin began to prickle with little shocks of fear. Was someone hiding in there?

Gray's flashlight moved slowly around the darkened room. I picked up a faint odor, sickly sweet and unmistakable. It smelled like my uncle Vito's butcher shop, a childhood memory that had been all but forgotten until now. At that moment, Gray's light hit my bed and caught a puddle of dark red blood that covered my pillow.

I heard someone gasp, realized it was me, and moved forward as Gray did, approaching the bed and the tiny figure lying on the pillow. It was a doll. Gray didn't attempt to touch the carefully arranged tableau, and held his arm out to keep me back.

"Don't come any closer," he cautioned. "I'll call the forensics people in a minute."

As we studied the scene before us, Durrell began to wail,

a high-pitched, single-noted howl of unmistakable fear. I bent down and attempted to comfort the frightened animal, but I found myself unable to look away from the bed. The doll on the pillow was fashioned from modeling clay, her hair made to look black and curly like mine. She was naked and posed so that she lay in the center of the pool of blood. A spot of the red liquid dripped realistically from a wound made by a tiny dagger stuck dead center in the doll's chest.

Without warning, Gray's pager went off, making us both jump. The shrill beeping seemed to echo in the high-ceilinged room, followed by Wendell Arrow's voice, clear and unhurried.

"Gray, give me a call ASAP," he said in his low, deep drawl. "I heard back from NCIS."

Gray reached into his pants pocket, pulled out his flip phone and hit a button. He paused, and then said, "Yeah, I've got something for you, too. Call the crime scene unit and y'all come on over to Sophie's house." He listened briefly to something Wendell said, flipped the phone shut and turned to me.

"Kind of spoils the evening, doesn't it?" I said. I tried to smile, tried to act like death threats were an everyday occurrence, because above all else, I didn't want him to see how scared I was. I didn't want him to think I was the kind of person who fell apart and needed the protection of a big strong knight in shining armor.

Gray frowned. "That's an understatement," he said, watching me. "Are you all right?" He gestured toward my bed.

I felt a wave of nausea wash over me, intensify and then recede.

"Yeah," I said, trying to keep the tremor out of my voice. "I'm just a little surprised, that's all. I didn't know Nick was the artistic type. Guess he learned that in prison."

"You think Nick did this?" Gray asked.

"Who else? I haven't been in town long enough to make

any enemies—well, other than Agent Cole, and she doesn't look like the artistic type, either. And Nick's car was found around the corner. I think everything that's happened in the past twenty-four hours is courtesy of my ex-husband."

"Even the woman in the backyard?" he asked.

I thought for a moment. Was Nick capable of murder? I closed my eyes, envisioning him as I'd last seen him, escorted from the courtroom after sentencing, his face contorted with rage and hatred. "Maybe," I answered, "but I don't see a connection there. The woman in the backyard didn't look like Nick's type, but then I guess I don't know what Nick's type is anymore."

"How did you—" He broke off, probably not wanting to ask, *How did you make such a foolish mistake?* or *How did you get taken in like that?*

"It's all right," I said. "You wouldn't be asking anything that I haven't already asked myself." I wandered a few steps away from the bed and pretended to examine the antique perfume bottles on my dresser. "I could say that I was young and too naive to know better, but that isn't true. I was twenty-six when I met him. And it wasn't love at first sight, either. I think I made myself fall in love with him."

Gray had turned to watch me, but hadn't moved from his post by my bed. "Why?" he asked.

Harsh truths are sometimes best faced and answered in the dark. For some reason I felt almost like I was sitting across from Father Thomas in the confessional booth of my childhood church, St. Mary of Everlasting Peace.

"I think I thought it was time to grow up," I said. "I was still living in my parents' home, working but not out on my own. I was tired of the slick men I'd been dating, the bad boys and the pretty men. I saw Nick and bought the package. I thought he was reliable—you know, steady and predictable."

"That must've been some act he put on," Gray said.

I heard a car pull up to the curb outside. Wendell Arrow arriving just in time to keep me from confessing to every sin of ignorance I'd ever committed in my life.

"Maybe I just wanted to believe in him, because when I look back, I see there were warning signs, some little but some not so little at all. Maybe I was too scared to try making it on my own." I shivered. "I hate to admit it, but I think back then I believed my parents when they said a woman needs a man to take care of her. But that was then…"

"And this is now," Gray finished.

"Yeah, this is now."

Before either one of us could say anything else, Wendell Arrow knocked on the front door, driving Durrell crazy. The moment was successfully broken. As Gray headed toward his partner, I lagged behind, staring at the doll on the bed and thinking how easily Nick had reinserted himself into my new life, ruining it as surely as he had ruined the old one.

I had wanted to tell Gray more. I wanted him to see and feel things as I had almost twelve years ago: Nick, short and plain, but somehow charismatically charming; the succession of men before him, predictable in their unreliability; and finally, my family, mired in tradition and unable to see my desperation. I wanted Gray to know where I'd been so he could see that I never intended to let myself get caught up in that kind of entanglement again.

I heard the two men talking in low voices, but as I entered the living room, they stopped.

"What's up?" I asked.

Gray looked at me, then back at Wendell. "The crime scene unit is en route," he said, his professional voice replacing the personal tone he'd used with me all evening.

Wendell looked ill at ease. He fidgeted with the pockets

of his suit coat, adjusted his tie and fingered the clip on his holster. "I'll just go out front and wait for them," he said. "I'll check the panel box after they dust it. Somebody probably just hit the circuit breaker. Shouldn't take no time at all to get the lights back on." He tipped his head briefly to me and was gone.

"What is it?" I asked. "There's more, isn't there?"

Gray was staring at me. Even in the darkened room I could see the somber expression on his face and feel the change in his demeanor.

"Sophie," he said, "we need to talk. How about we go sit at the kitchen table?"

I felt an uneasy caution spread through me, and protective walls slid into place around my heart.

"Sure. Good idea. Let's talk." I knew I sounded like a stilted version of myself.

I led him into the kitchen, following the beam of his Maglite, took a seat at the table and waited.

"We've got an ID on the woman in your backyard," he said. "Her name is Connie Bono." He looked at me, eyebrow raised, waiting for me to indicate that I knew her. I shook my head and he went on. "She played guitar in a garage punk band that was actually starting to make a name for itself. But she couldn't quit her day job on what the band made, so she supported herself dancing in a strip club in Chester."

"Chester, as in the suburb of Philadelphia?" Surrounded by oil refineries and the airport, Chester was a pretty rough neighborhood. I imagined the type of clubs where Connie Bono could've danced—rough biker bars with frequent fights and more drugs than alcohol.

"Yeah," Gray answered. "Chester, Pennsylvania." Then he dropped the hammer. "She was Nick's girlfriend. In fact, that was the address he gave his parole officer."

The familiar sense of dread overtook me. My hands began to shake and I hid them beneath the table so Gray wouldn't see.

"What else?" I asked, because there had to be more. With Nick there was always more bad news.

"Connie Bono's skull was fractured," Gray said, his voice even and unemotional. "She was hit with a tire iron. We recovered it yesterday in a Dumpster behind the public housing complex."

I shuddered. "God," I breathed, "that's awful."

Gray gave no indication he even heard me. "The tire iron came from the trunk of Nick's car. It was the same type of tire iron that comes standard with his Mercedes."

"So Nick killed his girlfriend?" Nick a murderer? I just couldn't see it, not yet. "You know this? You found his prints on the tire iron?"

Gray's eyes burned into me. "No, Sophie, your prints were the only ones we found on the murder weapon. There were smudges, but no other prints."

There, he'd said it. This was the bad news I'd seen sitting on his shoulders, the whispered information Wendell Arrow had passed on to him in the living room before I got curious and wandered out to see what they were discussing. Now there were doubts, suspicions that might have been easily laid to rest had I not been Nick the Criminal's ex-wife.

I could guess at the thoughts forming in Gray's head. First Nick betrays her, he'd think, and then he comes to town with his girlfriend. Maybe Sophie even invited them, luring them into her new neighborhood. Maybe she wanted to set it up so it would look like Nick did it. Maybe Sophie, the deranged ex-wife of a pervert, killed Nick, too. Or maybe she was so shocked to see Nick following her that she acted without really thinking. After all, Sophie's prints were all over that tire iron....

The more I tried to think for Gray, the angrier I became.

When I could stand it no more, I dropped my hands, palms down, onto the table. The sharp slap echoed like a gunshot in the semidark room.

"For as long as I have known Nick, he has been incompetent. He couldn't make it as an accountant, he couldn't make it as a criminal and he couldn't even make it as a husband. Nick couldn't change his tie, let alone a tire. So when that car had a flat three years ago, guess who changed it?"

I didn't wait for an answer. "Me. Stopped by the side of the road in a bad neighborhood at night, I changed that tire, all by myself. And did I call that man to come help me? No I did not. I didn't even have a cell phone back then because my husband was too cheap to buy one. He knew I was going to meetings and classes at night, but my safety wasn't worth the price of an emergency cell phone. I let him convince me that we were too poor. And you know what? We were. Don't you wanna know why?"

Again I didn't wait for Gray's answer. "Because Nick was using all of our money to buy cameras so he could spy on me and every other innocent woman he could find in our neighborhood. And when he ran through the decent women, he bought whores. I was too stupid to see any of it. So, yes, those are my prints on that tire iron. No doubt about it, but does that make me a murderer? I think not. It just makes me stupid and gullible."

"Sophie, I—" Gray said, but I interrupted.

"I don't want to talk to you anymore," I said. "Process your 'scene' and leave me alone."

I walked off, out the back door, across the porch and down the steps. There wasn't even anywhere for me to go, not really. I had to stick around. My home was a crime scene and I was a suspect.

Gray didn't try to follow me and I was surprised to find

that it hurt to suddenly find my world empty again. I could've made excuses for him, valid ones, too. He was on duty; the slamming doors of the crime scene van were proof enough of that. Still, I wanted to be trusted instantly. I wanted him to instinctively know that I was incapable of murder. I wanted a miracle, someone and something that didn't exist.

I don't know how long I stood in my tangled backyard. I was dimly aware of the sound of another car door slamming. I could hear voices and music thumping from cars that cruised past my street and headed into the projects. I could smell the honeysuckle and jasmine that bloomed on my back fence, their scents almost masking the briny salt air. And I could hear people inside my house, taking pictures, dusting for prints and talking to each other as they went about their jobs.

When I did hear the screen door softly slam on the old back porch and the sound of footsteps descending the steps, I didn't turn around.

"I couldn't sleep because I was so happy," Darlene said, sounding miserable. "I thought maybe you couldn't sleep, either, so I thought I'd drive by and just see." Her voice trailed off as she reached my side and stretched one hand up to rest softly on my shoulder. She squeezed gently. "I guess the night didn't end so good, huh?"

I didn't say anything.

"But Gray's here. He'll take good care of you. Nick wouldn't dare hurt you with him here."

"Gray thinks I killed that woman," I said softly. "He says she was killed with Nick's tire iron and that my prints were all over it. Oh, he'll take care of me, all right. He'll probably slap cuffs on me and read me my rights!"

Darlene wrapped her arms around me and squeezed softly. "Oh. honey," she whispered. "Gray doesn't think you killed Nick. He's smarter than that."

"I don't know about that," I said. "After all, he's not an architect."

Darlene giggled. "Rome wasn't built in a day," she said. "And he is a man. What do they know?" She breathed deeply. "I smell something wonderful," she said.

"I know. It's whatever that vine is that's blooming on the back fence."

Darlene sniffed. "No, that's not it." She inhaled, held her breath and then exhaled. "I think someone's smoking pot." She stopped, looked confused and then shook her head. "Whatever it is, it's making me hungry. Let's get out of here and go to the Waffle House."

That was my sister, always hungry. It didn't matter if she was happy or sad, angry or tired, the first thing Darlene turned to for comfort was food. Of course, Ma was responsible for that. It's the Italian way.

"I should stick around," I said. "I need to know what they find out. I need to find Gray and get this mess straightened out."

Darlene wasn't having it. "That is so like you. You're too responsible for your own good." She grabbed my arm and started pulling me toward the driveway. "Let him wonder. Vanish. If you're a suspect, act like one. Become a fugitive." Darlene giggled again. "Let him hunt you down. Let him push you up against his car and frisk you. Maybe he'll tell you to 'assume the position.'"

"Darlene, have you been drinking?"

She did a little dance step at the bottom of the driveway, twirling in her peasant skirt and pulling me with her. "No, girl," she said, "I am high on life."

"More like you are high on lust," I muttered.

The darkened street was empty. The police were all happily ensconced in my home, dusting and photographing themselves silly. Darlene and I crept down the sidewalk to her di-lapidated Chevy, giggling like teenagers sneaking out past curfew.

"Would you like to swing on a star," she sang softly.

"No, actually I would like to keep my feet on the ground," I answered. "Enough of this head-in-the-clouds business."

She fit the key into her ignition and cranked the engine. The car sputtered to life as she patted the dash and said, "Good girl!"

"Wait!" I cried. "Who's going to lock up the house when they're done?"

Darlene rolled her eyes. "Locking your house doesn't seem to be doing you much good," she said. "Maybe leaving it un-locked will change your luck."

I looked back up at the house and the figures moving around inside. "Relax, will ya?" Darlene said. "We'll be back long before they're done."

"What if we're not?"

Darlene sighed. "I'll call Wendell on his cell and tell him where we are, okay?" She looked over at me, smiled and pat-ted my knee. "Now take a deep, cleansing breath and release those toxins. You are such a bundle of nerves lately!"

"You think, Darlene? You think I'm under just a little bit of stress here?"

We were driving down the darkened street, turning toward the Waffle House. It seemed that every other person in New Bern had long ago gone to bed, and yet it wasn't even mid-night. Darlene hummed as if this was just an ordinary outing. Nothing seemed to bother her. Darlene was in love.

"Scattered, smothered and covered," she said after a few moments.

"Excuse me?"

"That's how I want my hash browns—scattered on the grill, smothered in onions and covered with cheese."

She looked at me, saw the expression on my face and reached with one hand into the depths of her mammoth straw bag. "All right, I'll call him right now and tell him where we are."

She acted like this was a big ordeal, but I knew her better than that. She was dying to call Wendell. As I watched, she punched one number on her phone and waited.

"You have him on speed dial?"

Darlene rolled her eyes. "Oh yeah, like I could memorize his number, then dial it in the dark while keeping my eyes on the road? I think not. This is the only practical way to do it."

"Oh yeah, what number is he on your speed dial?"

There was a slight hesitation. "One." She made an exasperated face at me. "Well, it's not like anybody else had that number. I was waiting. Arrow starts with *A*, the first letter of the alphabet, and one is the first—"

"Oh, can it, Darlene!" I said.

"Hey, honey," she said suddenly, her voice changing into sweetness overdrive as Wendell answered his cell. "Listen, I'm taking Sophie up to the Waffle House. She needs a little cheering up. You know, in light of what's happened and all."

Darlene listened for a long moment, then said, "Yes, well, Gray didn't make it any better by practically accusing her—" Wendell must have interrupted because Darlene broke off and appeared to be listening. "I know, but there are ways of asking questions without—" She listened again, her expression changing from one of pure joy to a concerned frown.

"You know, honey," she said, stressing the word honey until it sounded more like an insult than an endearment, "if I didn't know better, I'd swear you were on his side."

Great, I thought, now I was rocking Darlene's boat. I reached over and touched her arm, but she was talking again.

"Fine!" she said, her tone sounding curt and irritated. "Be

that way! But just you remember this, Detective Arrow, karma will win out and goodness prevail! You just wait and see. What goes around comes around, buddy!"

She shoved the phone back into her bag and took a curve so fast the tires squealed. We came to a halt right in front of the Waffle House entrance.

"What did he say?" I asked.

Darlene smiled, but it was forced. "He said he doesn't much care for waffles, and to tell you they'll wait until you get back to lock up."

"Darlene, what did he really say?"

Darlene gripped the wheel with both hands, unshed tears glistening in her eyes, reflecting the lights in the restaurant windows.

"Not a damn thing worth mentioning," she said, and burst into tears.

Chapter 7

Darlene dropped me off in front of my house an hour later. She wouldn't come in when she saw the unmarked car parked where Gray had left it. Instead she waited, motor idling, until she saw the front door open and Gray step out onto the porch. She drove off then, accelerating as she flew out of town, anxious, I figured, to put as many miles between herself and Wendell Arrow as possible.

Durrell shot past Gray, taking the steps at a dead run, barely able to control himself as he skidded to a stop at my feet. He flipped over onto his back and lay there wiggling and whining until I scratched his belly. At least someone was glad to see me, I thought.

"Oh, stop feeling sorry for yourself," I muttered.

"Did you say something?" Gray had moved from the front porch to the driveway, edging closer as I stooped to greet Durrell.

"No. I was talking to the dog."

"Can't say as I blame you," Gray said. "Right now I'm guessing you feel like he's the only one on your side. Well, him and your sister."

I didn't answer him. I straightened and looked him right in the eye, but I wasn't about to speak one unnecessary word to the man.

"Listen, Sophie," he said, "I'm sorry if I hurt your feelings but—"

I didn't want to hear this. "You were just doing your job," I said. "You were asking the questions that had to be asked. No big deal." I pushed past him and started up the drive to my house.

"Sophie, I—" Gray began.

"Detective, it's late," I said. "If you have more questions we can cover them tomorrow."

Durrell growled, keeping Gray from pursuing me.

"I don't think you should stay here alone," he said.

I turned around and faced him. He looked haggard and worn. For a moment I wanted to relent and be nice, but when I remembered that he wasn't entirely certain that I wasn't a murderer, I froze.

"Durrell's here for the night," I said.

Gray attempted to pass Durrell, but the dog growled louder, this time showing his teeth and placing himself between the two of us.

"He's just a little mutt," Gray said. "He won't stop someone who's serious."

Durrell must've understood because in one quick lunge he sank his teeth into Gray's pant leg and hung on for all he was worth.

Gray yelled and tried to pull the dog off, but Durrell stuck fast. A light went on in the house across the street and then in the house to the left of mine. Gray yelped again and I flew off the steps.

"Don't shoot him!" I cried.

That brought the neighbors out of their houses. Gray was shaking his leg in an attempt to lose Durrell, and hopping around on one foot.

"You're going to hurt him, Gray! He's just a little dog!"

"Sophie, you need some help?" one neighbor called.

I reached Gray and Durrell just as the dog's strength gave out and he surrendered his trophy. This coincided with a fierce shake of Gray's leg that sent the little dog flying into the front yard.

"You hurt him!" I cried, bending to retrieve the yelping Durrell.

"Hurt him?" Gray said. "Look at my pants!"

The neighbors were slowly closing in, murmuring angrily among themselves. The man next door stepped to the front of the little group, hands on his hips and an angry scowl on his face.

"Now look here, mister," he said, "you got no call to go kicking a harmless little animal. You'd best git!"

Gray turned on them, his badge flashing as he pulled his suit coat aside. "I did not kick that dog," he said. "I shook him loose, that's all."

"Police brutality," a tiny gray-haired woman called from the back of the group. "We're mad as hell and we're not going to take it!" she added.

"Well, I don't care if you are the po-lice," my neighbor said. "There's no call for cruelty to animals."

I looked down at Durrell, nestled in my arms, trembling. He looked up at me, his huge brown eyes shining, and I could've sworn he was smiling. He seemed to be enjoying every single moment of Gray's predicament.

"Good night, Detective," I said, my voice as firm as I could make it.

I whirled around and left him at the mercy of my angry neighbors. "Now that's karma for you, Durrell," I said. "What goes around just came around and bit Mr. Evans in the ass, huh? Tell me we can't take care of ourselves!"

Durrell moaned, content to lie in my arms and be carried inside. Once we were safely behind the thick wooden door, I locked it and watched from the front window as my so-called destiny started his car and slowly drove away.

A few minutes later, the house got spooky. Durrell and I decided not to sleep in my bed. The pillow and its grim warning had vanished, probably forever in the custody of the New Bern Police Department, but there was grimy graphite powder everywhere and the entire room was a mess.

"Durrell, this is a message from the Goddess," I said. "It's an omen telling me that the time has come to finish the master bedroom and quit sleeping in the dining room."

Durrell yapped once and I took this for agreement. I studied the room and the furniture in it. Up until this point in my life, I'd never really given it much consideration. The dresser and the bed were over 150 years old, brought to this country by my maternal great-grandparents. Babies had been born in that bed. People had taken their last breaths in that bed. Nick had slept in that bed. That alone was reason enough in my book to never sleep there again.

"Durrell, I'm trying to start a new life," I said. "This bed is part of the past. It has bad memories. Tomorrow we find a new one." Durrell didn't care about tomorrow; he was tired now. I pulled a quilt out of the closet, then grabbed a spare pillow and pillowcase. Tonight it was going to be the sofa.

We wandered through the house switching off lights—not all of them—and checking doors and locks. I peered out the kitchen window into the darkened backyard and imagined Nick hiding in the bushes, waiting for his opportunity to kill me.

"I think I could take the little shit if he ever showed him-self," I muttered to Durrell. Somehow talking to the dog made me feel less afraid.

"He's puny, you know," I added. "Couldn't be over five foot six, and he hasn't worked out or exercised in years. I figure one or two good kicks and he'd be a goner."

I began to wonder if he'd spent much time in the prison yard, working out with weights. I pictured all the tattooed men they always show on TV, and tried to imagine mild-mannered Nick, thick glasses and all, sweating as he pumped iron. I tried to envision him with muscles, transformed at age forty-nine into an Adonis. It was simply impossible. I could take Nick on my worst day and still not break a sweat.

Durrell and I curled onto my ancient couch and pulled the quilt up to cover us. I hit a button on the TV remote and flipped idly through the channels, surfing for background noise to keep me from imagining that every creaking board I heard was a burglar breaking into the house, armed with knives and guns.

We settled for a *M*A*S*H* rerun. Durrell seemed to iden-tify with Klinger, while I took more to Hawkeye. We drifted off into an uneasy sleep sometime after the third episode, right before Hot Lips kissed Radar and just after Klinger eloped with the colonel's horse.

I awoke to the smell of coffee—fresh, right-under-my-nose coffee. Durrell was gone, but Della was back, sitting in an armchair across the living room from me. She was sipping from a chipped mug and watching me.

"Jesus!" I cried, sitting upright. "How did you get in here?"

Della looked faintly surprised. "Well, the back door was unlocked and standing wide open," she said. "It wasn't too hard after that. Durrell was there waiting for me to let him out, so I opened the screen door and out he went. I figured you might want coffee so I just came in and made a pot."

"What time is it?" I asked.

Della shrugged. "A little after six-thirty, I'd reckon. Don't want to wait till it gets too hot to work. Best to start early."

"I locked that door last night," I said. "I checked it twice, too."

Della shrugged. "Well, it wasn't locked when I got here a little while ago." She frowned at me. "You know, you didn't wake up when I made the coffee, and you snore. A truck could've run through here last night and you wouldn't have known."

No, I guess not, I thought. "You didn't see anyone else around, did you?"

Della shook her head. "Nope, just Durrell." She looked around the living room. "You got a lot of work to do in here, too," she said. "And your carpenter won't be back anytime soon."

"Oh, yeah," I said, rubbing my face and reaching for the coffee mug she'd brought for me. I felt bad about forgetting the accident. "How is Clem? Was his leg broken? What happened?"

Della sighed. She was wearing the same jeans and tight T-shirt she'd worn the day before, and her hair was even stringier, if that was possible. "I'm going to tell it just like it happened," she said, her voice tired and thin. "Clem said it was my fault. He said I tripped over the ladder and that shook him off. But I swear I wasn't anywhere near that ladder. I had my back to him and I was working on that patch of ivy behind the garage."

She paused to take another sip of coffee, shaking her head as she did so. "It was probably Durrell what done it. He's clumsy as all hell, the worthless shit."

I stiffened. "Durrell was a big help to me last night," I protested, thinking of the way the dog's sharp little teeth had fastened on to Gray's pant leg.

"Anyhow," Della continued, "Clem took a god-awful fall. He was still knocked out when I got to him, but he wouldn't let me call the ambulance or nothing like that. I finally convinced him to let me drive him to the hospital and they admitted him."

"It was that bad?" I asked. Nowadays it took an act of Congress to get admitted to the hospital.

Della nodded. "Yep. He has a heart condition and they said his heart wasn't beatin' right. Then there was the concussion from the fall and his leg bein' broke in two places. As soon as he's stable enough, they're going to do surgery."

I felt awful. Santa Claus had been seriously injured working on my house. Maybe we were jinxed. Or worse—maybe Clem's fall hadn't been an accident.

Della brightened a little. "But don't worry," she said. "His wife is with him. And me and Durrell are going to finish clearing up the backyard today so we can start on the carpentry work tomorrow."

I couldn't quite organize my thoughts. It seemed to me that my new home was cursed. Dead bodies. Terrible omens and threats. Clem injured on the job. What in the world was going to happen next, and did I want to stick around to find out?

"Maybe we should hold off a day or two," I said.

This got Della's attention. "Oh, no," she said, sitting upright and leaning toward me. "We can't do that!"

"Listen, I know you could use the work, but—"

Della rushed on, interrupting me. "Lord, yes, me and Durrell could use the work, but that's not the only reason. You're just getting a little discouraged, that's all," she said. "It happens all the time in these kinds of projects. Things hit a snag or they don't go quite like you'd planned, so you think it's all a big mistake, but listen, if you give me two days to really get goin' here, I promise you, it'll turn around."

Della's face twisted into a mute appeal. Durrell picked

that moment to return, nosing his way through the screen door and running across the room to jump up onto the couch. Between the doggy kisses and Della's soft "Please?" I gave in.

"Two days. If nothing bad happens then we'll evaluate the situation, but if one more thing happens to jinx this project, it's over."

"Thank you!" Della cried, abandoning her coffee and jumping to her feet. "You won't be sorry," she added.

"Listen, before you start back, I need to ask you something."

Della froze halfway out of her seat and slowly sank back down onto the couch. "What?"

"Is there any possible way that what happened to Clem wasn't an accident?"

Della's face furrowed into a belligerent frown. "Hey, now wait a minute! Durrell and me may need the work, but we are not—"

"Not you! I mean, did you see anyone hanging around? Walking by? You know, someone who could've—"

"Oh, I see! Man, I thought you thought… Well, never mind. No, I didn't see anybody, but then, like I said, I was pulling vines and had my back to him."

I nodded and stood up. "Good. That's one less thing I have to worry about, I guess."

Della got up, too, eager to be off. "Durrell!" she called. "You lazy idiot! Get out here! We got work to do!"

Durrell started to ignore her, but when she whirled around and glowered at him, he changed his mind. With a sudden leap he flew off the couch and followed her to the backyard. His limp made him lurch like a drunken sailor, but he didn't seem to feel any pain.

I grabbed my mug and climbed the stairs to the second floor. The new central air-conditioning hummed efficiently, making the high-ceilinged rooms bearable in the midsummer heat. Today I was not going to be a victim. Today I was going to make a bedroom, come hell or high water.

I wandered to the end of the hall and stood there studying the huge master suite.

"The good news is that the floors are in good shape," I said aloud. "The bad news is…" I looked around. "Everything else." The walls were a filthy peach color, but the plaster wasn't bad. The windows were covered with twenty years' worth of grime. The closet probably housed dead animal carcasses beneath the piles of old newspapers and trash, and the adjoining bathroom was almost a total loss.

I wandered down to the kitchen in search of paper and pen to start detailing a supply list, and noticed the answering machine light blinking.

"What now, huh?" I groused, and hit the playback button.

"Ms. Mazaratti, this is Shirley Garwood at Duncan Elementary. The central office forwarded your résumé to me and I would like to speak with you tomorrow morning at 9:30, if that's convenient. I know it's short notice, but I'm trying to leave town for vacation and would really like to finish staffing the school before I go. The number here is…"

I scrambled frantically for a pen, scribbling her number on a piece of paper towel and then picking up the receiver to call the woman back. I'd gotten wrapped up in renovating my house and completely forgotten that I'd sent my résumé out to the school district's office. I reached the school's answering machine, confirmed my appointment and hung up. It was 7:15.

By eight, I was showered, dressed in a navy-blue suit and pumps, and ready to go bowl Principal Garwood over with my experience, charm and credentials. Then I remembered I had no car. I sank down into a kitchen chair and cradled my head in my hands. "Some days it does not pay to get up," I moaned.

I wasted another twenty minutes calling the insurance company and then the car rental agency. The rental agency had cars, all right, but they couldn't deliver one until after noon.

I grabbed the phone book and began looking up cab companies. "Shit! I'm not going to make it!" I said, letting the sound of my voice echo off the kitchen walls.

"Hey, watch the mouth, Sophia Maria!" Joey stood framed in the back porch doorway, his oldest, Emily, behind him. "What's the matter with you, a kindergarten teacher talking like a longshoreman?"

"Sorry, Em," I said, glancing at my niece. "I didn't know anybody was around."

Joey's shy daughter gave a tiny little grin that lit her eyes and just as quickly disappeared. Joey stepped into the kitchen and helped himself to a cup of coffee.

"What's with the drug addict you got working in the backyard?" he asked. "I thought we were gonna work on that, me and you."

"Joey, do not make assumptions like that. She isn't a drug addict. She's just down on her luck, so I gave her a job."

Emily returned, but didn't say a word. She was staring out the kitchen window, apparently making up her own mind about Della. "Cute dog," she said softly.

"See, Joey?" I said. "How can a girl with a cute dog be all bad?"

Joey sighed. *"Stunade!"*

I noticed Joey and Emily were both dressed in old clothes and wearing work boots and ball caps.

"You guys incognito today or what?" I said, indicating their outfits. "Is it Blue Collar Day at the college?"

"Hey!" Joey said. "Have some respect for my institution. It's summer. The boys left for camp yesterday and Angela's working. We're bored, so here we are, ready to help."

Emily didn't seem at all enthusiastic.

"You're not teaching summer school?" I asked my brother. "Must be nice!"

"I'm a college professor," he said. "Everybody knows we don't work. Besides, summer school doesn't start till next week. I'm taking a few days off."

I looked at Joey and knew he was lying. Joey can never look you in the eye when he lies. It's all that time spent as an acolyte. It ruins you for lying.

"Gray called you, didn't he?"

Joey studied the contents of his coffee cup. "I don't know what you're talking about, Soph."

"Joey, you already know what's in your coffee cup. Look me in the eye and tell me, did Gray call you?"

Joey exhaled loudly and looked up at me. "Yeah, so he called, but that isn't why I'm here. I'm here to help."

"All right, Joey," I said. "You want to help? Good, because I have a job interview in twenty minutes and I don't have a car. You can lend me yours. On my way back from the interview, I'll swing by Home Depot, pick out paint, a kit to turn that decrepit tub into a shower and a mirror. Then I'll come here, pick you two up and you can drop me and Emily off at the car rental place before you help Pa install the fixtures."

"Pa's coming?" Joey asked.

"I figure he will after you call him and tell him you need some help."

Alarm was beginning to grow in my brother's eyes. "What are you two gonna be doing while we're working?" he asked.

I grinned at Emily. "Shopping," I said. "I need a bedroom ensemble, new sheets, a comforter, pillows, curtains and any other doodads my niece and I come up with."

Joey took a big swallow of coffee. "All right," he said. "I give up. Here're the keys."

I snatched them out of his hand, grabbed my portfolio and ran for the door. I flew across town, turning into the parking lot behind Duncan Elementary School with only three minutes to spare. It was barely enough time to reapply my lipstick and certainly not enough time to deal with the man in the car that had suddenly materialized behind me.

I took my time pretending to inspect my appearance in the rearview mirror, hoping the guy was an employee and not what he appeared to be, which was trouble.

I looked up at the school. An elderly Mercedes sedan was the only car in the lot and it was parked right beside the front door. Principal Garwood was probably the only one working. I glanced in the mirror again and tried to determine the size of the man in the front seat, but he was just far enough away to make the details impossible. One thing was for certain, it wasn't Nick behind the wheel, not unless he'd grown both wider and taller.

I took a deep breath, closed my eyes for a moment and cleared my head. This was not necessarily a bad situation. I needed to find Nick. I needed to know what everyone seemed to be looking for and I needed to know who was looking. I could either wait for them to come to me or I could bait the trap and go on the offensive.

"No time like now," I whispered, and slowly opened the car door.

I stepped out onto the pavement, gazed up at the school and then deliberately avoided looking at the car behind me. I walked to the trunk of Joey's Toyota, unlocked it and raised the lid. It made a perfect cover for a mugging, keeping anyone inside the school from seeing me clearly and thereby giving my follower the opportunity to approach. I had no doubt that catching me alone was on the agenda.

I leaned deep into the trunk, well aware that the slit in my tight pencil skirt left plenty of leg exposed. I made a show of tossing things around and appearing to search for something with great concentration. I was prey.

I looked in the chrome reflection of the trunk lid, studying the car behind me. The driver's side was now empty. I saw him coming for me, moving quickly, and readied myself for the confrontation.

I waited until he was almost upon me before turning, my fingers laced together, arms held stiffly in front of my body, my elbows locked to form a human sledgehammer. I swung as I turned, bringing my fists up to hit him dead center beneath his chin. His teeth chattered as the blow caught him off guard, and the fight was on.

He had a gun but I had the training to disarm him and the adrenaline to complete the task. I grabbed his right forearm with both hands, twisted his wrist and turned into him, pulling his arm down onto my thigh, slamming his wrist sharply against the bone and then watching as the gun flew out of his fingers.

He was everything Nick wasn't—strong, mean and completely capable of killing me—but he was no match for a year of intense Krav Maga training. I jerked my knee up hard into his crotch, giving it every ounce of force I could muster, and brought him down to the hard surface of the parking lot. It was late June; the asphalt was smoking hot despite the relatively early hour, and my attacker shrieked as I grabbed a hunk of his hair and drove his head, face-first, into the gravel-and-tar griddle.

I straddled his back, my skirt forced to ride well up my thighs, and leaned forward to apply pressure to his carotid artery. It was, I'll admit, overkill, but I wasn't taking chances.

"Did Nick send you?" I asked.

The thug moaned and retched, sick from the blow to his testicles.

"Don't even think about hurling on my new pumps," I warned him. "I've got a job interview and you're making me late."

My captive said something unintelligible.

"Where is Nick?"

This time he made himself understood. "I don't know."

I laughed, the adrenaline rush bringing me close to hysteria. "Did he send you?"

"No!" This time it was more of a howl than a moan.

He was getting ready to fight again. I could feel the muscles tensing beneath me as he marshaled his strength.

"You don't want to do that," I said, rocking forward to grind his face harder into the ground. "Now," I said, feeling the fight ebb out of him, "if Nick didn't send you, who did?"

There was silence until I hit the painful pressure point behind his jaw with my thumb.

"All right, all right! Ease up! I'm just doin' what I get paid to do. I get a phone call from a guy. He says there's money in it for me if I come down here and get what you're holding for Nick."

"What are you looking for?"

"I don't know," the man whined. "He didn't tell me. He just said to watch for Nick and take anything he got from you. He said if Nick didn't show I was to put it to you until you handed it over. He said you'd know what it was."

I rocked forward on the man's head again, ignoring his shriek of pain, and leaned down close to his ear.

"This is your lucky day," I said softly. I reached out and touched the spot behind his jaw, waited until I knew he was losing consciousness, and then released my hold. "I could kill you and it wouldn't take any effort at all, but I'm gonna let you go on account of I want you to take a message back to your boss."

When the man didn't say anything, I continued. "Tell him to back the fuck off. I don't have what he wants and I don't know where Nick is. Tell him I'll kill the next one he sends."

The man moaned.

"Should I take that for a yes?" I asked.

Before he could answer, we were interrupted.

"What in the world is going on here?"

A tall, middle-aged woman holding a baseball bat in one hand and a can of Mace in the other stopped a few feet from us, watching warily as she slowly raised the spray and pointed it at my attacker's head.

"Ms. Garwood?" I asked.

"*Doctor* Garwood. And you are?"

"Sophia Mazaratti."

Shirley Garwood's eyes widened slightly and she nodded to the man on the ground. "And this gentleman?"

"I don't know. I think he wanted my purse, but don't worry. He realizes now he made a mistake, don't you?" I said, tightening my grip on his collar.

"Yes, ma'am," the thug moaned.

Dr. Garwood's finger tightened on the Mace trigger. "I'll call the police," she said. She turned to run inside, stopped and looked back at me anxiously. "Will you be all right if I do that or should I spray him?"

I smiled up at her. "We'll be fine," I said. "I handle these sorts of situations all the time."

She nodded. "I heard the Philadelphia schools were rough," she said. "I'll be right back."

When the principal was safely inside the building, I jumped off my attacker and pulled him to his feet.

"Get the hell out of here before she comes back," I said, "and make sure you tell your boss what I said."

The big man stumbled off, fell into his sedan and roared away just as the principal returned.

"They're coming," she said, her voice trailing off as she watched the Taurus spin out onto the street in front of the school.

"He got away," I said, brushing gravel off my skirt.

"Are you all right?"

I nodded. "You'd better call the police back and give them a description of the car. Maybe they can catch him. I think he was driving a late model Lexus."

Garwood nodded and dialed the number. By the time she'd finished, I had my portfolio in hand.

"Do you still want to interview me?" I asked, giving her my very best kindergarten teacher smile.

"Oh, absolutely, we could use someone like you around here!" She chuckled softly. "I hope you won't find us too boring."

I followed her into the school, smiling to myself. Boring…now, I could use a bit more of *that* in my life.

By the time I returned home from the interview, my house had been taken over by Pa and a crew of gray-haired men. Ma was in the makeshift kitchen, swearing at the microwave and hauling plastic food containers out of brown paper bags.

"Pezzo di merda! Figlio di puttana!"

"Ma!"

Ma shrugged. "You have no kitchen," she said. "How am I to feed so many people with no kitchen?"

"Ma, what people?" I asked. But the answer was becoming evident the longer I stood there. Pa's friend Mort trooped through the kitchen, trailed by two or three other men. They wore carpenter's belts and were laughing at something Mort had called over his shoulder.

Ma pointed to them. "There are at least six men up there with your father and your brother. And that device, that thing, that…" Ma's voice sputtered to a halt as she tried to conjure up the right description of my microwave. "We will have to serve antipasto and sandwiches." She said this as if it were an indictment of her talent as a chef. She threw up her hands. *"Marone a mia!"*

Emily walked to her grandmother's side, threw her arms around the little woman and kissed her cheek. "Don't worry, Grandma," she said. "Later we can have a party to thank them and you can cook and cook. I'll help you."

Ma has a soft spot for Emily. She smiled in spite of herself and turned to me. "You should take a lesson," she said, reaching out with the lightning quick hand to smack the air near my head. I ducked and ran, leaving her and Emily to their preparations, following the sound of male voices and the smell of fresh paint that wafted down to me from the second floor.

Pa was in the bathroom, leaning over the new toilet, seating it into its final resting place, an unlit cigar hanging out of his mouth. Joey, stripped to his undershirt, was down on the floor by Pa, caulking the area around the new fixture. An unlit cigar hung from the side of his mouth, too.

They looked up briefly when I stopped in the doorway. "Rough interview, huh?" Joey asked, looking at my torn hose and dirty clothing. "Must be a rough school."

"Flat tire," I said, not wanting to let Pa know about my earlier adventure.

"Joseph," Pa said, "pay attention. You're getting the caulk everywhere."

Joey looked away reluctantly, not ready to believe the flat tire story, and returned to caulking the toilet.

Pa watched as Joey worked, now and then nudging him if he thought Joey wasn't doing it just right. "The old guys were over at the house this morning when Joseph called," he said. "I brought some of them with me—hope you don't mind."

I looked over my shoulder and saw my bedroom transformed, with scraped and patched plaster and stripped wood trim. I felt a hard lump form in my throat and thought for a minute that I might cry.

"Pa, no, I don't mind. How can I ever thank them?"

Pa grunted. "You can say thank you and be done with it," he said. "Besides, it looked like rain. What else could we do? You got paint?"

"I forgot. I'll go after I change."

He straightened up and walked over to me, giving me The Look just like he had when I was back in Catholic school and he suspected me of not telling the whole truth.

"Sophia," he said, his voice stern, "I got to hear it from your brother about last night. This is a great disrespect to your father."

Great. Just great. I shot Joey a dirty look, but his back was to me. "I didn't want to call and risk getting Ma. She doesn't need to know about this. It'll worry her. You two didn't tell her, right?"

Pa looked as if he was going to whack me. "What, I look like suddenly I'm too stupid and senile to think?" Behind him I saw Joey's shoulders move up and down with suppressed laughter. He was enjoying my agony.

"No, Pa. Nothing like that, it's just that—"

"Fagetaboutit," Pa said. "I want to know when you're coming home tonight."

I sighed. "Pa, this is my home. I'm staying here. If Nick is behind this the police will find him before he can do any more damage. I'm fine, Pa."

"Where's the detective?" Pa demanded.

"Working, Pa. He's a cop, not a bodyguard."

Pa was coated in a fine film of dirt and sweat. His arms and shoulders, the muscles ropey with age, were still broad and strong. I knew where he was headed. If I didn't come home or come up with a plan, my father would move into my house and protect me himself. In fact, my father and all of his friends would become my new roommates.

"Pa," Joey said, "it's going to be fine." I breathed a sigh of relief, thinking that Joey was going to come to my defense.

"I talked to Gray this morning. He'll be here tonight as soon as he gets off work. We're going to stay a couple nights to make sure Sophie's all right."

Pa nodded. "And when you're not here and Gray's not here, I'll be here," he said, sounding like we didn't have an option. "Me and the guys, we'll be here."

"Pa, you don't need to do that. I'll be fine!"

He switched his unlit cigar from one side of his mouth to the other and gave me The Look again. "You need help, Sophia. Look at this place. It's a wreck! You got Nick chasing you down like prey and on top of that, you ain't got a job. You think about that, Sophia? What are you gonna do for money? You can't live on your looks forever. You need to be out hunting for a nice, safe teaching job, not hanging around this place getting in our way."

I gazed at my father and sighed. "I had an interview this morning, Pa. I'm looking! But you're right, I could use some help around here, I don't need bodyguards though. Just having people around will keep Nick from bothering me. He's really a coward, Pa."

Pa snorted. "You let me handle him, *cara mia*. He won't bother you no more after I'm done with him!"

He walked past us, out into the hallway and across to what was about to become my bedroom. "You guys up for a little guard duty?" he asked, then stepped inside the room and closed the door.

"Joey," I said, turning back to my brother, "you made that up about Gray and you taking shifts, right? You know I can handle this by myself. Don't sweat it."

Joey just stared at me. "No, Soph, I did not make that up. Pa's right, you can't stay here by yourself. That's why Gray and I worked it out. I knew you wouldn't move back home. You're too stubborn. What else was I supposed to do?"

Ma's voice came bellowing up from the first floor. *"Mangiamo!"* I was rescued from further caretaking by lunch. I followed my brother, father and the crew of old guys down the steps, thinking about my predicament. As I saw it, I really had no other alternative. If I wanted any chance at a new life I was going to have to find Nick Komassi and see that he went back to prison where he belonged. In order to do that, I had to prove Nick had killed Connie Bono and was now hunting me.

"I can do this," I muttered to myself. "I'll have it all wrapped up by tomorrow." Of course, I had no idea how I was going to accomplish this feat, but life was too short to spend it trapped under a self- and family-imposed house arrest.

Chapter 8

Pa and his old guys were in heaven. It was a love affair between them and my wreck of a house. As the day wore on, they found more and more to do. My kitchen became the central planning and recruiting hub, and old men flocked to my neighborhood, called by Pa or one of his cronies.

One new recruit, Alfonso, knew plaster. He arrived wearing the old guy standard uniform, a V-necked T-shirt, baggy chino pants, a worn leather belt and ancient work boots. The unlit cigar was an extra, provided by Pa.

Another old guy materialized and studied the wooden floors. His name was Frank and he looked like a hot dog—tall, thin and bald, with a ruddy complexion.

"We do the upstairs floors tomorrow," he said. He turned to Pa. "You'll need to rent a floor sander, only one if nobody else has floor experience." There was silence from the crew of old guys. Joey finally spoke up. "I don't have experience, but I'd like to learn." Joey had the muscle to help the old guys, and they needed him but would never have admitted it. Apprenticing him was the only way they could take him in and save face.

Frank studied Joey. "You don't fly hot when I tell you do it over or go slow, right? I don't need no hotheaded kids, now."

Joey, forty-two years old, clamped down on his cigar. "Yes, sir," he said, his jaw working overtime to keep his mouth shut. I figured a week working for the old guys was good for at least one book of poetry by next year. Maybe even a novel.

Pete, the landscaper, Pa's tennis buddy, came in from surveying my yard. He was a little man with a fringe of white, close-cropped hair that couldn't hide his tanned and freckled scalp. Pete laughed all the time and rode his ten-speed bike everywhere he went in Pa's neighborhood.

Pa saw Pete as a challenge. He felt Pete didn't accurately understand the great seriousness with which we should face life. Pa was always presenting some glum fact of their current reality to Pete and waiting expectantly for Pete's cherubic face to fall as he realized the gravity of old age. Pete never came through for Pa. He always saw the best in every situation.

"Sophie," he cried, stepping into the kitchen, "your yard is beautiful! My God, the plants you have out there. And that girl! Honey, she's working her tail off for you.

Pete took a long swig from a plastic cup of water and turned to me. "There are old rose bushes back there," he said, "lining the picket fence. I think if they're uncovered, they'll bloom. In fact, I think you should pull all that honeysuckle. Now the pachysandra in the front's another matter."

I must've looked dazed, because Pete nodded. "Don't worry. Della and I can handle it."

Outside, Durrell barked. Della yelled at him to stop and I

heard Darlene squeal. "Get down, you mangy hound! I do not like you! I don't like any dogs and I especially don't like you!"

Before I could intervene, Darlene flew in through the front door. She was wearing a swirl of blue colors, a multilayered paisley dress that gave her a gypsylike appearance. Long strands of colored beads and tiny bells tinkled as she moved quickly to shut the door behind her, closing out the offending Durrell.

"Is he always like that?" she demanded. "Does he do that to Joey and Pa? He doesn't, does he? It's just me he's after. That dog wants to eat me! He's vicious, I tell you. He ought to be locked up. That evil girl should be locked up along with him. She doesn't even try to control him."

"Darlene, if you would stop running from him, acting like a crazy woman, Durrell would leave you alone. The way you dart around and squeal, he thinks it's a game and you're playing with him."

"Bullshit!" Darlene said. "He wants to eat me."

I shrugged. Convincing Darlene that Durrell was basically harmless was an exercise in futility. Her mind was made up. "So, the workers are here today?" she said. She was progressing through the house toward the kitchen, in search of a late afternoon snack. She stopped in the doorway, taking in Pa and the old guys, then seeing Emily and Joey.

"Hi, everybody!" she called.

The old guys smiled, every single one of them.

"Mort, how's your wife?" Darlene asked. "Frank, are you wearing sunscreen when you go out? You know, with your skin type you're a prime candidate for melanoma." She beamed at sour Alfonso. "I hear you and the wife are taking the grandkids to Disney World. You are just the bomb!"

The old guys ate Darlene up with a spoon. She wandered into the center of the group, grabbed a cookie and managed to speak to and touch every man in the room. She beamed at them, honestly delighted to see them, basking in their attention and doling out plenty of her own.

Joey sidled over to me. "Next, she'll be signing autographed pictures so they can pin them up in their workshops."

Darlene walked past him on her way to the refrigerator. "I heard that, Joey," she said in an undertone. "You just wish you charmed them like I do, don't you?" she whispered, the smile never leaving her face.

"Bite me, Darlene," Joey said, and smiled just as sweetly.

My sister poured herself a tall glass of milk, took my arm and pulled me into the living room.

"I have been giving the situation a great deal of thought," she said. "And now I have a plan." Darlene paused for effect. "We need to have a séance."

"What?" This was *so* Darlene.

"I'm serious," she said. "There is a disturbance in the energy. Someone must've died here with unfinished business."

I thought of Connie Bono. "Of course they did, Darlene. Have you forgotten the body in the backyard?"

Darlene shook her head. "Not her," she said. "I mean, sure, she's got things to tell us, but that's not where the disturbance is coming from." Darlene closed her eyes and swayed gently back and forth for a few moments. Her eyes popped open and focused on my face.

"Sophie, you are such a literalist. If you can't see it, you think it doesn't exist. I'm telling you, we need to contact the afterlife, and if you don't do it with me, I'll do it by myself." She looked around the room as if scouting a location. Her eyes settled on the fireplace.

"Okay, Darlene, we'll have a séance, but in the meantime I need to find Nick."

"That shouldn't be too hard," she said.

I gave her the evil eye. "You think?" I said. "The police can't find him. His parole officer can't find him. I don't expect the spirit world to have much luck, either."

Darlene rolled her eyes at me. "Not the spirits, stupid. They're for finding dead people."

"Then why do you think it won't be hard to find Nick?" I asked.

Darlene sighed, looked over her shoulder toward the kitchen and pulled me closer to the fireplace.

"Because I saw him this morning as I was leaving for work. That's what I've been trying to tell you."

The fact that Darlene had tried no such thing was beside the point. "What do you mean you saw him? Did you talk to him? Are you sure it was Nick?"

Darlene nodded. "It was Nick, all right. I'd recognize that sleazeball anywhere. He was parked down the street from Ma and Pa's place, watching it. But when I drove by and saw him, he took off."

"Did you call Wendell? Did you warn Ma and Pa?" The idea of Nick stalking my parents terrified me. I never expected him to go after them.

Darlene pulled herself up straight and gave me her haughty act. "I am not calling that Wendell Arrow," she said. "He isn't at all who I thought he was. And I didn't tell Ma and Pa because he's looking for you, not them. Besides, they'd just freak out and Pa would kill Nick if he saw him."

"And that would be a bad thing?"

"Well, yes," Darlene said. "Pa would have a criminal record. His karma would be forever twisted. We can't have that. The Virgin Mary can't give you immunity from homicide. Pa would take the universe into his own hands if we didn't watch him."

"You're sure it was Nick?"

"Absolutely," Darlene said, "one hundred percent positive."

"What was he driving?"

Darlene closed her eyes, screwed up her face as she concentrated and seemed to think for almost two minutes. At last her eyes opened and she looked at me.

"I don't know," she said. "It was a car and it was a sort of royal blue. Oh, and it was dented up pretty much."

"That's beautiful, Darlene. That is *so* helpful. I'm sure we can narrow that down and find him immediately."

Darlene stamped her foot and glared at me. "I am not a mechanic," she said. "I am a professional therapist."

I counted to ten and let the car question drop. "All right, so Nick is in New Bern and he's looking for me. Why did he kill his girlfriend?"

Darlene was poking around the fireplace, testing the bricks with her fingertips and running her hands along the wall.

"Maybe they were spying on you and Nick realized he wanted you back," she said. "Or maybe because he found out she lied to him about her breasts."

"Darlene, shut up! What are you doing?"

She straightened and looked over her shoulder at me. "I am searching for secret passageways. These old houses had them, you know."

"Darlene, this is a cottage. Secret passageways are found in big houses, like mansions and castles."

"Well, I was just trying to help," she said. Her feelings were obviously hurt. "You never know."

I tried to smile. "No, you never know."

"Never know what?"

Darlene and I whirled around at the sound of Gray's voice. He stood in my front doorway, a small duffel bag in hand. He smiled when I looked at him and I felt my insides begin to melt.

"What can we do for you, Detective?" I asked.

My tone unsettled him. He looked around and seemed, for once, uncertain. "Didn't Joey tell you I was coming?"

"Joey did, but I told him that wouldn't be necessary."

Gray advanced a few steps into the room, moving toward the spot where Darlene and I stood.

"Sophie, I want to do this."

Darlene sighed, as if this were the culmination of a life's dream on her part. "That is so…wonderful," she breathed. "I wish a man wanted to protect me."

I stepped on her foot and glared at her. Had she forgotten that Gray and Wendell thought I had murderous potential?

"Ouch!" Darlene cried.

This brought Joey to the doorway. "It's about time you got here," he said to Gray. He looked at me and added, "Della said to tell you she's going home. You can pay her at the end of the day tomorrow."

Gray smiled at Joey and came even farther into the room. "Sophie says she doesn't like the plan," he said.

"She likes the plan just fine, don't you?" Pa stood in the dining room doorway, his dark eyes focused on me, waiting for me to deny it so he could pack me off to his house.

They were all looking at me, waiting for me to say something. The way I saw it, I had no choice but to go along. I shrugged. "I was just saying that it would be a huge inconvenience for Gray."

"So then you could come home," Pa said.

"It's no trouble, really," Gray said. "This is a good place for me to be, in terms of getting this case settled. Maybe Nick Komassi will come snooping around and I'll be here to talk to him."

"Then it's settled," Joey said. "Good, because me and Emily have to head home and, Pa, I know you gotta get all these guys back."

Joey hustled everybody out the door, but returned within a minute, sticking his head inside the doorway and giving me a meaningful look.

"Hey, Soph, maybe you can tell Gray about your job interview," he said. "I'm sure he'd like to hear all about it."

When Gray looked interested, Joey threw his parting shot. "Yeah, Gray, it must've been a hell of an interview because she came back with her clothes all dirty, saying she had a flat tire. Funny thing," he said, pausing to look at me. "My spare tire hasn't even been used! Imagine that!"

Before I could kill him, he was gone, leaving me alone with Gray.

"Did something happen, Sophie?"

I forced a long deep breath into my lungs and exhaled softly. If I told him, he'd side with Joey and Pa, wanting me to go home and stay "safe" while the big, strong men dealt with Nick. And it's not like I could help the investigation by telling him. I didn't actually find out anything he and the FBI didn't already know. At least, that's how I saw it.

"Okay, okay," I said, and sighed again. "I didn't have a flat tire. I saw a stray dog get hit by a delivery truck. The dog took off into the woods, but I knew he was hurt, so I followed the poor thing."

Gray's eyebrow rose into a skeptical arch. "But you didn't find him, huh?"

I shook my head and smiled the kindergarten teacher smile. "No. I was such a mess! I just couldn't bring myself to tell Joey I was chasing a hurt dog. He would've given me hell about trying to put a bleeding animal in his immaculate car."

"You're sure that's all it was?" he asked.

"Yep. That's all it was."

Gray and I were facing each other across the living room. I sat on the sofa and he took the wingback chair. Neither of us spoke. I looked around the room, letting my attention slowly settle back on him. He was watching me, still trying to decide whether or not he believed me. His blue-gray eyes seemed electrified with intensity, as if he were trying to communicate something without speaking.

I met his gaze and held it for a moment, then broke the silence. "About yesterday, I know you had a job to do," I began. "I know that's what you were trying to do."

He nodded and seemed relieved. "I didn't mean to—"

I interrupted. "Misunderstandings happen when two people don't really know each other well, don't you think? And since you know a lot about me maybe I should know more about you. Don't you agree? I mean, I should know so that I can communicate with you more effectively and avoid situations like the one we had yesterday. I mean, if two people have a common ground and understand where each one is coming from, then they have a better working relationship." I was babbling. Why was I babbling?

Gray's face relaxed into a warm smile that lit his eyes and softened the hard angles of his jaw.

"Sophie, you don't need a reason to ask me about myself. All you have to do is ask. Now where would you like to start? Let's see…how about this? I was born about ten miles from here—"

"Tell me about your girlfriend," I said, interrupting. As soon as the words left my lips, I wished like hell I could've taken them back. Nothing like looking obvious. "I mean, you know about my ex, so…"

I was relieved when he stopped me. "What girlfriend?"

"Joey said you had a girlfriend. He said she comes to watch your games." I could've shot myself for even asking, but on the other hand, I felt a foolish flicker of relief start in my chest. Maybe there wasn't a girlfriend, after all.

Gray's brows furrowed even more before the lights went

on. "Oh, he must've meant Tina." He grinned. "Yeah, she's hot all right, but she's not my girlfriend, she's my sister. I don't have a girlfriend at the moment."

I nodded, hardly daring to believe what was both my good fortune and deepest fear: this man was absolutely available. I closed my eyes for a second, muttering my mantra silently. *Like a fish needs a bicycle.* Then I stopped, realizing that I was smiling, and forgetting for a second the man who sat across the room watching me.

"More questions?" he asked, his voice suddenly husky, deepening just as his eyes seemed to darken with both intent and interest.

"Oh, right," I said, trying my best to sound like a cheery kindergarten teacher. "I have lots of questions. For example, where did you go to—" I broke off when I saw him move.

He pushed himself up out of his chair, striding toward me with a purpose that was all too clearly communicated when he stopped just in front of me, grabbed my hands and slowly pulled me to my feet.

He cupped my jaw in his hand, tilted my chin and stared deep into my eyes. Without another word, he lowered his head and kissed me. His lips were soft, gentle at first, but then as he felt me respond, his hand moved to cradle my neck. He pulled me close with a hunger that took my breath away.

It was a long, slow kiss that kindled feelings I thought were long forgotten, if indeed ever experienced. When he drew back, he regarded me with a warmth and concern that overpowered me.

"Does that answer any of your questions?" he whispered.

I felt need and longing rise up through my body, as if coming from some deep and unfathomable place inside myself. In that one instant, the Sophie Mazaratti that I wished to become was born. I slowly stretched my arm out, bringing it up along the side of his face, letting my fingers stroke the sharp angle of his cheekbone. I smiled as my hand circled his neck, pulling him back down to me, watching as his face drew closer and his lips parted. And then the new Sophie Mazaratti kissed Gray Evans right back, with all of the passion and desire that had been waiting forever to bubble up and escape.

"Yes," I said at last, "that answers quite a few questions."

Gray smiled and pulled me even closer. "Good," he said. "I am all for open and honest communication."

He was pulling me down onto the couch when the bullet tore through the window, passing right through the spot where we had been standing and slamming into the wall next to the dining room doorway.

"Shit!" He shoved me down onto the floor, covering me with his body. "Damn!" He was feeling for his holster and not finding it. "I left the fucking gun in the duffel bag! Stay here!"

Gray pulled the heavy coffee table across my body like a barricade, yanked the lamp cord out of its socket and began doing a frog crawl across the room in the general direction of his bag.

I heard the zipper slide and the sound of him fumbling around in the darkened room for his weapon. Without a word, he was on his feet and gone, running toward the back of the house. I heard the soft click of the back door and knew he was outside.

I couldn't just lie there and wait to see what happened next. I rose up, crouched low and looked around the dark room for a weapon. Nick Komassi was about to learn just how much his ex-wife had grown up since he'd been gone.

I snatched a candlestick off the mantel and made my way toward the door, staying low and away from the front window. In the distance I heard a siren start up and begin moving toward the house. Outside there was absolute silence and then the sound of muffled footsteps crossing the front porch. I gripped the candlestick tightly, bracing myself in the first defensive Krav Maga stance Vinny had ever taught me.

My heart was beating so hard I figured even Nick would hear it. I crept toward the front door and stopped. The doorknob rattled softly. I held my breath, raised the candlestick and got ready. The door began to give and slowly open.

The sound of footsteps, running along the far side of the house and down the narrow passageway that separated my house from my neighbor's, stopped the intruder's progress through the front door.

"Tony," a low voice called. "Cops. Let's go."

The front door clicked shut, someone ran to the edge of the porch and then I heard a dull thud as the intruder jumped, landing beside the living room window. Who was Tony? I wondered.

"Shit!" a male voice called, not Nick. "Down the side. Go out the back way!"

I didn't wait. I ran out the front door and down the steps, chasing the intruders around the house. Car doors slammed somewhere behind me and the blue lights of an arriving patrol car lit the path as I ran. Where was Gray?

"Stop! Police!" a male voice yelled in the distance. It was not Gray. Another set of footsteps pounded somewhere behind me.

Where was Gray? I felt my heart clutch and the blood rush to my ears as I darted along the house and burst out into the backyard.

"Gray?" I called.

I sprinted up the porch steps and hit the outside light switch. The area around the porch and the top of the driveway were illuminated in an instant, but Gray was nowhere to be seen.

I heard something rustle behind the garage and heard a soft

moan. I went toward the sound without even considering that it might not be Gray. I knew it was him. He was trying to move, struggling to rise as I reached him.

"Wait," I said, kneeling down beside him. "Let me help you."

"Sophie, look out!"

I barely had time to react. A shadowy form tore across the backyard heading straight for us. I half rose from my crouch, stepped forward and tucked my body into a low, tight ball. The man flew into me before he could stop himself, hurtling over me and landing with a loud thud on the ground a few feet away from Gray.

I sprang up and lunged for him, just missing his leg as he rolled, stood and ran off into the alley. A cop in uniform, running hard, came racing around the house and stopped, gun drawn and trained on my body.

"Freeze!"

"Wait, she's the home owner," Gray called.

The officer kept his gun on me, but reached with his other hand to pull his flashlight from his equipment belt. The beam passed over me to the spot on the ground where Gray sat, struggling to rise to his feet.

I went to him, kneeling down and holding out one hand to keep him where he was. My hand traveled up the side of his arm, across his shoulder and toward his head. He was bleeding and my fingers came away covered in the warm, sticky liquid.

"You're hurt. Sit still. Did he shoot you?"

Gray moaned and tried to stand despite my attempts to keep him down. "No. There were two of them. I came out, saw the one guy running and started to take off after him. Something hit me as I passed the garage, and that's all I remember."

He looked at the officer who stood in front of us and said, "Check the alley." When the man had gone, Gray reached up and felt the back of his head. "Shit, that hurts like a son of a bitch!"

Blue lights from another squad car lit up the driveway as more units began to arrive. Gray managed to stand and walk out from behind the garage, leaning on me for support. When he saw a K-9 officer standing beside the car with his German shepherd, he stopped, identified himself and then broke away from me to approach the car on his own.

The first officer returned, out of breath and gesturing toward the public housing complex that stood a short distance away from my house.

"I chased them as far as Front Street," he panted. "There was a car waiting so I lost them."

"You get a license number?" Gray asked.

The officer shook his head. His silver nameplate identified him as L. Reid. "No. It was a black sedan, maybe a Ford, with tinted windows."

"You get a look at the guys?" Gray asked.

By now both officers were staring at him. I stepped up behind him and touched his arm. "Gray, you're bleeding. You'd better get that looked at."

He shrugged it off. "It's nothing. Just a scalp wound. I'm fine."

Officer Reid and I exchanged glances. Gray was going to need stitches and X-rays, a fact that seemed obvious to everyone but Gray.

"Did you get a look at the men?" he continued.

The K-9 officer moved toward the side of the house with his dog. I noticed him talking into his radio and hoped he was calling an ambulance.

"You know, I thought heading toward the Projects, they'd be kids, a break-in, but these were older white men," Reid said. "I'd put them in their mid-thirties, one pretty skinny but muscular, wearing a dark T-shirt and black pants. The other guy was shorter, kind of squat. I'd say he went about five-eight but was built like a pro wrestler. He was carrying a sawed-off shotgun—at least that's what it looked like. I never did get very close."

I started to tell Gray about the man at the school but stopped when I saw that he was in too much pain to focus. His features were pinched and his skin was almost white.

"Do you want to finish this inside?" I asked. "It might be easier to write up your report at the kitchen table. Maybe you'd like some water or coffee." I directed this remark to Officer Reid, because I knew if I asked Gray he would say no, he was fine.

The young guy didn't pick up on it. He deferred to Gray.

"I could put a bandage on that wound while you start the report," I said pointedly.

The EMS squad turned the corner and pulled up in the middle of the street, lights flashing but no siren on, probably in an attempt to keep a low profile. It didn't matter; the neighbors were all outside, anyway.

"Sophie," Bill, from next door, called. "Pretty soon we won't have to bother turning on the TVs anymore. We'll just come outside every night and wait!" The guy was starting to grow on me. "Really, are you all right? I called when I heard the shot."

"I'm fine, Bill. Thanks. I keep trying to top each night's performance, but I don't know, this may be as good as it gets."

Bill shook his head, and his partner, a slim man with tight jeans, moved up beside him. "Just so you don't go into reruns," Bill's partner said. "I just hate summer reruns."

Bill shushed him and said, "Seriously, Sophie, if you need anything we're here."

His partner nodded. "Yeah, honey, stop by for a piña colada later and bring the boy toy with you."

I laughed and turned back to Gray. His face had gone completely white. As I watched, he suddenly seemed to sink. I reached for him just as his knees started to give. Officer Reid moved forward, catching Gray's other arm. Together we helped him down the driveway to the waiting ambulance.

Gray tried with every fiber in his being not to give over to the pain and blood loss. He bit his bottom lip, tried to remain conscious and tried to walk. I knew better than to show any emotion. I knew he needed to stay strong.

"I think it was the shock," he murmured.

"Shock?" I echoed.

"Yeah," he said, his voice barely audible. "I knew you wanted me. I just didn't know he did, too." He sighed. "So many people, so little of me to go around."

"Hey," I said, in an equally quiet voice, "he's going to have to take a number. I think I'm ahead of him."

We reached the ambulance and the waiting stretcher as Wendell Arrow stepped out of his unmarked car and walked quickly toward us.

"You finally had enough of him, huh?" he asked me. "Hell, you could've just called. I would've come and dragged him out."

I looked at Gray. His eyes were closed and I wasn't sure if he was even conscious. "May I ride with him?" I asked.

Wendell looked around, took in the scene and nodded. His expression was grave and his eyes full of compassion as he looked from Gray's still face to mine. "Yeah, go on. I'll tend to things here. I'll call Darlene if you want, get her to come over and lock up. We'll ride out to the hospital as soon as I clear things here and check on his status."

An hour later I was sitting on a cold plastic chair in a sterile cubicle, separated from the rest of the emergency room patients by a thin yellow curtain that stopped two feet from the floor.

I sat there, motionless, listening to the sounds of the emergency room world. A baby cried, an old man coughed with a dry hack that ended in a long choking gasp for breath, two women in the cubicle next to mine discussed "pain in the female area," and down the hallway another woman laughed, her voice carrying all the way from the nurses' station.

What if he isn't so lucky next time? a little voice inside my head asked. *What if you fall in love with this man and he gets killed trying to save the world? What will you do then?* I felt myself begin to shiver. I was freezing. The only warmth in the entire room came from the hot tears that finally began, spilling over and running down the sides of my face.

Chapter 9

Darlene arrived before Gray made it back from his CT scan. I recognized her as she paused outside the curtained examination area, her unmistakably big toes unpainted and wiggling in her Birkenstock sandals.

"Number two?" she muttered to herself. "Or did she say three? They don't number the flippin' things, so how do you tell? Do you count from down there or up here?"

"Darlene," I said, pulling open the curtain, "in here."

"Good gravy," she said. "I thought they'd swallowed you guys up forever." Then she caught sight of the empty gurney. Her eyes widened. "Oh, my God! He's not—"

"No, Darlene, he's not dead. They're doing tests."

Darlene snorted. "Well, you can't blame me for wondering. I mean, look at you, your eyes are all red and puffy, fourteen hundred tissues by your side. I thought—"

I raised my hand like a traffic cop. "All right, it's okay.

He's having a CAT scan. Where's Wendell? I thought he was coming."

Darlene's face softened. "He had to answer a page. He should be here any minute." Without probably even realizing it, she broke into a broad smile. Somehow Darlene had fallen back in love with lonesome Wendell.

"So you two straightened things out?" I asked.

Her smile widened. "He apologized, and anyway, once he told me Gray was hurt and you needed me, I knew he had come to his senses." She glanced toward the hallway, looking for Wendell, and then leaned in toward me. "He's a Libra. I should've realized. They're so full of indecision. He was probably just thrown off by everything happening so quickly. It's his nature, you know. He needs to be kept on track."

Oh, that would be the blind leading the blind, I thought. "Well, I'm glad it worked out."

Darlene swept the crumpled tissues off the chair next to mine and into a trash can. She sank down onto the hard plastic seat and sighed gratefully. "I needed that," she said. "I've been standing up all day." She stretched her feet out in front of her and studied them. "Let's go get pedicures this Saturday," she said. "I want some color down there. I want—" she leaned out and made another quick scan of the hallway "—I want sexy toes," she whispered, her eyebrows wiggling with the sheer wickedness of her thoughts.

There was movement in the hallway as an orderly turned the corner, pulling Gray on a long, slender gurney. His eyes were open and his color was better. As they passed the nurses' station, a doctor fell in behind them.

"All right," he said, sounding cheerful. "No fractures, just a concussion." He leaned over Gray and glanced toward me. "Gave your fiancée quite a scare there, fella!"

"Fiancée?" Darlene and Gray both said in the same breath.

"Oh honey," I said, jumping to my feet, "that must've been some whack you took if you've forgotten about the wedding next week! You know," I added, "they usually don't let nonfamily members back with the patients, but when I told them about the wedding and said we were as good as married, they let me in."

"Oh, my God!" Darlene cried. "I am so happy for you two! Did you hear that, sweetie?" Darlene turned to the arriving Wendell and clutched his hand. "Sophie and Gray are getting married!"

Gray looked at me, his eyes twinkling, understanding the situation immediately. He grinned broadly, grabbed me and pulled me down into a long passionate embrace that included a very thorough kiss and an overly familiar pinch of my posterior.

"Honey," he said, "there is no way on this earth that I could forget our upcoming nuptials." He smiled up at the doctor and winked. "We're planning a very large family, you know."

The doctor laughed. "Well then," he said, "we'd best get you sewn up so you can get to work, especially with that wedding only a week off." He shook his head. "You know, a police officer's wife has to have nerves of steel, just for rare occasions like this one."

Gray nodded, searching my face, obviously taking in my swollen, bloodshot eyes and red nose. "Oh, she's a brave one," he said softly. "They don't come much stronger than Sophie."

A nurse came in with a tray and looked at Wendell, Darlene and me.

"I think you three better wait outside," she said with a smile. "Sometimes these hero types are the biggest babies when it comes to stitching them up."

Gray moaned. "You are going to deaden it before you start sewing, aren't you?" he said. I looked at him. His eyes were sparkling again.

"Nope," she said, placing the tray down next to the doctor.

"A big he-man like you can take a little bit of pain. It builds character."

Dr. Davis chuckled. "Jean just loves to torture her patients," he said, lifting a syringe.

Jean shooed us off. The last thing I heard her say was, "Hey, Doc, let's have a little fun and embroider our initials at the bottom. Gray wouldn't mind that, would you, hon?"

Twenty minutes later the door to the emergency room swung open and Gray emerged in a wheelchair, propelled by the nurse and clearly not happy about his confinement.

"I can walk, you know, Jean. You don't have to follow protocol with me. I'm in and out of here all the time."

"And this time you're out of here in a wheelchair," she said, her tone not allowing any margin for error on his part.

"Car's right out front," Wendell said.

The doctor stopped me as our little procession headed toward the exit. "I gave him something for pain," he said. "But in a few hours it'll wear off and he might get uncomfortable." He handed me a small bottle. "These are for pain. Now I want you to watch him tonight. Wake him up every couple of hours. If you can't rouse him, we'll need to get him back in. Okay?"

He patted me on the shoulder and I nodded. "Thank you," I said. But he was already gone, walking through the swinging doors and on to his next patient.

I turned away and hurried to catch up with Gray and the others. I didn't figure it was going to be difficult to wake Gray up every couple of hours. I didn't think there was any way in the world I would sleep, not with all that had gone on. I was too wound up.

Wendell and the nurse got Gray settled into the back seat of Wendell's unmarked Lincoln. Once Darlene and I climbed inside and the doors closed, Wendell looked in the rearview mirror.

"Where to, boss?" he asked.

Gray was starting to feel the effects of the shot Dr. Davis had given him. His eyes drooped and he had to work hard to focus on the mirror in front of him.

"Sophie's house," he said. "I gotta watch out for her."

"You sure?" Wendell asked. "I don't think you'll be doing too much watching tonight, pal."

"I said, Sophie's house!"

Gray seemed confused but determined. Wendell noticed and took over. "Right, Sophie's house." His eyes shifted from Gray to me. "You all right with that?" he asked. "I can stick around and make sure nothing happens."

I shook my head, noting his own bloodshot eyes and the lines of fatigue that deepened his already worried expression.

"We'll be fine. I'll call if I need you, and I'm sure my house is now one of the most patrolled homes in New Bern. Don't worry about a thing."

Gray's head slumped over onto my shoulder and he began to snore softly.

"You party animal," I whispered. "You hunka, hunka burning love. I'm going to throw you in my bed and take you like a wild animal." I added this last part secure in the knowledge that he was out of it, smiling with the sheer relief of knowing that he was going to be all right.

"I love it when you talk dirty," he answered softly, and then collapsed back against me, this time asleep for good.

I turned and stared out the window into the inky darkness. I hadn't thought Nick would find me in New Bern, and now I was beginning to wonder how he had. "If I were Nick," I breathed to myself, "how would I find me? Where would I be now?" That was really the key, to think like Nick.

"Darlene," I called softly.

She turned around in her seat. "What?"

"Tomorrow, can you call some of the family up north? I want to know if anybody saw Nick after he got out of jail. I want to know if he asked any of the relatives where I moved to or what I was doing now."

She smiled. "Good plan."

"I think we should start asking about Connie Bono, too. I want to know how long she was seeing him, how serious it was, all that."

Wendell appeared to be concentrating on his driving, but he was listening to us, too. "Let me know what y'all find out, all right?" he said.

Darlene smiled knowingly and nodded. "So we'll be your snitches then, huh?" she said.

I closed my eyes and shook my head slowly back and forth. How did my sister manage to make her way in the world knowing as little as she did about reality?

Wendell was spared a long explanation by our arrival at the house. The crime scene van was gone but traces of their presence lingered everywhere inside and out, in the swirls of graphite powder, the yellow crime scene tape and the detritus of yet another investigation of a crime at my house. Every light in the house was on and a marked squad car sat idling on the street in front of the house.

Darlene and I raced ahead of Wendell to find fresh sheets and clean up my makeshift bedroom before he reached us with the semiconscious Gray in tow.

"All right, buddy," Wendell said, lowering Gray down onto the bed. "Let's make you comfortable."

Gray sighed and smiled. "Comfortable. Okay."

Wendell pushed Gray gently back onto the bed and helped me undress him. By the time we'd finished, Gray was snoring softly.

I walked Wendell and Darlene to the door and practically

pushed them out. "Go home," I said. "You both look exhausted and tomorrow's another day."

When they'd left, I slipped into the dining room and stood in the semidarkness, waiting for my eyes to adjust. Gray slept in my old double bed, nestled under one of my grandmother's quilts. His face was pale again and dark shadows rimmed his eyes. I tiptoed across the room, pulled a chair up next to the bed and settled in to watch him sleep. At some point, I fell asleep myself, awakening to the early morning sunlight filtering through the slats in the window blinds and the gentle sound of Gray's even breathing. I had a crick in my neck. A thin line of drool had dried on one side of my chin, and I knew I'd been snoring. I could feel my hair sticking out at odd angles all over my head and I felt the distinct need for a shower.

I walked into the living room, pulled back the curtains and surveyed the street in front of the house. The squad car that had been parked there was gone.

"It's not like I'm the president," I muttered. "They can't leave a car in front of the house at every citizen who has a little trouble. I can handle Nick Komassi or anyone else, for that matter." I was talking louder now, as though actually having a conversation with someone.

"Come on," I told myself. "Let's get some coffee and go to work." I walked through the dining room, past the softly snoring Gray, and on into the kitchen. I fumbled around making coffee, then pulled my old address book out of a drawer and flipped it open to the F page. I was going to start hunting Nick the same way he appeared to be hunting me.

I picked up the cordless phone, stepped out onto the back porch so I wouldn't awaken Gray, and punched in Gina Foucci's number. On the fourth ring a breathless voice said "Hello?" and panted into the receiver. Gina was fresh from the treadmill, if I knew her.

"Gina," I said. "Guess who?"

There was the briefest pause, then, "Oh my God, Sophie! Are you back?"

I smiled and took a deep breath. Gina, the girl voted "Most Likely to Tell All" in my neighborhood, was open for business. Anything I said could and would be used against me in the court of public opinion and gossip. Gina Foucci was the presiding judge, and everyone else in South Philly would be the jury.

"Listen," I said, "I need your help. You're the only one I can turn to."

I heard the slight anticipatory intake of breath as Gina paused, ready to receive the holy sacrament of new dirt. She didn't even question why I'd suddenly want to talk after avoiding her like the black plague for months.

"Well, Sophie, you know I'd do anything within my power to help," she said, her voice thick honey. "You've been through just the most awful time. I tried to call you after Nick got, well, you know, but I guess you weren't up to taking calls. I mean, what a shock!"

"Exactly," I said. I pictured Gina, frosted blond locks pouffed up into a tousled mass of wild bed hair, clutching her cordless phone and pacing around her tiny row house in neon-pink workout clothes. I could imagine her reaching for a cigarette and a Diet Coke.

I gave her what I knew she wanted. "It was awful, Gina," I said. "I just couldn't talk about it for the longest time. I mean, I had no idea about the things Nick was doing!"

"I know," she said. "To think that man was skulking around, looking through all our windows at night, taking pictures and posting them on the Internet! Selling videos of all kind of lewd acts, too! I don't know how I escaped becoming one of his victims!" The distinct tone of regret was unmistakable. "I'm just so thankful he didn't post any pictures of me, naked and exposed for all the world to see."

That couldn't have been further from the truth. Gina would've loved the drama. It was probably her secret fantasy to appear in the centerfold of *Playboy* magazine. She exercised, tanned and oiled her body like a machine. Her nails were manicured once a week. Her clothes, mainly spandex numbers, left nothing to the imagination. Gina was a natural born exhibitionist.

"You are so absolutely right," I said, trying to interrupt her train of thought. "Gina, did you know he actually hired prostitutes as models and, well, actresses in his porno flicks?" I didn't give her the chance to answer. "Worst of all, Nick was actually dating one of them! Some girl named Connie Bono."

Gina sighed heavily. "Sophie, that's old news. You poor, poor thing, you didn't know about Connie? Why, he was seeing her and a couple of other girls long before he got arrested."

"I didn't know," I said, waiting for Gina to enlighten me.

"Sophie, Nick's out of prison, you know that, right?" She took a long drag on her cigarette. "He moved in with her and her two roommates. She's in this retro, all-girl punk band. She lives with a couple of the other group members."

"Punk band?" I echoed. "I thought punk went out in the eighties?"

"Oh, honey, believe me, Nick's gone way downhill. You should see them. Those girls are tattooed, pierced, pale-skinned skeletons. I'm just sure they're all using drugs." Her voice dropped lower. "Connie strips in this sleazy bar, too. I've heard all those girls turn tricks. Sophie, you're just lucky he got busted when he did. Imagine the diseases you could have gotten."

Gina stopped here, the question unasked, waiting for me to confirm or deny my health status.

"Oh my God, Gina," I breathed, trying to sound as innocent as possible. "You mean the whole time he was in prison, Nick was still in contact with that girl?"

Gina snorted. "Yeah, and not just her. Connie's band was Nick's little harem. The way I hear it, he was doing them all. Of course, he was paying the rent, so I guess they wanted to keep him happy. I mean, yeah, they talked like they were one big family, like they were all in love, but who would believe a bunch of crap like that?"

I didn't have to pretend I felt sickened by what Gina was telling me. My stomach lurched, rolling and heaving toward my throat. Nick was much sicker than even I had imagined.

"You mean he was supporting them from prison?"

Gina coughed lightly, choking on her Diet Coke, I guessed. "Oh, absolutely," she said. "What? Don't tell me you didn't get anything in the divorce settlement. That slug! Honey, that ex-husband of yours diversified. He went from porn to drugs to gambling. At least, that's the word on the street. Of course, I never gossip, so I only hear these things in passing."

"Gina," I said, striving to sound earnest, "I think Nick's followed me to North Carolina."

I waited for her response. The "You mean Nick followed you to New Bern?" told me all I needed to know. If Gina Foucci knew I'd moved to New Bern, it was all over South Philly. I don't know why this surprised me.

"Well, I'm not positive it's him," I said.

"It's him, all right," Gina said. "And don't you fall for it, either."

"Fall for what, Gina?"

She sighed. "I don't want to hurt your feelings, Sophie, but if Nick shows up and says he loves you or he's a new man and wants you back, he's lying. He's looking for a place to hide."

"What, prison wasn't good enough?" I asked. I glanced up

at the clock over the sink. Nine-thirty. Pa and the old guys would be arriving soon.

"Sophie," Gina said, "Nick's made a lot of enemies up here. People are hunting for him. In fact, the list of people looking to pay him back is so long it would be easier to list the one or two who don't want a piece of him. Now, what I really want to know is…who are they? Do you know?"

The questions were starting, which meant she was out of information and looking for more. "What?" I said, loudly. "Gina, speak up. I can't hear you." I took the phone and banged it against the counter, whacking it hard. "Gina?" I called. I opened the refrigerator, shoved the phone into the bucket of ice cubes and twirled it around. "Gina?"

I heard her faint voice calling my name. "Sophie, there's something wrong with the connection."

"Damn it!" I cried, opening and closing the freezer door quickly. "Gina, I'm losing you. Wait, I'll call you back."

I left Gina in the freezer for a few more minutes, then retrieved the frozen phone and returned it to the hook.

"Not bad," I said to the empty kitchen. "I could be a detective. There's nothing to it."

Feeling full of myself, I poured a tall mug of coffee, slipped past the still sleeping detective in the dining room and headed upstairs to take a well-deserved shower. Twenty minutes later I was still standing in the shower, the water now lukewarm, raining down on my shoulders. Beyond the opaque white curtain, Bruce Springsteen sang "Thunder Road," his gritty voice booming and echoing off the white tile walls.

I was working on a plan. It was time to lure Nick out of his hiding place and into broad daylight. I had to figure out a way to let him know that I wouldn't kill him on sight. I had to make him believe that I'd had a change of heart and would be willing to hand over whatever it was he wanted from me. Now how was I going to accomplish that?

I stood in the shower thinking and still didn't have a solid plan when the warm water ran out. It would come to me, I felt certain. Perhaps after I investigated the health and well-being of the man sleeping downstairs in my bed I would feel further inspired. I let my thoughts turn to Gray as I dried my hair and carefully applied just enough makeup to look as if I wore none at all.

I replayed the memory of his kiss over and over in my head, wondering if there might be a repeat when I went downstairs to make breakfast. It was a tantalizing escape from my current Nick reality, and before long I was rushing into my clothes in order to pursue the sweet, new fantasy.

I hurried down the steps, practically running in my haste to get to Gray. But when I reached the dining room, the bed was empty. A note lay on his pillow. "I got a page and had to go. Thank you, Sophie. I'll check in later. G."

"Oh, isn't that just great!" I said to the empty room. "I'm up all night and what do I get? How's that for a one-nighter, eh?"

"I didn't figure you'd be too happy about it," a female voice answered.

I looked up, shocked to find anyone in the house, and saw Della leaning in the doorway, coffee mug in hand.

"I saw that note, heard your shower running and thought, damn, now that would piss me off but good!"

I opened my mouth to say something, anything, but no words came out.

Della shook her head. "You know, I think you must have bad-picker genes. I mean, I can't help but hear what your family says about that ex-husband of yours and well, this note sure sounds like you struck out again. You know what I mean?"

Pa, Joey, Emily, Mort and the rest of the crew arrived then, interrupting us and saving me from saying "What in the hell were you doing in my house, reading my note?"

Della, trapped by the entrance of the others, turned back into the sullen, guarded girl the others knew, and did her best to become invisible.

Pete walked right up to her, smiling and touching her shoulder. "Hey, beautiful," he said, "you ready for a day of dirt digging and manure slinging?"

Della had to look up then. She gave the tiniest hint of a smile and nodded softly. "Sure," she said, and followed him through the crowd to the backyard.

"She's shy," Emily said, looking after her.

Takes one to know one, I thought, and nodded. Joey was watching me from across the room. He was pretending to listen to Frank give instructions about sanding the floors, but I could tell his mind was elsewhere. I knew as soon as he found a way, he'd be on me about whatever it was that was bothering him.

Pa and Mort cornered me as I was attempting to slip out of the kitchen.

"Sophie," Pa said, grabbing my elbow and propelling me forward. "Come in the living room a minute. Mort and me got something to say."

It wasn't as if I had a choice in the matter. The two of them had me pinned between them and they didn't ease up until I was sitting on the sofa and they were standing in front of me.

"Now," Pa said, "we've got a problem." He glanced at Mort. "I don't want this getting back to Darlene or your mother. I told Wendell, but I want you to know about this, too." He looked over his shoulder, like he was checking for eavesdroppers. "Mort, here, works up at the security hut, you know, at the front gate to the neighborhood?"

I nodded and smiled at Mort. Cute. Old guys on patrol, watching the neighborhood and protecting their own, as if they could really stop an armed intruder.

"Well, for the past couple of mornings, early, around 6:00 a.m., Mort here has seen the same beat-up blue Ford sitting in the same spot off Bounty Court. The first day, he says he didn't think nothing of it, thought the guy was fishing the canal. But yesterday, Mort notices the guy's got a pair of binoculars and from where he's sitting, Mort thinks he's watching our house."

Mort nodded, like Pa was doing a fine job of speaking for him.

"Now I ain't taking no chances, Sophie, so I show Mort a couple of pictures of Nick, from back when you two was together. Mort thinks the guy in the car is Nick."

"That's right," Mort said. "I can't be positive, but I'm pretty certain it's your ex-husband."

Pa nodded his head in Mort's direction. "He's former ATF, you know. If anybody should be able to make an identification on a suspect, it would be him."

I looked back at Mort, figuring him to be closing in on eighty, and tried to imagine him bringing down dangerous fugitives in the Bureau of Alcohol, Tobacco and Firearms. He was wearing khaki shorts, white crew socks and standard issue sneakers. His white hair stood in rumpled shocks that, along with his mustache, made him look more like Einstein than Elliot Ness.

Then I looked closer. Mort was packing heat. He was wearing a Hawaiian shirt over his white T-shirt, and unless I was imagining things, he had a black gun strapped to his belt, almost hidden because it was positioned so far toward his back.

"Mort," I said, "is that a gun you're wearing?"

Mort beamed. "Standard issue Glock 9 mm, semiautomatic," he said. "Some scumball makes a move on you or your family here, and I'll ventilate him."

I felt my eyebrows go up and knew my mouth was hanging open. I looked at Pa. "*You're* not carrying, are you?" I asked.

Pa shook his head and the regret was unmistakable. "They got a waiting period. I won't have mine for two weeks," he said.

"But, Pa, you don't even know how to shoot a gun, do you?"

He frowned at me. "Sophie, I was in the service for four years. What do you think?"

"Pa, you were in the Coast Guard. What would they do with guns?"

He pulled himself up straight and glared at me. "It's all relative, Sophie."

"Relative?"

"Yeah, you're my kid and Ma's my wife and ain't no asshole going to mess with my family. It's relative. I operate a weapon relative to the level of distress I feel over this schmuck you married causing us such angst."

I stared up at him and tried to figure out when my father had learned the word *angst* and started thinking of himself as a vigilante.

"What are you trying to say here, Pa?" I asked.

Mort took over. "What we're telling you, honey, is that you should not worry about your family, or yourself, for that matter. We know the police are trying their best to catch this…pervert, but we're not going to leave it all up to them. They're understaffed. Their response time is slow, especially out in the country."

Pa broke in. "We're just going to institute a little neighborhood watch, that's all. We're going to watch our neighborhood and your house. You know, Sophie, there's lots of us ex-military types in the Neuse Harbor subdivision. We take care of our own."

"Yeah," Mort added, "and our own's own, too."

I jumped to my feet. "No, no, no," I said. "One of you will end up getting hurt. Worse, some innocent civilian could get hurt. That guy might not even be Nick. Let the cops handle it."

Mort and Pa looked wounded. "Sophie, we're not senile. We're not dead. When we say we're going to up the ante on old Nick, that's just what we mean. If he comes skulking around the neighborhood, we're going to set him straight about a few things and hold him until the police can come pick him up, that's all."

Joey hadn't stopped frowning since he'd arrived. He wandered into the living room now and stood there like a younger version of Pa, dressed in the same standard issue khaki shorts and T-shirt that Pa and his crew wore.

"All right," I said, hopping up off the sofa. "I'll let you two get on with the shower then."

I looked at Pa and saw him nodding his approval. Joey wasn't to know about the old guy militia.

"We're going, we're going," Pa said. He and Mort stood up and headed for the upstairs. "Little girl," Pa called to Emily, "come with me. I gotta read something on this paint can and I forgot my glasses."

Emily followed them, humming some unrecognizable tune to herself, filled with a twelve year old's self-importance at being able to help her grandfather.

That left me with scowling Joey. He waited almost two seconds before launching in on me. "So what went on here last night?" he demanded.

"Gray got hit on the head by—"

"Not that, Soph, I know about that. Gray called, and after him, Darlene called. I managed to piece that part together. What I want to know is, did this have anything to do with whatever it was that happened yesterday—you know, when you tried to pass off that bogus story about a flat tire?"

Joey might have said more, but Frank came puffing into the living room, struggling to carry a huge floor sander.

"Hey, hey, hey!" Joey called. "Wait! I got that." In three steps he crossed the room, grabbed the machine and hefted it into his arms. Then, with Frank behind him, my brother vanished upstairs.

I stood still for a minute, listening to the sounds of people working on my house and trying to adjust my thinking. "You should be so grateful," I whispered. "You have friends and family who want to help you."

Yeah, the other side of my head answered, *and an ex-husband who wants to kill you.*

"But I've got protection," I reminded myself. "A detective is working on my case. And I can take care of myself. I know Krav Maga. I am not a fainting flower."

I stepped into my temporary bedroom and began ripping the sheets and blankets off the bed. I couldn't wait to get a new one. How could I start a new relationship with an old bed? Maybe Darlene had something with her karma idea. Maybe it was for the best that Gray hadn't lingered this morning.

If we'd pursued my fantasy in this bed, who knew what could've happened? Oh no, this would never do. I would never be able to reinvent myself in Nick's tainted bed. A feeling of revulsion and shame washed over me, old baggage returning to haunt my new life. Something drastic had to happen to change my karma. I didn't just need to rid my life of Nick Komassi, I needed to rid my life of everything that reminded me of him and the pain he'd caused.

I went to the bottom of the steps and called up to Emily. She came bounding down moments later, all energy and exuberance, just the shot in the arm I needed.

"Hey," I said, "We didn't get a chance to do our shopping yesterday. Let's go now. I want to get some paint and build a bed."

Emily's eyes widened. "Cool. What kind of bed?"

I took her into the kitchen and showed her a picture in a magazine. Bright panels of gauze hung down from a pole that ran the length of a sofa.

"I want to take that and make it into a frame that surrounds all four sides of my bed."

"Like a queen's bed," she breathed. "Aunt Sophie, you are way too cool!" She grabbed her backpack purse off of the counter and turned, ready to go. "What are we waiting for?"

I snatched the car keys off their hook and followed my niece out the door. Emily seemed to come alive when it was just the two of us. She giggled, talked about boys and teased me considerably about Gray Evans. She absolutely loved the rental car, and who wouldn't? I'd upgraded to a metallic red Shadow Eclipse convertible.

The car flew down the road into town, barely able to contain its horsepower to a smart ten miles over the speed limit. The radio throbbed with the mating-ritual, rock-and-roll station that Emily picked and just had to listen to at top volume. We sang along, with her knowing every syllable and me making up new words, cruising into my new town without a care in the world.

I didn't notice the black sedan following us until we turned into the Lowe's parking lot. Even then, I wanted to dismiss it as coincidence, but I didn't. We parked near the exit doors. The sedan parked a discreet distance away. When we got out of the convertible and headed inside, the sedan's occupants stayed put.

Emily and I stepped into the cavernous warehouse and instantly became lost in the possibilities. At one point, as we consulted a cute, teenage boy about building a canopy frame, I thought I saw movement out of the corner of my eye.

I turned, glancing over my shoulder between the shelving

into the next aisle. A shape wearing dark clothing moved slowly down the row, casually inspecting pieces of PVC. I could only see him from the shoulders to about midhip. He was wearing dark clothes.

"Aunt Sophie!" Emily said, her tone letting me know that my attention was needed by her new pal, the teen idol who was attempting to assist us.

"I'm sorry," I said, turning back to them. "I just remembered something I need. Em, honey, are you following what he's saying? Do you think you could stay right here and get the rest of the instructions?"

My niece looked at me like I'd grown two heads. But I could tell she was pleased I'd given her a shot at the Holy Grail. She nodded and the boy began patiently explaining how to screw the wooden dowels together.

I took off after the man in black, cutting over two aisles and doubling back to come up behind him as he pretended to study brass elbow joints in the plumbing department. I studied him for a brief moment, realizing that he was exactly the same size as the man who'd accosted me at Duncan Elementary School. His hair was now shorter, but after the hair-pulling he'd received from me, I couldn't blame him for shearing it short. Today he wore black jeans and a black T-shirt, hardly an adequate disguise considering I'd promised to kill him if he returned.

He was doing a very good job of appearing fascinated by the plumbing fixtures, bending down to study the boxes that just happened to be placed directly in front of the aisle where Emily stood talking to the young clerk.

I could've sworn the man didn't even know I was coming up behind him, but I doubted that to be true. After all, he was hired help. He stalked and bullied people for a living.

I eased into position and with a quick move that worked just as well as it had in training, I grabbed his right thumb and twisted until the man dropped to the ground, screeching like a banshee.

"Shut up!" I said. "What are you trying to do, draw a crowd?"

I flipped him over to face me and realized he bore no resemblance to my former adversary.

"Lady, what the hell are you doing?"

The black T-shirt had writing on it: Hoyt's Plumbing. The pocket on his left side had his name embroidered in neat white letters: Hoyt.

I dropped his hand like a hot rock, the shocked expression on my face mirroring his own.

"Oh God, I am so sorry! I thought you were stalking us!" I pointed through the shelving to the spot where my niece had been standing. "Someone has been following us and we were right there and you looked like…"

Hoyt stood up and backed away, obviously terrified. "Lady, I don't know what you're talking about!"

"Aunt Sophie!" Emily ran up to stand by my side. "What's wrong?"

Hoyt, angry now, answered for me. "Your auntie's seeing little green men," he said.

Sweet, shy little Emily transformed into a volcanic eruption right before my eyes. "You leave my aunt alone!" she said. "Stop bothering her!"

We were drawing a small crowd, including the teenage boy who'd been helping us.

"Is he bothering you, Emily?" the boy said. "Security!" he yelled. "Aisle five!"

"She's crazy!" Hoyt insisted. "That lady threw me to the ground and was about to kill me! She attacked me!"

"Oh, please," a female clerk said. "Look at her. That bitty thing? She couldn't hurt you! Ain't that just like a man to blame it on the victim!"

The crowd was about to turn ugly. Hoyt, seeing the handwriting on the wall, turned and quickly started walking toward the exit, finally breaking into a full run as Emily's knight in shining armor took off after him.

"Come on, Auntie," Em cried, "I want to go home! I'm scared!" And as I watched, a lone tear escaped and ran down her cheek.

"You poor baby!" the clerk gushed.

The manager arrived then, accompanied by an overweight, out of shape security guard. In the ensuing frenzy of explanations, all of them wrong, I turned to reassure poor Emily. To my surprise, she winked.

"And then the man had the nerve to say this little, bitty woman attacked him!" I heard.

"Well, I'm sure I could've taken him in a fair fight," I said.

Not one soul believed me. By the time the story had been told over and over again, there was a mass agreement that I had narrowly escaped death. The manager, sensing a possible lawsuit, insisted on giving us the bedding for my new bed. He promised to have the mattress and box spring delivered to my home within the hour and escorted us to the convertible, apologizing the whole way.

The sedan that I'd felt sure had been following us was now gone, leaving me to feel six kinds of stupid. Emily, however, was absolutely thrilled and couldn't wait to tell her father about our great adventure.

"Em, let's not tell your daddy about this, all right?"

It took a stop at Dairy Queen, two CDs and the promise of a new outfit to buy Emily's silence, but all in all, I considered it well worth the price. I cringed every time I imagined the joy my brother would take in telling his friend, Gray, how his ferocious sister had attacked an innocent plumber in the local hardware store.

Chapter 10

Emily and I took our time driving across town, enjoying the feel of the warm summer sun on our skin and relishing the rented convertible. The radio played the Dixie Chicks singing "You Can't Hurry Love," and Emily and I sang along. As my house loomed into view, I saw the bedroom set delivery van leaving. Then I saw that an ambulance blocked the driveway. A police car sat behind it, lights flashing. Any sense of peace I'd found at the arrival of my bed vanished as I pulled up to the curb and saw a stretcher being wheeled down the driveway.

Gray and I arrived at the same time, coming from opposite directions and reaching the ambulance just as the doors were closing.

"What happened?" Gray asked a uniformed officer.

The cop, a middle-aged man with thinning hair, looked up from his clipboard. "We're not real sure," he said. "It's a gunshot wound. The guy got hit in the leg. There was a lot of blood, but he'll be all right."

I strained to see past the two men into the back of the ambulance, my heart racing.

"Sophie!" Pa stepped off the porch, with Joey and Mort right behind him. Della walked down the driveway, talking earnestly to another uniformed police officer. Her shirt and overalls were covered in blood.

I stepped past Gray and looked into the back of the ambulance. Pa's friend Pete, the landscaper, lay on the stretcher, his eyes closed and his lips drawn in a painful grimace. His face was white and still. As I watched, an EMT began hooking him up to an IV.

Joey reached my side and grabbed my arm. "He wasn't doing anything, Soph. He and that girl were in the backyard, pulling up a tree stump or something. She said the shot came from behind the fence, maybe near the Projects."

Joey's face was grim and he looked very angry. "Son of a bitch, Nick," he swore. "I hope they find that little bastard before I do."

"Joey, they'll find him. They have to find him."

I looked around. Pa was heading for his car, probably on his way to Pete's wife and take her to the hospital. Emily stood on the sidewalk, tears streaming down her face, as Mort and Frank tried to comfort her. Gray looked past the responding officer, watching Della give her statement to the other uniform. His eyes met Joey's and a look passed between them that frightened me with its intensity.

"It was intentional, wasn't it, Joey? It wasn't just a random shot from the Projects. It's Nick, isn't it?"

Joey turned to me. "*Stunade!* Of course it was Nick! Why's he doing this, Soph? What does he want? I mean, if he wants to kill you, what's he doing shooting defenseless old men? If he wants something you have, why doesn't he come and get it like a man?"

This was entirely my fault. Pete had stepped into my world, a world Nick wanted to destroy, and now he was a victim.

Della, obviously shaken, walked away from the police officer and up to where I stood with Joey. Durrell, for once, was nowhere in sight.

"I don't know what happened," she said, in a dull flat tone. "Pete and I were trying to get this stump out of the ground. He said maybe if I reached over and wrapped the chain around the root we could run the other end to his Jeep and pull it out that way."

She was staring sightlessly at a spot on my driveway, as if seeing the scene unfold as she spoke. Her thin bony arms were wrapped tight around her sides and she shivered as if she were cold. She was in shock.

"Della," I said, "why don't you come inside and tell me about it."

She didn't appear to hear me. "I reached down in front of him, you know? I had just hitched it tight when I heard a loud crack. Of course, I knew right away what it was. So I looked up and Pete was gone. There was blood everywhere. I tried to put pressure on the wound, but blood kept on coming up through my fingers…."

Her voice trailed off as she stared down at her hands. Pete's blood had dried, staining her skin and covering her clothes.

"Come on, honey," I said. "Let's get you cleaned up."

Like a child, Della let me lead her inside. I took her into my bathroom, turned on the tap and led her through the motions of washing the blood from her hands and arms. I grabbed one of my T-shirts and a pair of shorts from my room and offered them to her. Instead of taking them, she stood staring at me with a puzzled expression on her face.

"Go on," I said. "Put them on. I'll be out in the kitchen. Come out there when you're dressed, and don't worry about your dirty things, I'll get them later."

I put the clean clothes on the counter behind her and touched her arm. Her skin was ice-cold.

"Della? Have you had lunch?" I raised my voice slightly, commanding her attention.

"I think so," she answered at last.

"Good, then I'll get you something to drink."

The girl nodded slowly. "Do you have any Jack Daniels?" she asked.

"Sure. Just get changed and come on out when you're ready."

I left her there, fairly certain that she was capable now of dressing and following my directions. I walked out to the kitchen, my mind going in a thousand directions at once. I opened a cabinet and began pushing past canned goods, reaching for the liquor that stood on the shelf behind them.

I pulled down two bottles, Jack Daniels and Wild Turkey, and was pouring two shots when Joey found me.

"Who's that for?" he asked.

"Della."

"And the other one?"

"Me." I turned, pulling down a third shot glass. "You want one?"

Joey raised an eyebrow, glanced at the two bottles and said, "Sure. What the hell? Make mine a Turkey."

"Joey," I said, handing him his shot, "I'm done waiting on the police. I'm going to hunt that son of a bitch like prey. I was married to him for ten years. If anybody can find him, it ought to be me."

He held the glass out, waited for me to take mine, and when I did, lifted his to his lips and drained it with one quick swal-

low. I did the same, then reached for a bottle of water that sat
on the counter.

I drank, passing it to him when I'd finished. He looked at
me and shook his head. "I don't know what to tell you, Soph,"
he said. "I'd say don't do that, it's a stupid idea, but you
wouldn't listen, and besides, I think you're right. You do know
him like nobody else. And he's not going to go away, that's
clear. It's like his stink follows you, even here."

Joey looked at the Wild Turkey bottle, but he wasn't really
seeing it. He was thinking. I tried to second-guess him.

"I can't go home to Ma and Pa's if that's what you're thinking, Joey," I said. "He'll follow me there. He could hurt them,
trying to get to me." I swallowed hard. "I can't go anywhere
because he doesn't care who he hurts trying to get to me. I
can't believe this is happening. I can't believe Nick turned so
bad. I gotta stop him, Joey."

Joey shook his head again, nodded toward the bottle and
handed me his empty glass. I set mine down next to his and
poured.

"You didn't want to see what Nick was before," he said.
"To be honest, none of us saw this coming. The pervert part,
I could see that, but this—"

He broke off as Della wandered into the kitchen wearing
my clothes. I turned around and handed her a shot glass. It
was gone before I could reach the water bottle, and her arm
was outstretched, indicating she wanted more.

"You sure?" I asked. "I mean, you don't look so good. You
look pale."

Della's eyes, flinty hard, met mine. "I can handle it fine,"
she said.

Joey didn't say anything. He took his glass, raised it
slightly in my direction and swallowed the amber liquid without so much as a trace of expression on his face. I knew he

was looking at Della and thinking junkie. Joey wasn't one to go back on a first impression.

Della drained her glass and set it down on the counter. "I'm going home," she announced.

"Where's Durrell?" I asked her.

The girl shrugged. "I haven't seen him all afternoon. Maybe he ran off." She didn't seem too concerned about her dog, but I attributed it to the shock of the afternoon's events. "If he shows up, can you keep him for me until morning?"

"I don't know if I'll stay here tonight," I answered. "But if he shows up, I'll feed him and let him in." Something about Della bothered me, teasing my unconscious and trying to break through into a recognizable thought. What was it?

She was moving toward the back porch when a uniformed officer stepped through the screen door and stopped her.

"Ma'am," he said, "Detective Evans would like you to come downtown and look at some pictures. He said we'll get you back to your vehicle or take you home later, whichever is more convenient."

Della was obviously unhappy at this turn of events. "I just want to go home," she said.

The officer nodded. "I know, ma'am," he said. "But if we can get your input while your memory's fresh, it would sure help. My car is right outside."

Della didn't really have an option. She was going to go with the police officer one way or the other, and as I watched her accept this fact, I also noted a flicker of fear cross her face and just as quickly vanish.

The screen door slapped shut behind Della as she followed the police officer to his car. Joey looked over at me, about to say something, but I raised my hand. "Don't say it," I said. "Just don't say it. You're probably right, but I have bigger fish to fry right now."

He shrugged. "I wasn't going to say anything about her. I was going to say that I'm going to help you find him, Soph. You may be all tough with your martial arts crap, but he's got guns and he's not working alone. For what it's worth, I'm helping you."

I looked at my college professor, poet brother and saw the determination in his eyes. It meant everything to me.

"Thanks."

Joey nodded. "Where do we start?"

I shrugged. "I need to give it some thought," I said. "I'm going to sit here at the kitchen table and come up with something. All I know for certain is what I'm not going to do."

Joey's eyebrow lifted. "Yeah? What's that?"

"I'm not going to run."

Joey nodded, but didn't say anything. I couldn't tell what he thought, but knowing him like I did, I figured he was trying to formulate his own plan.

"It's like this," I said. "It doesn't make sense that all of these things are happening because Nick wants revenge. He's not like that. I mean, he'd talk about it, maybe even map it out in his head, but Nick was never much for direct conflict. He's sneakier than that. He's also too cheap to pay to have me taken care of. There's got to be more to it than this."

"Like what?" Joey asked.

"Like maybe that stupid FBI agent was right, maybe Nick left something or hid something before he went to prison and maybe he's come back looking for it. Maybe he thinks if he scares me badly enough, I'll hand it over when he comes looking. Or maybe Nick's trying to scare me away from here so he can search the house."

Emily wandered into the kitchen, her eyes red and swollen. Mort hovered behind her, obviously trying to take care of her, and almost overwhelmed himself.

"When who comes looking, Aunt Sophie?" she asked, her voice hoarse from crying.

"Joey," Mort said, interrupting. "You should take your little girl home. This is no place for her."

My brother went to his daughter, slipped his arms around her and pulled her close. "Baby," he said, his voice a husky whisper, "I'm sorry. I wasn't paying attention. Let's get you home."

Emily lifted her head from his shoulder and attempted to smile. "Oh, Daddy," she said. "You were just trying to take care of Aunt Sophie. I'm not neglected. I'm not a baby! I'm almost thirteen."

Joey looked like Pa. His face darkened, his chest seemed to expand, and he became the man and not the son or the brother. He was in charge and he was going to protect his family.

"This is not the place for you or your aunt, but I can't make Aunt Sophie listen to me. I'm not her father. But you," he said, "are my little girl and you are going home, right now."

Emily had no intention of fighting her father. I saw her arms tighten around his waist and heard the small sigh of relief. Mort nodded his approval.

"I'm going to the hospital," he said. He looked over to me. "Your pa and I will get things situated there and then we'll come back."

"Mort," I said, "I think it would be best if you didn't. I might not even be here and if I am, I'll be fine."

Mort frowned. "What do you mean, you'll be fine? You don't have protection. The cops said all they were going to do is beef up their patrols."

The lie came easily. "Gray and Joey are taking turns staying here," I said. "It's Gray's night."

Joey glanced over the top of Emily's head. "Gray feel up to that?" he asked. "'Cause I can stay."

"It's all taken care of," I said, and prayed he wouldn't check.

Emily tugged at him. "Detective Evans won't let anything bad happen," she said. "Let's go, okay?" She looked at me, her expression apologetic. "I mean, if you're sure, Aunt Sophie?"

I smiled. "Go on, all of you. I'm fine." I pushed them out of the kitchen and followed to watch them leave. Gray was deep in conversation with a crime scene technician. I saw Joey hesitate, note that Gray was busy, and continue on. Mort never stopped in his hurry to reach his buddies at the hospital.

I headed back inside and busied myself washing the shot glasses and thinking. What kind of information would Nick have about a murder? Pictures? Something written down? Who were the men in the black sedan and how did they fit in with Nick? Why were they looking for him? If they worked for Nick, wouldn't they know where he was?

I glanced out the kitchen window and saw Gray moving toward the back porch. His head was bent and he appeared to be deep in thought. I stood there watching him, taking in the way the white cuffs of his dress shirt stood out against the deep tan of his skin, and the way he walked with a sure purpose, moving like an athlete.

A few minutes later he was standing next to me, his strong hands wrapped around a coffee mug. I felt the warmth of him, inhaled the scent of his cologne and tried out the idea of him as a constant in my life. He fit with me, I realized, and this thought comforted me in a way that nothing else had. Maybe Darlene's dreams of destiny and permanence weren't such bad thoughts, after all. Or maybe the presence of death and evil made me long for a connection to something good, like a loving partnership shared with the right person.

"You left before I could check on you this morning," I said. "How do you feel?"

Gray smiled. "Got a hell of a headache, but I'll be all right. I'm sorry about running off. Agent Cole needed to see me and said it couldn't wait. I didn't want to barge in on you in the shower or I would've said goodbye in person."

I found myself wishing he had barged in, but didn't say it. "Is there any news about Nick?"

Gray shook his head. "Not yet." He put his coffee cup down on the counter and smiled apologetically. "I have to get back to the office, but someone will be here, in front of the house, until I get back."

I nodded and tried to smile, but my head was in a thousand places and words wouldn't come.

"I want you to lock all the doors. Pull the blinds and stay away from the windows. I don't think he'll risk showing up again, especially with marked units riding by every few minutes, but I also don't believe he's thinking too clearly—not when he risked shooting in broad daylight."

"Right," I mumbled. Maybe the two shots of Wild Turkey were having their effect. "I'll stay inside. There's a lot I can do around here."

Gray lifted my chin with one finger and stared into my eyes. "Why don't you take it easy instead?"

I nodded. "The way things are, I don't figure I'll be alone for too long. Darlene's bound to pop by, and Pa will be back from the hospital soon."

"Sophie, you don't need to try and act tough with me," Gray said softly. "I already know how brave you are."

I looked up at him. "You think I'm brave, huh?"

He chuckled softly. "Sure you are. But you can be plenty brave and still feel scared." The initial desire I had felt for him deepened into an almost unbearable ache. "I'll be back as soon as I can," he said, and was gone before I could answer him.

I went through the house, locking doors and pulling curtains, thinking about Nick and wondering where I would've hidden something I didn't want anyone to find.

Darlene found me two hours later, hot and sweaty from a household search and a wrestling match with the contents of my dining-room pseudobedroom. She stood on the front porch, dressed in another long flowing skirt, her hair pulled back into a French braid and her cheeks flushed with the late afternoon heat.

"What happened to you?" she asked, brushing past me and making a beeline for the kitchen. "You look awful."

"You're just in time," I told her. "You can help me move the bed I'm making upstairs."

Darlene poked her head back out of my refrigerator and smiled. "Aha!" she cried. "It's come to that, has it?"

I felt my face turn scarlet. "What in the world are you talking about?"

Darlene bumped the refrigerator door shut with her hip. In one hand was a bottle of water, in the other a package of sliced cheese and a plastic bag of sliced ham.

"I am talking about the fact that your ex-husband is hunting you like a wild dog and instead of being the overly responsible, perhaps even obsessive-compulsive person I know you to be, instead of freaking out and becoming paralyzed with fear, you are moving your boudoir upstairs and making plans to seduce Gray Evans." She held up an arresting hand and added, "Don't even try to deny it. I know the look when I see it."

"Darlene, for your information, I was looking for something. When I couldn't find it, I decided to build my new bed upstairs. For safety purposes, of course. It's harder to shoot me from the street if I'm on the second floor."

Darlene calmly rolled ham up in a cheese slice and regarded me with a knowing look. "Honey, you need to loosen up. Gray wants you and you want him just as bad. What's wrong with admitting it?"

She leaned against the newly installed refrigerator and

smiled. I opened my mouth to say something, anything, and couldn't make the words come. I wasn't about to tell her I was hunting for Nick's evidence. "Timing," I said finally. "The timing is wrong."

Darlene rolled her eyes. "Don't you know anything? Haven't you read about the baby booms that happened in the sixties nine months after the Bay of Pigs Invasion? Everybody thought they were going to die, so what did they do?" Darlene nodded smugly. "That's right, they screwed their collective brains out! Making love is a life-affirming activity. It flies in the face of death and danger. It's man's way of insuring that the human race will continue."

"Darlene, I am not trying to get pregnant! I am just trying to move my bed to a safer location. I'm not saying I don't want to consider a relationship with Gray. I'm just saying that I have to take care of this business with Nick first."

Darlene put down her water bottle and shook her head.

"Sophie, you can't hunt Nick twenty-four hours a day without ceasing. I think what you really want is a guarantee that Gray is the right man and he won't hurt you. Sophie, they don't hand out guarantees like that. You go after Gray and I can promise you right now, you'll get hurt." Darlene's eyes softened. "Love always hurts. But love also heals and nurtures. Love takes the best and worst of everything and whops you upside the head. It fills you and completes you, all right, but it also drains you dry."

"Then why do it?" I heard myself ask, drawn in despite myself. "Why set yourself up to feel all that?"

Darlene smiled her serene Mistress of the Universe smile. "Because we can't help ourselves." She motioned toward the boxes in the living room. "Now let's get to it."

The twinge of anticipation that hit my stomach only confirmed what Darlene was saying. I did want Gray Evans. I

wanted to feel his skin against mine, but more than that, I
wanted to feel him in my heart and in my life.

"Damn!" I said.

Darlene smiled and pushed away from the counter, brushing her hands off on her skirt as she moved past me. "Come
on. Let's get that bedroom in order," she said. "This could take
a while."

Chapter 11

Nick had been everywhere. The irony of it was that if I hadn't given in to my active fantasy life and Darlene's insistence, I might never have known. She was the one who dragged me down into the basement looking for gauze curtains that had been packed along with the rest of my nonessential belongings, and stored out of the way of the renovations.

The two of us stood on the steps overlooking the dim, musty cavern and stared at the chaos sprawled below us. My carefully packed and labeled boxes had been ripped open and the contents strewn across the hard-packed dirt floor. The furniture carefully placed alongside one bone-dry wall of the cellar, waiting in alleged safety for the day when the floors would be refinished and the rooms ready for their contents, now lay in a haphazard pile. Drawers had been pulled from empty chests. Doors had been jerked open to cabinets. My life had been pawed through and trashed.

Darlene and I reached for each other, the way we did as kids watching scary movies on TV. A million thoughts ran through my head. I'd just been down here! Everything had been in order then. How had he gotten into the basement and gone through my things without us hearing him? Why had he done this? What did he want? And worse, was he still here?

"Nick, you lowlife son of a bitch, I know you're in here. Now come out where I can see you!" I started forward, peering behind the furniture and trying to see into every dark corner.

"Nick?" Darlene asked. "You think he's in *here*?" She sniffed the air, as if she could actually smell the creep. "Could he have done this while we were upstairs?"

"I was down here two hours ago. It wasn't like this. If it's not Nick then it's someone who wants what he left behind." Frustration swept over me, overwhelming me with an anger that burned deep in the pit of my stomach.

"Darlene, that stupid FBI agent must be right. Nick hid evidence in a murder investigation somewhere in our house before he went to prison. Hell, maybe Nick even committed the damn murder! Maybe all the accidents and warnings were his attempt to scare me away from here so he can get into the house and find it. Maybe that's why those men are looking for him—maybe they want what he hid."

I finished my search of the basement and returned to Darlene's side. "Well, nobody's here now."

She surveyed the scene around us and nodded slowly. "Do you think he found what he was looking for?" she asked.

I shrugged. "I don't know."

As I moved closer to the wall, I felt fresh air hit my ankles. I stepped closer, looking for the source of the breeze, and found it almost immediately. The door leading to the backyard was securely locked, but a small window had been jimmied open, leaving its broken frame to swing softly in the cross draft.

"He got in through there," I said, pointing the window out to Darlene.

"It doesn't seem big enough," she said, squinting in the dim light.

"Yeah, but Nick's not a big guy," I said. "Maybe he lost weight in prison. Even if he didn't, there's plenty of room for him to get through."

I stepped onto the soft dirt floor that rimmed the back half of the cellar and picked my way through clothing and kitchen utensils to reach the window.

"See?" I called to Darlene. "The dirt's kicked up a little right underneath it, and the wood is splintered where he broke the latch. I wish I knew what he was looking for."

Darlene nudged an overturned box with her big toe and quickly drew her foot back.

"What if it's, like, a trophy?" she said.

"A trophy?"

"Yeah, you know, like a serial killer's trophy. They take souvenirs from their victims, you know, like ears or fingers."

"Oh, please! Nick wouldn't touch—" I broke off, realizing that the Nick Komassi I knew was obviously capable of doing lots of things I hadn't anticipated. In fact, I didn't know Nick very well at all.

I stooped and picked up a box of broken Christmas ornaments. I straightened and looked at the chaos around me. Searching felt so pointless and yet we had to do it. We had to try every possible lead or else Nick would continue to plague me.

"Darlene, I doubt we'll find body parts. Nick took dirty pictures. We're probably looking for photographs."

My sister raised a skeptical eyebrow, but she joined me in the search, the pointless, frustrating quest that left us filthy, cob-web-coated and sweaty. Worst of all, we came up empty-handed.

"I give up," I said. "There's nothing here. We might as well finish the bedroom while I think about it. Maybe something will come to mind while we work."

Darlene pushed her bangs out of her eyes and smiled. "Now you're talking."

I yanked the curtains we'd originally come looking for out of a box marked Linen Closet, and followed Darlene back up the stairs. "Thanks for helping me look," I said.

"I live to serve," she called over her shoulder. "On to the boudoir!"

"Bedroom, Darlene. It's a bedroom."

"Whatever."

We left the basement. I closed and locked the door behind us, then as an added precaution, pulled a kitchen chair over and wedged the back of it under the doorknob.

Darlene rolled her eyes. "It needs a dead bolt," she said.

"This'll have to do for now."

Darlene picked up a glass from beside the sink and balanced it carefully on top of the diamond-cut doorknob. The flat edge was just long enough to support the glass.

"If we're going to invent a home security system," she said, "at least be a little creative. Now if he turns the knob, the glass will fall and break. You'll hear it and call 9-1-1."

I rolled my eyes. "Or the glass will fall, we'll call the police and it'll all be for nothing."

"Work with me here, Sophie," she said. "It's part of the process. It's better to be safe than sorry."

"Whatever," I said, doing my best imitation of her.

We climbed the stairs to my new bedroom, each carting items from my dresser and closet. For the next two hours we worked side by side, united in the effort to create something new and wonderful. I tried to focus on Nick and his search of the basement. What was he looking for?

Darlene and I threw quilts and comforters onto the new mattress and box spring. We draped gauzy curtains across the windows and piled pillows all the way across the bed. Darlene arranged the lighting, insisting on a pink lightbulb for the bedside table.

"Pink makes you look younger," she insisted. "I think I have one. Wait right here."

She vanished, the front door slamming behind her as she ran out to her car. Only Darlene would travel with pink lightbulbs, I thought. She returned with a brown paper bag, smiling triumphantly.

"I was going to take this home to my house," she said, "for the same reason. I can stop on my way out to the subdivision and buy a replacement. I think you might need the pink light before I do."

"Darlene! You'd think I was..."

Darlene raised an eyebrow. "Well," she said, "aren't you?"

I couldn't look her in the eye. I felt myself blushing, and worse than that was the little smirk that crept across my lips, no matter how I hard I bit down on the inside of my cheek to stop it. Darlene was right and I was only making a bigger fool of myself by denying it.

Darlene saved me. She pretended to straighten a pillow and, with her head turned, said, "Make sure you lie on your back."

"What?"

Darlene dropped the pillow pretense and turned around, her eyes sparkling. "Well, at your age, I'd be thinking that you'd want all the help you can get from gravity."

"Darlene, what are you talking about? And what about my age? I'm only thirty-six."

"Muscle tone doesn't last forever, you know. All's I'm saying is, you should lie on your back as much as possible. It smoothes the lines out so you look younger. If you're on top looking down at him, well, there's no telling what body parts will be sagging and drooping. First impressions are everything, Sophie!"

"Oh, my God," I said, getting her now. "Darlene!"

She held up her hand. "Don't bother thanking me," she intoned solemnly. "After all, it's what I do."

The doorbell rang, startling us and preventing me from killing my sister. "It's him," I said.

"Well, it certainly isn't Nick," she answered. "He doesn't ring doorbells. He just slithers under the door and makes himself at home."

I felt the shiver of revulsion ripple over me as I headed down the stairs. Darlene must've felt the same way I did. She was muttering under her breath, but all I heard was the occasional "bastard" and "no good son of a bitch."

I stopped suddenly on the last landing and Darlene ran into me, almost propelling me down the remaining four steps.

"What's wrong?"

"Listen, if that is Gray, don't say anything about the basement. Let me tell him later."

Darlene nodded. "It'd be a shame to go to all this trouble only to ruin the mood with bad news. All right. I'll keep a zipped lip."

"Thanks, Dar," I said, and really meant it. "I owe you."

"Use the light and lie on your back," she whispered as we approached the front door.

"Darlene!" I peeked out through the peephole and saw Gray jab impatiently at the doorbell again. "It's him," I whispered.

"I told you Nick wouldn't ring the doorbell," she said.

I unlocked the door and swung it wide. Gray smiled. "What took you so long?"

"We were changing a lightbulb," Darlene answered. "And

now, if you two will excuse me, I have to return to the store and buy a replacement bulb before I head home. I'm seeing Wendell later."

Gray frowned, trying to make sense of Darlene, but she didn't linger to field questions. She was out the door and down the driveway before he could turn to me and say, "Lightbulb?"

I shook my head and grabbed his hand, pulling him inside the doorway. "Never mind," I said. "It would take too long to explain. So, what are you doing here? I thought you'd still be at the station or following leads."

The unmistakable odor of Chinese food began to permeate the room, and as I watched, Gray brought a brown paper bag from behind his back and held it out to me.

"I've done all I can tonight. They'll page me if something comes in. I thought you might be hungry," he said. "I didn't know what you'd want, so I got a little bit of everything. You do like Chinese food, I hope?"

I was ready to rip the bag out of his hand, but managed to restrain myself. "Love it," I answered.

He smiled. "I do like a woman with a healthy appetite."

Somehow I no longer felt he was talking about the food. Perhaps it was the chemistry that had invaded the room, drawing me to him, making me aware of every detail of his appearance, filling me with an anticipation that far outweighed my hunger for lo mein.

"Plates," I murmured. "We need plates." I turned and walked away from him, stopping a few feet from the entrance to the dining room and looking back to see what was keeping him from following me.

He hadn't moved at all. He was watching me, the smile on his face slowly vanishing as his expression changed to one I couldn't read. He turned and carefully placed the bag on the table beside the door.

"Come here," he said.

It was the tone, the urgency and strength that made me move without question toward him, walking right into his embrace. His arms opened enough to fold me tightly against his chest, and then locked with equal intensity. When he bent his head to kiss me, I melted into him, exploring his mouth with my tongue, hungry for the taste of him.

We stood by the front door, and then leaned against it as his kisses grew into a fire that weakened us both. I felt his tongue searching my mouth, promising me more, and then demanding the same in return.

My hands slid up his body, wrapping around his back and pulling him into me. I felt him grow hard, heard the low moan in his throat, and knew with certainty that the Chinese food would grow cold sitting on my table. I wanted Gray Evans as I had never wanted any man. The feelings that surged up inside my body were totally foreign and frightening in their intensity.

His tongue found my ear, circling the outer rim, darting behind and around, resting briefly on the fleshy lobe before I felt the sharp pain and pleasurable sensation of his teeth nibbling, teasing and insisting.

I felt my nipples grow taut, hardening as I brushed against his chest. My head swirled as Gray moved, touching me, tasting me and driving me slowly out of my mind.

"I want you," he whispered. "Now."

I felt my body answer him. I told him everything he wanted to know without uttering a word. I reached for his hand and turned, leading him toward the staircase, not sure that we would even make it to the landing before I had to tear his clothes off and see him standing in front of me, naked and hardened with desire.

I walked up the steps, my fingers fumbling to undo the buttons of my shirt. I pulled it off and tossed it over the rail as we moved. That stopped him. He grabbed me, swinging me sideways into the wall, pinning me as his fingers reached for the clasp of my black lace bra and undid it.

As the flimsy garment gave way and fell across my shoulders, he yanked it off, his eyes riveted to my breasts.

"God, yes," he whispered, and took my nipples between his fingers, rolling and pinching them into tight balls of sensation. He bent his head and slipped one bud into his mouth, sucking and running his tongue over the ultratender tip.

I slid my fingers across his temples, down his neck and across his shoulders, pulling him to me and then pushing him away with almost one movement.

"Not here," I whispered.

Gray raised his head and smiled into my eyes. "Sweetheart," he murmured, "it will be here, there and everywhere I can take you. It will be tonight and tomorrow and next week." His blue-gray eyes deepened into a smoky dark gray. "This may be the first time, but it will not be the last."

My heart pounded. My knees felt as if they would give way. I wanted him everywhere—inside me, on top of me, behind me. I wanted all of him. I wanted to sink into him and give myself up to him. I wanted to make him sob with pleasure and groan with the agony of wanting me. I wanted all of him and I wanted it now.

I grabbed at the navy-blue T-shirt he wore and yanked it out of his waistband, pulling until he had no choice but to raise his hands and bend to let me tug it off. I tossed it aside and stopped, staring at the man who stood before me. Even in the dim light of the stair landing I could see the sheen of his tanned skin and the firm definition of muscles well accustomed to exercise and activity.

He saw me watching him and smiled. "Will it do?" he asked.

I ran my fingers across the fine hair that covered his chest and abdomen, marveling at the soft, feathery feel under my fingertips. I reached up and touched one nipple, felt it tighten, and then sucked the tip into my mouth, doing to him what I had felt him do to me.

I heard his sharp intake of breath, felt his hands tighten around my waist, and tried not to let go as he pulled me into him.

"You've made your point," he whispered. "All right. Not here."

He scooped me up in his arms, effortlessly carrying me the rest of the way up the stairs and down the hallway to my new bedroom. He lay me down on top of the quilts, capturing my wrists with one strong hand and pulling my arms up over my head. With his free hand he began to explore my body, trailing his fingertips across my cheek, down my neck and over my breasts, circling my stomach and dipping below the waistband of my jeans.

He released my hands and unzipped my jeans, pulling them off with a swift and practiced motion. He stood there at the foot of my bed, examining me and taking in every detail before returning to lie beside me. He touched every inch of exposed skin, following his fingers with his tongue and bringing me as close to the edge of control as he could without tipping me over. Somehow the man knew just where to draw the line, just how to bring me quivering to the point of no return.

"Please," I heard myself beg.

He smiled softly. "Please what?" he whispered.

"Please," I said again. I squirmed, struggling to get out of his grasp, longing to do the same things to him that he was doing to me.

"Do you like it when I do this?" he asked, flicking his tongue over the tip of one nipple.

"God, yes!" I cried softly.

"How about this?" His tongue traveled the length of my

stomach, edging its way ever closer to the center of my body, skirting around and then teasing the inside of my thighs. "Do you like this?" he whispered.

My body was exploding with the waves of desire that built, one after another, threatening to overwhelm me with their intensity. It took every ounce of willpower I could find to push him away.

"Not so fast," I whispered. I slid back from him, rising up on my elbows and resting against the mound of pillows that Darlene had taken such care to arrange. Gray gave me a puzzled look, tilting his head to one side and waiting.

I nodded my head in the direction of his legs. "Stand up," I said. "Right there, at the foot of the bed."

Gray smiled and did as I asked. I took my time, studying the tall, lean torso, savoring the way the whorls of hair disappeared below his waistband, and letting my gaze become a caress.

"Take them off," I said, indicating the worn blue jeans.

The game was on. Gray slowly unbuttoned the top button of his pants, his eyes never leaving mine, his look a challenge. Who would last the longest? Who could prolong their desire, lengthening it into an almost unbearable tease of longing and sexual desire?

Gray's fingers caressed the next button, easing it open, revealing a flash of gray briefs beneath the denim. His eyes never wavered. He slid his fingers slowly down the line of his fly, opening each button with slow, deliberate care. It was an invitation.

With elaborate ease, he worked the jeans down over his slender hips, letting them fall down around his ankles as he slowly stepped out of them and stood before me in gray silk boxers. They barely contained the bulge that grew as he stood and hooked his thumbs under his waistband, pulling the sexy underwear slowly down past his thighs.

He stepped out of them and straightened, unselfconscious, totally aware that I was watching him and staring at the erection that indicated just how aroused he was.

He smiled. I smiled. He waited and I slowly licked my lips.

"Come here," I whispered.

"My pleasure," he said softly.

"Oh, no," I muttered under my breath, "I believe the pleasure will be all mine."

Gray lowered himself onto the bed, covering my body with his. His tongue found the tip of my collarbone and he slowly began working his way up my neck, sending electric shocks throughout my body as he teased and flicked his way toward my lips.

I was losing what self-control I had, giving myself over to his knowing touch while still trying desperately to keep some part of myself insulated and protected from the feelings that accompanied Gray's lovemaking. I wanted him but I didn't want to lose myself to him.

Gray moved down my body, his tongue everywhere, his fingers slipping between my legs, teasing and investigating, entering me with a sure, deft touch that made me cry out with pleasure.

He lifted his head then, looked up at me and smiled slowly. Still watching my face, he lowered his head and let his tongue begin to follow his knowing fingers.

I shuddered, my hands reaching reflexively toward his head, caressing him as his tongue found every tiny, desire-filled spot. I felt my back arch as I moved into him. I moaned, calling his name softly as my body gave up every secret it possessed.

"Please," I heard myself whimper. "Don't."

His tongue insisted. His fingers moved deep inside me. I lost track of time and place and everything else but the feel of him slowly bringing me closer and closer to a shattering climax.

He felt it, too. He brought me time and again to the edge, only to back off at the final moment, waiting, then building again.

I pulled at him. I begged. "Please. Now. Inside me. Please." But it was no use. Gray Evans was on a mission to make me lose my mind, and I was his hopeless prisoner.

Just as I thought it would never end, he raised his head, looked at me and said very softly, "Let go, Sophie."

I felt tears well up in my eyes. I wanted him. I wanted this, and yet part of me wanted to shield myself from such emotion.

"It's all right," he whispered. "I'm not going anywhere. Let it happen, Soph."

He waited for a brief moment, searching my face for some sign, some signal that I had heard and understood him. Then, apparently satisfied, he lowered his head again and I felt my body sing beneath his touch. This time, as Gray worked his careful magic, I forgot to think, forgot to protect myself and indeed forgot everything but the pure desire that swept throughout my body.

He felt the climax coming almost before I did, and murmured something soothing as my body arched against him again, racked with the building waves of pleasure.

"Now, Sophie!" I heard him say. I called his name and the world exploded into a tidal surge of color and longing.

I grabbed his shoulders with an urgency that would not be denied now. I pulled at him, calling his name and begging as he hovered over me. I felt my body lunge to meet his, and gasped as he entered me, hard and forceful, his own desire making him take me with an urgency that stole my breath away.

"Sophie, Sophie, Sophie," he cried, using my name to punctuate his thrusts, driving deeper inside me as his desire mounted.

We moved together, each feeling the surge of pleasure building, our bodies communicating in a timeless bond of need and longing. I watched his face, feeling him swell inside me as he came closer and closer to climax. With a cry, Gray thrust into me and exploded, taking me with him over the edge.

He collapsed against me for a long minute, holding me close and murmuring my name over and over, whispering it into my hair and kissing me softly as the insistence in his voice slowly subsided.

"Are you all right?" he asked, finally.

I giggled, but it was muffled by the weight and size of his body. "I'm fine," I managed to say. Fine was an absolute understatement. I was beyond fine. I lay there in a sweaty embrace, totally sexually satisfied, and he wanted to know if I was all right? I was so all right.

I stayed there, pinned beneath him, planning my return assault on his body. Perhaps Gray thought he could get away with driving me crazy, perhaps he was naive enough to think that he was the only one with a tongue, perhaps he even thought me incapable of sending him right up the wall of desire only to leave him there, begging as I had for completion. I chuckled to myself.

Gray stroked my hair tenderly. "Are you laughing?" he asked.

I smiled. He rose up on his elbows and looked down at me, concern replacing complacency. "You're not crying, are you?" he asked.

I smiled up at him and gently pushed him away, rolling him over onto his side and following him, until I was on top of him, resting my head on his strong chest.

"Crying? No, honey, I'm not crying…but you might be."

He frowned, but when I lowered my head, running my tongue down the side of his neck, I heard him sigh.

"Oh," he murmured, "so that's how it is, eh?"

I nibbled softly on the bud of one nipple and let my fingers range slowly down across his stomach.

"Yeah," I said, "that's how it is."

I believe he moaned then, but I was too intent on my explorations to really listen. Gray Evans had met his match, and I intended to show him just exactly how well suited we were.

Chapter 12

Late that evening, we settled on pizza. The Chinese food, cold and congealed, languished at the bottom of my trash can, sacrificed for a noble and very worthy cause. We sat, Gray barefoot, wearing his jeans and T-shirt, and me in a thick, terry-cloth bathrobe, on the couch in the living room, the pizza box open between us, pizza slices balanced precariously in our hands. We wore the happy but exhausted expressions of new lovers. I smiled continuously, never taking my eyes off of Gray, and was rewarded by seeing the same satisfied and happy look mirrored in his eyes. Was it any wonder, then, that I temporarily forgot the destruction in my basement?

I remembered as the last pizza slice disappeared. I stiffened, looked toward the kitchen and said, "I need to show you something."

"Again?" he asked, licking the last bit of sauce from his fingertip. He smiled, running his tongue slowly around the edge of his lips, his mind a million miles away from Nick and the events that had thrown us together.

I brushed the crumbs from my lap and stood up. "Come on. It's downstairs."

Gray stood up, his smile vanishing as he realized that I was serious.

"Darlene and I found it when we were moving my bedroom," I said, leading him through the dining room and toward the basement door. "She thought I should show it to you as soon as you got here, but I wanted a little time to think about it. I thought it could wait."

I moved the chair away from the door and stopped, my hand poised over the doorknob. "You do understand that, don't you?" I asked. "I guess I figured that every time the crime analysts have been here, they've left without any significant information, so I didn't think this time would be any different. Besides I think it's Nick. He's looking for something."

Gray stretched out a hand, resting it gently on the nape of my neck. "Sophie, what is it?"

I turned the knob, pulled open the door and fumbled for the light switch. "I think Nick broke in. He busted out a pane in one of the basement windows, undid the latch and got in that way. It must've happened late this afternoon because I had been down there looking for something earlier."

I led Gray down the steps. When we reached the landing I stopped, so he could look over into the dimly lit room and see the state of devastation that I had seen earlier.

"Jesus! Sophie! You thought it could wait? Damn! Call 9-1-1. Tell them to send an ambulance. Sophie, Jesus!"

I pushed him aside and peered over the edge of the railing. Lying below me, sprawled out on top of a pile of winter clothing, was my ex-husband.

"Oh, my God!" I cried. "What's he doing here?"

The two of us ran down the steps. Gray reached him first, kneeling and touching his neck for a pulse.

I stood beside him, trying to believe that the unconscious figure at my feet was really Nick and not a hallucination.

"Call 9-1-1," Gray said. "Hurry. There's a pulse but it's shallow." He moved Nick slightly, enough to reveal a nasty bruise that had swollen into a goose egg on the side of his head.

I turned and ran for the stairs, climbing them and emerging into the kitchen, the vision of Nick burning its way into my permanent memory bank.

When had he gotten back inside? I grabbed the phone and dialed. When the 9-1-1 operator came on the line, I gave the address, told her there was an unconscious man in my basement, and hung up. I flung ice cubes into a towel and ran back down the steps to Gray and Nick.

"I don't know if he's going to make it," Gray said as I handed him the ice.

I looked at Nick and saw how pale he was, how shallow and reedy his breathing had become, and how different he looked from the man I'd last seen in a Philadelphia courtroom a year ago.

"Stay with him," Gray directed. "I'll go upstairs and wait for the squad."

"Gray," I called softly as he turned away.

"What?" His look was almost impatient.

"He wasn't here earlier. Believe me, ex-husband or not, I would've told you if I'd known…."

Gray's expression softened. "Soph, I know that. We'll sort it out later." He turned and took the steps two at a time, leaving me alone to wait with Nick.

I looked down at the man who had so completely ruled my life for the past twelve years, expecting to feel the familiar surge of revulsion and fear, but finding instead that all I felt was pity.

While he had assumed gigantic proportions in my mind, he was in reality a small man, thin and wiry, not at all muscular. Nick had aged in prison, well beyond his forty-nine years. His hair had turned completely white, but not an attractive, brilliant white. It was more mottled and yellowed, like newsprint left out in the sun for too long. His face was thinner than I remembered and his cheekbones were sunken and hollowed. Deep lines bit into his face and dark circles rimmed his eyes.

Nick was wearing cheap clothing, polyester pants and a thin rayon golf shirt, the colors faded from many washings. There was a sour smell about him, as if he hadn't bathed or even bothered to change his clothes in quite some time.

"Nick," I murmured, "what happened to you?"

The man lying on the floor couldn't answer me. I heard the sound of an ambulance siren wailing in the distance and found myself murmuring a quick prayer for Nick. Whatever he'd done to me, I couldn't find it in my heart to want him to die. Nick had problems, there was no doubt about that, and deep in his heart, he may have intended to kill me for whatever imagined wrong I'd done him by testifying in court. Still I couldn't believe he'd carry out his threats in reality.

Once upon a time I had loved him. I now knew my instincts were probably all wrong. I had wanted to save him from himself and that was an impossible task. Nick obviously didn't want to be saved. If he had, he'd have saved himself.

A vision of Connie Bono, dead in the backyard, popped into my head. Then I thought of my father's friend Pete, lying white-faced on the stretcher as he was loaded into the waiting ambulance. Finally I remembered Gray, knees buckling with the pain of his head wound, blood running down the side of his face. Who was I trying to fool? Nick Komassi, the man I was feeling sorry for, was probably every bit the cold-blooded killer. What delusion made me think he hadn't been planning to kill me off, as well? Hadn't he as much as promised that before he went to prison?

A cold chill swept through me as I looked back at my former husband. How could I have been so wrong about him?

The sound of Gray and the EMTs walking overhead interrupted my thoughts, bringing me back to the here and now. I looked up and saw the shaft of light from the kitchen widen as the door opened and the crew began their descent into the basement.

I looked back at Nick and then at the window just above where he lay. Had he fallen? Was that how he'd hit his head, or had someone else hit him and pushed him through the small opening? If Nick wasn't the victim of an accident, then who'd hit him and why had they done it?

In the next few minutes Nick was loaded onto a stretcher and taken away. Police officers and crime scene technicians once again invaded my home. The man who'd held me in his arms only an hour before turned back into a New Bern police detective, all-business and very far removed from the teasing, playful lover I'd pulled up the stairs and into my bed.

Gray stood on the landing overlooking the basement, talking in low tones to his partner. The two men surveyed the scene, Wendell frowning and Gray looking impassively at my strewn belongings. Below them, crime scene investigators once again spread their graphite powder everywhere, dusting for prints and photographing every tiny corner of the musty cellar.

I turned away from them and withdrew to the kitchen to make coffee. It promised to be another long night. I peered through the kitchen window, trying to see to the back of my yard, wondering if anyone was out there watching me. I leaned closer, focusing and squinting out into the darkness, so intent upon ferreting out the details that I completely lost track of my surroundings. I shrieked when Durrell's cold, wet nose hit the back of my leg.

A nearby officer stuck her head in the kitchen, withdrawing when she saw me kneeling to pat Durrell. He was licking my hand, his tail wagging at a furious pace.

"Where'd you come from?" I asked.

Durrell grinned.

"Bet you're hungry, huh?" I asked.

Durrell barked and turned circles around his tail, prancing over to the refrigerator and waiting for me to serve him.

"Okay," I said, pulling open the door and inspecting the contents. "We have a slightly aged package of sliced ham, some provolone cheese and a small container of leftover chicken Scapaletti."

I chopped the ham and cheese, added a spoonful or two of the pasta and chicken, then poured water into a second dish and set the meal down in a corner. Durrell, without a backward glance, rushed the bowls and forgot all about me.

"Where's your mother?" I muttered under my breath. Della hadn't returned after Pete had been taken to the hospital, and now here was the long-lost Durrell. That seemed to be the pattern with the two of them. Durrell wandered off without much of an attachment to his owner and she did the same to him.

"You're feeding that mangy hound?" Darlene cried, entering the kitchen from the dining room.

Durrell lifted his head and barked ferociously at my sister.

"Get him away from me! He's violent! He's probably got rabies!"

Darlene stood in the doorway, holding her broomstick skirt up around her knees, obviously terrified of the little dog. She had painted her toenails in wild, bright metallic colors that stood out in vivid relief against the pale white skin of her feet and legs.

"You paint them like that for Wendell?" I asked.

Darlene favored me with a withering glare. "His pager went off just as he was about to discover them," she said. "Your ex-husband is ruining my love life!"

"Yours! What about mine?"

Darlene rolled her eyes. "Well, you were married to him. I'm just an innocent bystander…a frustrated, innocent bystander, I might add."

I heard a commotion in the living room and the sound of a familiar raised voice cursing in Italian.

"You didn't," I said to Darlene.

She shrugged. "What could I do? You want them to find out from a stranger that Nick was half-dead at your house? You want to face Ma and Pa after they see it on the morning news? All's I did was call and tell them not to worry. Can I help it they took it upon themselves to show up?"

It was too late now. Ma and Pa were right behind Darlene, pushing past her impatiently. Pa was loaded down with armfuls of brown grocery sacks. Behind him, Joey carried more grocery sacks, looking as if he'd been pulled straight out of bed without benefit of a comb or fresh clothing.

"Shit," I heard him mutter.

"Where is he?" Ma asked. There was no doubt whom she meant.

"They took him to the hospital, Ma. He got knocked out."

Ma set her bags down on the kitchen table and looked around. Durrell had returned to eating, but still managed to utter a low growl now and then. Pa and Joey set their bags on the counter and looked longingly at the coffeepot, while Ma took stock and prepared to issue orders.

"Maybe they'll take him to jail where he belongs," Pa groused. "Then maybe we can get a decent night's rest!"

Joey ran his hand through what hair he had left on his

head and looked up at the cabinet where I kept the Wild Turkey.

"All right," Ma said. "Pa, boil a big pot of water. Joey, put them groceries away. Darlene, get some milk and sugar out for the coffee and put out spoons and napkins. Sophie, I need a big stockpot."

Ma was beginning to move, reaching with a knowing hand into a sack and pulling out a bag of onions and peppers.

"Thank God you got the stove in," she said. "How many we got here?"

"Ma, you don't gotta feed them," I said.

Ma whirled around, knife in hand, and I jumped back. "You don't *gotta* feed nobody," she said in a dangerous tone, "but that's what you do. You show some respect for them what's helping you."

"Okay, Ma, okay." I held up my hands and backed off. "I think there's about twelve here."

"Go tell them there will be food in a little while, but for now there's coffee and pastries." Ma was giving me The Look, like she might leap out and beat me if I didn't move fast enough.

"On my way," I said.

"And put some clothes on," she called after me. "You look like *una puttana.*"

I looked down and realized I was still in my bathrobe and naked under that.

"Ma, I was asleep when I—"

How Ma knew, I'll never know. "You were sitting on your couch eating pizza with that detective," she said calmly. "Don't try and bullshit me, Sophia. I got eyes."

I stopped, my hand on the doorknob to the basement, and looked at my mother. She was staring at me with a carefully neutral expression.

"Wear something appropriate to the hospital," she said.

"What?"

Ma's eyes darkened. "What? Your husband lies in a hospital bed and you don't go to see to him?"

"Ma! He's my *ex*-husband. He tried to kill me! Why would I go to the hospital?"

Ma stiffened. "You go, Sophia. It is the right thing to do in the eyes of God! You go pray for his immortal soul." Ma's eyes narrowed slightly and she looked over her shoulder to make certain no one could hear what she said next. "You go to pray, yes, but you go to find out what the son of a bitch was doing here, too!"

"Jesus!"

Ma lunged and I flew down the basement steps, almost colliding with Gray and Wendell.

"There's coffee upstairs," I said. "Ma insists on feeding the world, so prepare yourselves."

Wendell smiled and started for the kitchen. Gray touched my arm, detaining me while Wendell went upstairs to make points with Ma.

"I'm going on to the hospital," he said. "If he's conscious we'll try and get a statement. Either way, I think this may mean we can wrap it up around here. Nick won't bother you anymore."

I nodded. "I'll go with you."

Gray frowned. "I don't think that would be a good idea."

I shrugged. "Me, either, but Ma's on my back. She says I need to go pray for his immortal salvation, and as she was holding a cleaver when she said it, I figure it's just easier to go make an appearance. Maybe he'll talk to me before he talks to you. He may hate me, but he hates police officers more."

"Sophie, the man was tracking you like prey. He's killed one woman already. You don't owe him your sympathy."

I looked away, staring at a spot on the floor in front of me. "I know." I lifted my head and looked into his eyes. "But what if you're wrong? Nick can't speak for himself. What about the bump on his head? What if he didn't kill Connie? What if it was the other men?"

Gray sighed. "Don't start making up stories to fit the moment," he said. "The truth is usually the most obvious answer, and Nick has a history with you."

"But not a violent history."

Gray grabbed my arms, spun me toward him and brought his face close to mine. "Wake up, Sophie," he said, his voice sharp with frustration. "He threatened to kill you in an open courtroom and now he's out of prison and tracking you. The man is violent. And what about the guy who did this to him? What if he comes after you?"

I jerked away from him and started up the stairs. "I'll drive myself."

"Damn it, Sophie!"

I walked slowly up the stairs to my room, grabbed a towel and headed into the bathroom for a shower. I didn't need Gray to take me to the hospital. All I needed from him was to feel understood, and that was something he couldn't give me. In his mind, Gray probably thought he was taking care of me, protecting me from a man who wanted to harm me. How could I blame him for not appreciating my situation?

I ducked my head under the warm soothing water of my new shower.

When I returned downstairs to the kitchen, Ma was holding court. Gathered around her at the table were EMTs, crime scene technicians and assorted police officers, many more than had been in the house before.

Gray wasn't among them. He had left without me. I leaned against the counter, watching the others banter back and forth.

One young female EMT was earnestly consulting Ma about her own mother, asking advice on how to handle some situation or another. Ma, with uncharacteristic gentleness, patted her hand and spoke in a whisper, shaking her head slightly from side to side.

Joey stood up and came to join me, pouring fresh coffee into his mug. "Gray left," he said.

"I know. He doesn't get Ma wanting me to go see Nick."

Joey sighed. "Me, either. The son of a bitch should lie there alone and contemplate his own eternal damnation. I don't like it."

I shrugged. "Doesn't much matter. It's easier to just go and get it over with. With Ma, you choose your battles. Besides, maybe I can get him to tell me something."

I slipped out while the others told stories, walking down the driveway to my rental convertible and wishing like anything that I was on my way anywhere other than the Craven County Medical Center.

I picked up the black sedan in my rearview mirror about a block away from the house. At first I thought it was Gray's unmarked car, but one headlight strayed slightly to the right and there were no telltale antennas sticking up over the trunk. I tried turning down several side streets, running a yellow light and varying my speed, but the car kept pace with me.

I reached into my purse and fumbled for my cell phone and realized that in my haste, I'd left it behind, securely attached to its recharging station.

"Shit!" I whispered.

I studied the car in my rearview mirror as we pulled to a stop at a red light. Two men sat in the front seat. I toyed with the idea of jumping out of the car and confronting them, but quickly discarded the idea as foolish. I drove on toward the hospital, figuring they'd leave when they saw me park and go inside. I was wrong.

At the very next red light they rammed me from behind, throwing me forward and triggering the air bag.

Before I could regain my senses, they were out of their car and running up to my convertible. I attempted to raise the car's top but I wasn't fast enough. When I leaned on the horn, one thick arm reached over and grabbed my hand, pulling it away with a painful wrench. They were on either side of me, one sitting in the passenger seat and one standing by the driver's side. Couldn't anyone see us?

"Get out," said the man hovering above me.

"Now," said the man seated to my right. The small black gun in his hand made arguing pointless.

I shook my head, still trying to clear the shock of the impact from my stunned body. The tall man standing by my side bent down to open my door. He reached into the car, grabbed my arm and yanked. I cried out as a shiver of pain ran through my elbow and exploded into my shoulder.

"Quit stalling," he said, his voice thick and nasal.

Within seconds we were moving toward their car. In a few moments, I would be stuffed inside the trunk, a prisoner. No one would know where I was. No one would be able to help me then. Where the hell was all the traffic when you needed it?

I was thinking in overdrive. I couldn't let them put me into their car. If they managed to get me into the trunk, chances were I'd never escape. With two of them holding guns on me, all the Krav Maga in the world wouldn't keep me from getting shot.

"What do you want?" I asked, stalling for time.

The shorter man nudged my side with his gun. "Where is it? Did Nick get it or do you still have it?"

Headlights turned onto the street behind us and I had the distraction I needed.

"Tony, move it!" the tall guy barked. "Get her in the car! We got company!"

There wasn't going to be a better opportunity. I moved, breaking free of them as the oncoming car approached. I ducked and ran, zigzagging toward a clump of bushes, expecting to hear the whine and ping of bullets flying around me. If I made it to cover, I could jump out and signal the car as it drew closer. If that failed I could run deeper into the darkness.

The vehicle in the distance suddenly put on a burst of speed and headed directly for my assailants' sedan. It was impossible that the driver didn't see the two cars stopped in the road. They were blocking the street, the black sedan sitting just behind my red sports car. Nonetheless the newcomer drove on, gaining speed.

I reached the bushes and crouched behind them, watching as my two assailants tried to start their car and move it out of the path of the oncoming vehicle. The other driver had to be drunk.

As I watched, the speeding car, another black four-door sedan, hit my captors' car. There was a horrible wrenching sound of metal hitting metal. The impact threw my empty convertible into the intersection of the busy Neuse Boulevard, causing the few cars already in the roadway to swerve violently to avoid it. Surely someone would stop and help now.

Horns blew. Voices yelled. The driver of the second black car threw his vehicle into reverse and started slowly backing up. Then the driver did the unthinkable. He revved his engine and prepared to ram the car once again.

As I watched him line his sedan up directly behind his intended target a lone arm appeared from the passenger-side window of his car, gun in hand.

I ducked down and heard the initial salvo. Bullets hit metal and I risked a quick glimpse at the roadway. I could see the second car's driver well enough to note the startled expression on his face as he threw his vehicle into reverse again. I'd never seen him before.

Sirens wailed. Another round of gunshots erupted and the second sedan took off, flying backward down the street, squealing tires as it turned suddenly and fled the scene. Tony and his companion sat up in their seats, cranked their battered car and rocketed out of the intersection and onto a side street.

I was forgotten.

Blue lights and sirens exploded into the intersection, surrounding my car and blocking traffic in all directions.

"Hertz isn't going to be happy about this," I said, crawling out of my hiding place. I stood on wobbly legs and attempted to brush dust from my clothing. I looked at my poor car, camped forlornly in the middle of the road, and said a prayer of thanks. "There but for the grace of God," I murmured, and started walking slowly toward the waiting police officers.

Chapter 13

It was after midnight when I reached the hospital. The attempted abduction and subsequent accident investigation had taken over two hours, and I was becoming known in New Bern as a one-woman disaster, responsible for keeping much of the city's police force on its toes.

Several of the officers who responded arrived with traces of Ma's handiwork on their uniform shirtfronts. Once they'd been assured that I wasn't hurt, and had ascertained that the men who'd attempted to kidnap me were long gone, they relaxed. They soon had the traffic officers acquainted with my talent for attracting danger and my mother's talent for preparing homemade Italian food. The scene was taking on the air of a street party when Gray Evans arrived.

He stepped out of his car looking like a thundercloud. "What happened?" he demanded. Then, almost as an afterthought, it seemed, he said, "Are you hurt?"

Once he'd been reassured, the cop in him reemerged. He listened. He wrote notes. He shook his head and walked over to the skid marks in the street.

"I don't get it," I said, when he rejoined me. "I swear there were two black sedans and it looked like the second one intentionally rammed the first one."

"Huh," Gray snorted. "And they wanted to know if you had 'it' or Nick had 'it,' right?"

"Yep. And one of the guys called the other one Tony—you know, like from the other night?"

He nodded. "Well, let's get you home," he said.

"Just drop me off at the medical center," I said. "Joey can come back for me later."

The temperature in the air around us seemed to drop by twenty degrees.

"All right," he said. "Let's go."

We didn't speak on the short ride to the hospital. He pulled up in front of the emergency room door and said, "He's in Neuro-ICU and still unconscious. I doubt they'll even let you see him. This is pointless, Sophie. He's in a coma."

I shrugged and reached for the door handle. Part of me wanted to turn and beg him to understand. But I held back, thinking that if he were the right guy, he'd know. He'd understand completely. Darlene and her big ideas! Whatever in the world made me think there was such a thing as destiny?

I opened the car door, thanked him politely for the ride and closed it softly behind me. I didn't look back as I walked toward the E.R. entrance, but it wouldn't have mattered. As the E.R. doors began to shut behind me, I heard the roar of his engine as he drove off.

The only thing that distinguished Nick's bed in the ICU unit from that of any other patient's was the cop parked outside the cubicle. The guy was young and sleepy, and sat slouched down in his uncomfortable blue plastic chair, a bored expression on his face.

"You're Mr. Komassi's wife?" the nurse asked.

"Yes," I lied. A half truth told for Nick's eternal salvation. After all, I meant well.

The nurse studied me intently, probably wondering if I was a criminal like Nick, or what made me foolishly stand by a wanted felon. She was middle-aged, a washed-out blonde carrying an extra fifty pounds. The fluorescent lighting gave her skin a sallow, dimpled cast. The pale lipstick she wore didn't help, either. But her eyes held that spark of compassion I associated with good nurses, the ones who still cared despite the era of managed care and insurance cutbacks.

"Mrs. Komassi," she began, "I didn't know you were coming or I would have asked the doctor to wait."

"It's all right," I said, attempting to soothe her. "It's late. I didn't expect to see him."

The nurse went on, almost as if she didn't hear me. "I would've asked him to stay, given the gravity of Mr. Komassi's condition."

Now she had me. "Was his skull fractured?" I asked.

The nurse—Lomax, her name tag read—shook her head. "There was some swelling of the brain," she said. "But the main issue seems to be his liver."

"His liver?"

She nodded. "I suppose you're aware that with hepatitis C, the liver can sometimes be critically compromised."

"Hepatitis C?"

Nurse Lomax frowned. "You didn't know?"

I shook my head. "I don't think he did, either," I answered.

The nurse stared at me. "Maybe that's why it's gotten to this point," she said. "Mrs. Komassi, we won't know until the test results are returned, but…" Here she looked at me with a practiced, grave expression. "The doctor doesn't think your husband is going to pull out of this. The head injury compounded by what was already a life-threatening liver complication may just be too much for him."

I felt the breath whoosh out of my chest, felt the sledge-hammer punch of unexpected grief tighten my heart, and futilely tried to control my shocked reaction.

"Oh, no," I said. "No."

Nurse Lomax rounded the corner of her nurse's station and led me quickly to a vacant, blue plastic chair. She knelt by my side and laid a reassuring hand on my knee.

"I'm so very sorry to have to tell you like this," she said. "It must be a horrible shock."

I nodded numbly, staring at the squares of linoleum on the floor in front of me.

Nick was dying. The thought echoed through my consciousness, resonating against the wall of denial my heart put up as protection. Nick was dying.

"May I see him?" I asked after a minute.

"Sure." Nurse Lomax stood up, waited for me to stand and then walked toward the cubicle where the police officer slept.

Nick lay hooked to tubes and machines. His face was drawn and his complexion pale and, as I now noted, yellowed.

"Hello, Nick," I whispered, leaning down close to his ear. "It's Sophie."

There was no response.

"He can hear you on some level," Nurse Lomax said. "Go ahead and talk to him. He might regain consciousness, but only for a little while."

Before he died? I wondered.

"If he does come out of it," she continued, "the police have asked that we let the officer outside know, so he can write down anything Mr. Komassi says." The nurse frowned, as if irritated by this imposition on her patient. "I'm leaving it up to you," she said. "Let him know or not."

I turned away from her and focused my attention back onto Nick. I stroked his arm lightly, swallowed a painful lump in my throat and began to talk, just like old times, only not.

"Oh, Nick," I whispered. "How has it all come down to this, huh?" I looked at the monitors, listened to the quiet beeps for a moment and then went on. "Ma made me come," I said. "Well, she didn't *make* me, I suppose. I guess I would've come anyway, especially with you so…sick. But you know Ma, always taking care of the world."

I looked down at the pale little man on the bed and wondered how I'd ever seen him as a powerful figure in my life.

"I don't know you anymore, Nick," I said. "And I guess I never really knew you, but you know what? You don't know me, either. Not now. Not like I am now."

I raised my head defiantly. "You're an asshole, Nick Komassi, a bully and an asshole."

The heart monitor went crazy, beeping suddenly as Nick's heart rate spiked and his eyes fluttered. He heard me.

"Okay," I said, "just calm down. I didn't mean it." Then I stopped myself. "Wait, I did, too, mean it! I meant every word I said. You made my life a living hell. You cost me my home in Philly. I moved because of what you did, Nick."

The monitor soared again and Nick moaned softly, but I couldn't stop now. "And you know what, you son of a bitch? I'll still pray for your fucking salvation. You know why?"

"Beep, beep, beep!" Nick's monitor answered.

"Because I'm a better human being than you, Nick."

My own words stopped me, because if I'd just made that

statement, how could I be a better human being? Better human beings didn't believe they were better human beings, they just were. You didn't hear the Virgin Mary spouting off how good she was for having Jesus, did you?

"Okay," I said. "That was wrong. I'm not better. In fact, I'm actually stupid."

Nick moaned, scaring me. I looked out at the nurse's station, saw Nurse Lomax watching the readouts at her terminal, and figured she was on top of the situation.

"I'm stupid because here I am, with you maybe dying, wanting to make peace with you, you son of a bitch. I don't want you burning in hell and me not having had my say with you. If you're going to die, I don't want you going to hell on my account alone." I felt tears running down my cheeks, saw them drip onto the sheet that covered Nick and saw the wide splotches spread into large circles.

"I couldn't save you, Nick," I whispered. "Why wasn't I enough for you?"

I felt strong hands slip over my shoulders gripping me and pulling me gently back against a solid wall of muscle.

"Aw, Soph," Joey said softly, "come here."

I turned and buried my head against my brother's strong chest, sobbing as if my heart were breaking, which in a way, it was.

"He's dying. I couldn't stop him from doing those awful things and I can't stop thinking that if I'd been the right kind of woman, he wouldn't have acted like that. Joey, what did I do wrong?"

"Soph, you listen to me," Joey said, his voice strong and tough. "This hasn't got anything to do with you. Nick chose his life. Nick had his shot with you and he blew it. The son of a bitch walked away from everything that was good and decent in his life. He chose to stay sick."

"No," I sobbed. "If I'd seen...if I'd known the signs, I could've gotten him help. I let him destroy himself, Joey."

"No!"

The weak voice coming from the bed startled us both. Nick's eyes were open, focused uncertainly on my brother and me. He frowned, seeming not to know where he was, but aware only of the conversation happening in front of him.

"Sophie," Nick croaked, "I didn't want bad things to happen to you."

I was aware of Nurse Lomax moving around her station, reaching out to adjust something on a screen. I looked up at her and nodded, but didn't try to alert the police officer. Lomax stayed where she was, signaling me with an imperceptible nod. She knew and she wasn't telling, either.

Nick shook his head slightly. "What happened?"

I stepped closer to the bedside and leaned down close to him. "I don't know," I answered. "We found you in my basement. Either you fell or someone hit you."

Nick's eyes widened, as if seeing something behind me that frightened him. I looked over my shoulder and saw nothing, then turned back to him.

"Are you hurting?" I asked. "I can get you something for pain if you are."

He shook his head. "No. I don't want anything for pain. I need to talk to you. I don't have much time." His voice had a hysterical quality to it, rising sharply as he spoke, and frightening me even more.

"What is it, Nick?" I asked.

His gaze returned to me, relaxing as he saw me standing there beside his bed. "I did something really stupid. I thought I was being smart, but it didn't work out too well."

"Who are the people in the black cars, Nick?"

"What black cars?" he asked.

Behind me I heard Joey's sigh of frustration. We both recognized the trace of the old Nick returning, the elusive, evasive con artist.

"What do they want, Nick? What are they looking for?"

Nick's eyes closed and for a moment I thought he was unconscious again.

"Nick!" I said sharply. "They think I have it. They ran me off the road on my way here. Now what do you have that they want?"

Nick's eyes popped open again. His face twisted as a spasm of pain shot through his body, and he groaned.

"It was an accident. I was making one of my movies, only nobody knew I was there," he said softly. "That's when it happened. A guy comes outta nowhere and wastes this other guy and I got it all on tape."

"You witnessed a murder."

Nick closed his eyes and nodded. "I didn't know who it was at the time. I didn't know what it was worth." He tried to laugh, but the sound died in his throat. "I would never have done time if I'd known what I had."

"Nick, you saw someone murder an FBI agent."

"Yes," he whispered. "I know that now. It was mob—"

Nick broke off, choking and gasping for breath. Joey touched my arm, his expression close to panic. "Should we call the nurse?"

Nick stopped coughing as suddenly as he'd started. "Don't do that. I'm not done."

"Nick, maybe you should rest awhile."

His eyes widened. "I told you. I don't have time. I need to tell you the rest."

"Nick, who wants the tape? Someone followed you down here, didn't they?"

He grimaced, either from the pain or from the effort to talk.

"I was stupid. I trusted the wrong people. I thought I could sell it to the guy who pulled the trigger, maybe get enough money to leave the country, but Connie double-crossed me."

Joey and I had to strain to hear him. His voice was barely loud enough to rise above the quiet hush of the machines that monitored his vital signs.

"She was supposed to meet me at the gate the day I got out, but the bitch took my car and took off. She was gonna beat me to it."

"Where is the tape, Nick? Where did you hide it?"

Nick smiled. "Where nobody but you would ever find it," he murmured. "It was too simple, just like ABC, like a kid's coloring book. I fooled them."

His eyes closed and he appeared to be sleeping. Joey frowned down at him and shook his head.

"What in the hell is he talking about?" he asked.

I shrugged. "I don't know. That's Nick for you, never gives you all the information you need, always holding back something important."

Nick's eyes were open again and he was listening. "I treated you so badly, Sophie," he whispered. "Don't worry, Connie paid me back."

"Nick, did you kill her?"

He shook his head.

"Who did?"

"I don't know," he moaned. "Tony? Kathy? I just don't know. Sophie, they won't stop until they have what they want," he said, his voice pitched high with panic.

"Nick, who is Kathy?"

He didn't seem to hear me.

"It's a fucking war, Sophie. Connie was such a fool. You don't play with the mob, Sophie. They don't play."

"Who, Nick? Who?"

"Where's Kathy?" Nick asked suddenly. "She brought me here and then she left. Maybe she killed her."

"Kathy who? Nick, who is she?"

His head dropped back against the pillow and his eyes shut. "May God have mercy on my soul," he murmured. "I'm going to hell."

Joey and I crossed ourselves reflexively and bowed our heads. When I finished, I looked up and found Gray Evans leaning in the doorway. His face was lined with fatigue and there was no warmth in his eyes, no sign that he even recognized me.

"Forgive me, Father, for I have sinned," Nick whispered, then lapsed back into unconsciousness.

I turned to him, reached into my purse for my Rosary beads and touched Joey's arm. The two of us murmured the familiar words, "Hail Mary, full of grace…" but Nick never responded. He was lost somewhere between our world and the next, scared and in pain.

I didn't need the pressure from Ma to pray for Nick's soul. The forgiveness and compassion came without effort. I reached out and touched his shoulder, as if willing some energy to pass from my body into his. I tucked my Rosary beads up under his pillow and leaned down to whisper into his ear.

"I'm going to call your brother, Nick. Try and hang on, okay?"

Nick's breathing never changed. The heart monitor beeped steadily and without any of the spikes I'd seen earlier. Joey and I bowed our heads, prayed silently for a few more moments and then turned to go. Gray Evans had vanished from the doorway as suddenly as he'd appeared; in his place stood his FBI counterpart, Agent Cole.

I attempted to walk past her and on toward the elevators, but she moved, putting herself between me and the metal doors. Given our last encounter, I figured she was a slow learner.

"Move."

"I need to know what he told you." Cole was attempting to stare a hole through me, giving me her best shot at intimidation.

I stared right back at her and said nothing. I didn't trust her. Would she still think I was in on it? Agent Cole blinked. "You'd think, after all he's done to you, that you would want to be more cooperative," she said finally.

I pushed my way past her, reaching the bank of elevators just as one slid open. Joey and I stepped inside, half expecting the agent to stop us, and feeling relieved when she didn't. Joey leaned back against the wall, closed his eyes and sighed.

"I'm just glad you didn't decide to kick her ass again," he said. "I'm way too tired to pull you off her, so it would've wound up being a homicide. Then Ma would've killed me for letting you kill an FBI agent, and Pa would've killed somebody, anybody, because he missed the boat on getting Nick."

"And all of this because you're tired?"

Joey nodded. The elevator doors slid open, discharging us into the front lobby. "Yep," he said. "That's family for you. They'll kill you."

I ignored my brother, picked up a pay phone and dialed Nick's brother's home number without having to search my memory for it. Some things just stick in your mind without rhyme or reason.

We returned to an empty house. Joey walked inside with me, checking every nook and cranny, offering to stay if I needed him. I shook my head, smiled and pushed him out the door.

"The police are watching the house," I told him, noting the dark circles under his eyes. "I've got more dead bolts on the doors now than I had in Philly. Go home. Get some sleep."

He was too tired to argue. I stood in the doorway, watching him walk away from me, and was suddenly overwhelmed by the urge to see his face just one more time before he left.

"Joey!" I called.

He turned, looking alarmed.

I raised my hand and smiled. "I just wanted to say thank you. I didn't want you to leave without me saying it."

He shook his head, relieved. "Soph, you don't have to thank me."

I looked at my big brother and smiled even though it was all I could do not to cry. "I know that, Joey. What I'm saying is I love you, and given Nick's condition, and the shock of it all, I think I need you to hear that I love you and I am grateful for all you do for me."

Joey didn't tease me. He nodded and stood there in the driveway, his hand resting on the roof of his car.

"Joey, there just aren't any guarantees in life," I said. "I want to make sure the people I love know how I feel about them."

He nodded. "I know, Soph. So tell Gray, all right? I don't think he knows where he fits with you. I think if he knew, he wouldn't have a problem with you and Nick. You see what I'm saying?"

That was Joey, half-dead on his feet and still giving me advice, only now I didn't mind it at all. My brother was right.

I nodded. "I'll talk to him in the morning," I said. "Right now, I'd better get the FBI off my ass. I'm going to call Agent Cole. At least she can't arrest me over the phone."

Joey lifted his hand, waved it in my general direction and got into his car. A moment later I watched as his taillights vanished around the corner and I was alone again.

I closed the door, turned the dead bolt and took one last glance out at the street through the living room window. No black sedans. No police cars, either. I wondered where Gray had gone and when he'd return, or even if he'd return. I closed my eyes and leaned back against the door, remembering the way the evening had started.

The flood of images rushed up to meet me, cycling rapidly through the evening and ending with FBI Agent Cole's icy eyes staring at me from the doorway to Nick's ICU cubicle. I felt tired and numb inside, too tired to figure it all out. All I wanted now was rest.

Instead, I pulled the FBI agent's card from my pocket, dialed the number and when she answered, began telling her everything Nick had told me.

Chapter 14

The shrill ringing of the phone awakened me at seven the next morning.

"I took the day off," Darlene said. "I thought you might need me."

I rolled over, phone in hand, and buried myself between two twin piles of pillows. I lay there with my eyes closed, surrounded by the lingering scent of Gray's cologne. I inhaled deeply and tried to go back to sleep.

"Sophie!" Darlene yelled. "Wake up! I'm coming over. I'm bringing bagels."

I moaned. "Let me sleep, Darlene!"

"Get in the shower," she instructed. "I'm leaving my house now. We've got to head over to the hospital. What if Nick wakes up and starts talking? What if somebody tries to get to him? Now move it. I'm on my way!"

The phone went dead and I stayed where I was, breathing

Gray and trying to pretend Darlene hadn't called. But my brain took over, making sleep impossible as it began chugging like a small train climbing Mount Everest. Darlene was right. We needed to get to the hospital. I threw the covers back and sat up.

On the best days, I am not a morning person. On other days I'm not even certain I belong to the human race. Today I was brain dead and unable to kick-start myself into anything more than a stupor.

I didn't bother waiting for a complete pot of coffee to brew, choosing instead to fill my mug from the thick stream of the first part of the brew and cut it with hot water. I wandered back upstairs to take a shower. I stood under the spray with my eyes closed, wishing for another four hours of sleep.

The water coursed over my body, beating on my back. Slowly I began to put the pieces of yesterday into place. The harsh reality of Nick lying in an ICU bed and not expected to live brought me back to a full awareness of my day's agenda.

I heard sounds coming from the kitchen and assumed Darlene had arrived. "Put cream cheese on mine," I yelled, turning off the water. I stepped out of the tub and turned to grab a fluffy yellow towel. Thinking Darlene might not have heard me, I wrapped a second towel around my body, twisted the first up to cover my hair, and started down the stairs to call to her again.

"Hey!" I yelled over the banister. Someone was moving in the dining room, opening and closing the drawers of my antique sideboard.

"The silverware is in the kitchen," I called. When no one answered me, I continued down the stairs, little prickles of alarm creeping up the back of my neck.

As I rounded the landing and descended the last four steps, Della walked out of the dining room. Durrell was following her, sniffing at her heels.

"You didn't answer the door so me and Durrell came on in to make sure you was all right," she said. "Need a refill on your coffee?"

Della looked like she'd been shopping at a thrift store. She was wearing a faded pair of men's jeans that had to have been two sizes too large, and an oversize cotton dress shirt in a faded shade of burnt orange. Her hair was a rat-tailed mess and she looked like she hadn't slept at all. But her appearance wasn't what caught my attention, it was the way she talked. Yesterday, shocked by Pete's shooting, Della had stopped talking like a country bumpkin. Yesterday, she'd spoken like someone who'd had a good education, and her enunciation had been polished, without a trace of an accent.

"Help yourself," I answered, but I watched her, feeling a wave of suspicion waft over me. Why look for a coffee mug in the dining room drawers? "I see Durrell finally turned up," I said.

Della looked down at the dog as if she hadn't realized he was in the room.

"You haven't been at the hospital with Pete all this time, have you?" I asked. I realized that in my rush to check on Nick, I'd forgotten all about Pete.

Again the blank look and another long pause before she answered. "No. I left after his wife got there. I guess I just forgot about the dog. That shootin' shook me up right much. I just went on home."

I nodded and would've said more, but Darlene, with her usual good timing, chose this moment to come walking in with a bagful of bagels.

"Get that dog before he bites me!" she shrieked. Durrell was still standing by Della's side, showing no signs of movement, but he did grin.

"He won't bite you," I said. I looked down at Durrell. He

grinned up at me like this was a big game and he was ready to play. "Go on, Durrell," I said. "Tell the nice lady how friendly you are."

Durrell spun around and growled in Darlene's direction. She yelped and made a vain attempt to scale the countertop. Della leaned down and yanked on his collar.

"Come on, mutt," she said. "We got work to do." She looked up at me and attempted a smile. "We'll start on the front yard if it's all the same to you."

"Della," I said, "you look done in. Why don't you go home and rest up?"

She shook her head vehemently. "No, me and Durrell need the money."

Durrell sighed, looked up at me and grinned.

"Dog food, huh?" I asked him.

"Rent money," Della answered, and signaled to Durrell. "Come on, mutt." They walked back through the house and were out the kitchen door before I could offer Della a bagel. Darlene watched her leave and rolled her eyes.

"I'm telling you, she's bad news. Bad Karma. She's a drug addict or something, and just look at that dog. You ever see a dog like that?" Darlene was opening the bag of bagels and pulling out a tub of cream cheese.

She started rummaging around, opening the kitchen cabinets and drawers and peering at the contents. "You don't own a toaster?" she asked finally.

"It's in the basement with the rest of the kitchen stuff. I didn't unpack it."

Darlene sighed. "What? We're supposed to eat them raw?"

"Darlene, they're not raw. They're cooked. They're just not toasted, that's all. Use the oven."

Darlene straightened up from her inspection of my drawers and cabinets; in her hand was a pink piece of paper.

"Okay," she said. "You want proof she's on drugs? Look at this." She extended her arm and shoved the paper in my direction. It was one of the flyers Della had printed up to advertise her home repair business.

"Look," Darlene said, "she didn't even put her phone number on it. If you were a potential client and you *did* want to hire her, how would you find her?"

I stared at the paper and then back at Darlene. "Okay, so she's not a rocket scientist. At least she works hard when she's here. That's all I ask."

Darlene was slathering cream cheese on a cinnamon raisin bagel. "How would you know?" she asked. "She's always taking someone to the hospital. She can't work a day without someone getting hurt or shot at."

I frowned at my sister. "That's not her fault," I said, but a flicker of doubt sparked and kindled into suspicion. What had Della been looking for when I'd come downstairs?

Darlene turned around, a smear of cream cheese dotting her nose. "Oh, isn't it? You ever think it's her karma attracting all that negative energy?"

I shook my head and started toward the bag of bagels. There was definitely something strange about Della and now I was beginning to worry about it.

"That girl wouldn't have a job working anywhere if she hadn't been walking down the street and bumped smack into you." Darlene laughed. "She probably spotted you from a block away and said, 'There's a sucker—let's go get her to hire us.'"

"Darlene, that's cruel."

My sister rolled her eyes again and bit down on her bagel. For a moment there was silence as she chewed, then she was at it again.

"I know people," she mumbled, her mouth full of bagel, "and I'm telling you, I don't trust her." She held up her hand like a traffic cop, warding off any further discussion of Della's karma. "Never mind about her for now. We have bigger fish to fry."

Durrell interrupted us, barking like a maniac as someone opened the screen door and stepped up onto the back porch.

"Well, at least you got a doorbell out of the deal," Darlene grumbled.

I stood up, expecting Joey or Pa, and found Gray standing in the back doorway. He looked like hell. Dark circles rimmed his eyes, he needed a shave and his clothes were wrinkled, like he'd slept in them, or worse, not slept at all.

"I wanted to let you know we caught the two men who hit your car last night," he said. His tone was terse and clipped, as if issuing a report to a hostile press. "Danny Cassiano and Mel Turantino. Those names ring any bells?"

I shook my head. "Should they?" I asked.

Gray shrugged, noticed Darlene and nodded to her before turning back to answer me. "They're from South Philadelphia," he said. "They've got arrest records as long as your arm. I talked to the police up there. They said both men work for the Lombardo crime family. They're mob-connected enforcers. All their arrests are on assault charges, but nothing ever seems to stick, or if it does, the most they've ever gotten is probation."

"Did they say this Lombardo sent them?"

Gray's expression was completely devoid of any emotion. "They're not talking, so we're working it from the Philadelphia angle."

"That would be you and Agent Cole?" A wave of unexpected jealousy swept through me. I had become an outsider. He was now keeping details to himself, sharing them with her and treating me like a civilian, or worse, perhaps a suspect.

"Yeah," Gray answered. "Cole said you called her about Nick."

He didn't thank me for passing on the information, or apologize for thinking I only wanted to see Nick because I once loved him, but his tone had softened.

"So do you know where those two guys are now?" I asked.

"Yeah, we found them. They're locked up for the moment, but they've got lawyers. They'll be out on bail by this afternoon."

I felt my heart jump, thudding against my rib cage. What would stop them from trying again? I poured a cup of coffee and took it to him.

"And the guy in the other car—have you found him?"

Gray stretched out his hand and took the mug from me. His fingers brushed mine and he pulled his hand away, almost as if I'd burned him.

"No, we're looking, but there wasn't much to go on. They found the car he used abandoned behind a warehouse across town. The tags came back stolen. As for the other two, they know we're watching you. They'll be twice as reluctant to come after you now."

This didn't comfort me. The police had practically surrounded me for two days and still these men had found a window of opportunity. These guys wanted Nick's tape badly enough to risk almost certain capture. I couldn't really believe that they were scared off by a small-town police department. On the other hand, perhaps it would give me the opportunity to set a trap of my own.

Gray's pager sounded and Darlene jumped. He pulled it out of its holster and gazed down at the tiny panel.

"I've gotta go," he said. He barely glanced at me before he turned and walked away, but the look in his eyes told me everything I needed to know. There was a distance between us now, a gap created by my past life.

"Wait!" I called, hurrying to follow his long-legged stride across the porch.

I grabbed his arm and tugged him around to face me.

"You don't understand," I said, and then stopped as the words caught in my throat, the guarded uncertainty in his eyes holding me at bay. I was an unknown again. All we had in common were a bunch of traumatic events tied together by one short, sweet night, a night that had ended all too soon.

"I have to do this," I finished. "He doesn't have anyone else and I need the closure."

Gray nodded and started to turn away.

"He told me that he filmed the murder of the FBI agent," I said, and watched as Gray turned back, interested now. "He said it was a mob killing. He hid the video, but he wouldn't tell me where. He said it would be easy for me to find, but he wouldn't tell me where it was and he passed out before I could get it out of him. I think he wanted to sell it, but his girlfriend Connie double-crossed him and was trying to beat him to it when she got killed. You wouldn't have gotten that out of him if I hadn't gone to the hospital. I told Agent Cole everything he said—doesn't that count for anything with you?" He didn't answer, instead he went on as if we were colleagues, not lovers.

"So it's a tape, not pictures, and he hid it somewhere he thought would be easy for you to figure out."

I nodded, feeling a slow burn begin as I saw his attitude toward me warming. It was okay for me to get information out of Nick, but if I was merely praying with him or offering the man support as he lay dying, then I was back to being the enemy.

Gray's expression softened, but as he reached out to touch me, I backed up, out of reach.

"I'll let you know if he says anything else before he dies, Detective. Have a nice day."

I turned away from him and walked back into the kitchen,

closing the door firmly behind me. A few moments later, I heard the dull roar of his unmarked car pulling away from the curb.

Darlene didn't say a word as I walked past her and up the stairs to my room. When I returned, dressed and ready to go, she had cleaned the kitchen and was sitting quietly at the table.

"You ready?" she asked.

I nodded, still not sure I could talk without starting to cry. Darlene seemed to understand and didn't press me. We rode to the hospital in silence and once we arrived, I turned my attention to Nick.

Nick Komassi died at 3:52 a.m., August 3, without ever regaining consciousness. He died gently, slipping away in the last moments of a quiet, still night and leaving before dawn could usher in another beautiful summer morning. I had been with Nick for the final day of his life, and in that time, I had found the closure I so desperately needed.

Darlene and I left the hospital as the tiniest red sliver of the returning sun nudged the last star into a full retreat. The rain had ended and the clouds were gone. It was going to be a lovely day.

We stood outside the hospital doors, taking in deep breaths of fresh air and trying to find our bearings. Darlene was smiling to herself and humming something softly under her breath.

"Want to sleep at my house?" I asked. "It's closer than driving all the way back out to your place."

Darlene shrugged. "Might as well. I'll see how I feel when we get there."

We found her car and drove slowly away from the medical center. I knew I was tired. I could feel the fatigue slipping into my awareness, but I also felt light and as if I were almost floating in a fog of some kind. The world had changed so much for me in the past twenty-four hours. I almost couldn't imagine it ever feeling normal again.

The weight of Nick and the battle we had waged over the past few years had lifted. What had once almost consumed me now was gone. I wondered what I would do with so much empty space in my life. No more anger. No more fear. No more waiting to see what horrible thing Nick would do next. All I felt now was this strange lightness. I was a different person, changed and released from a burden that had seemed to cover every aspect of my life. What would happen now? Who would I become now that I was truly free?

Pa and Mort met us as I pulled into my driveway. The two old men stood side by side, each cradling a mug of coffee, dressed in their old guy uniforms of white T-shirts and baggy khaki trousers. Their faces wore the stubble of an interrupted night's sleep and their eyes were bloodshot with fatigue and worry.

"You had company last night," Pa said.

"Yeah, but don't worry," Mort added. "We got here and secured the perimeter. Them bastards won't be back on my watch."

Darlene smiled. She thought this was cute, I could tell.

"What happened?" I asked. My newfound peace evaporated instantly, replaced by the familiar, heart-pounding anxiety that had become my everyday reality.

Pa rubbed his hand over his chin, then up through the fringe that he insisted was hair.

"Mort, here, has a police scanner set up in his bedroom. When he heard the dispatcher call in a possible prowler at your address, he phoned me."

Mort smiled broadly. "Yeah, you never know when them things'll come in handy," he said. "I bought it last week, you know, just in case. Boy, I'm glad I did, too."

Pa nodded. "Yeah, if Mort hadn't called me, I wouldn't have known a thing. They could've come back. As it is, you got some damage, but mainly what you got is a mess."

Mort shook his head. "Vandals," he said. "Vagrants. Drug users. Friends of that scumbag, well…that's what they was if you ask me."

I approached the back door, dreading what I'd see inside. My house looked like TV news shots of tornado damaged mobile homes. They had started in the kitchen, tossing drawers out onto the floor, breaking my teddy bear cookie jar, and proceeding with reckless abandon throughout my house.

Mort and Pa followed me while Darlene plowed on ahead, running up the staircase and calling back down over the banister. "They were up here, too."

I felt sick inside. The fatigue of a sleepless night mixed in with the pain of Nick's death, the distance with Gray and now the devastation of my home. It was more than I could absorb.

"Don't worry, honey," Mort said. "We got round-the-clock watches set up. Frank and Joey are coming on at eight. Joey says to tell you his wife and daughter are coming, too. They're going to help clean up while you get some shut-eye."

"I'd take you home to Ma," Pa said, "but you won't go, will you?"

I could only shake my head. No, I wouldn't run away, never again. I was going to stay right here. I was going to figure it all out somehow and deal with it, but I wasn't going to leave.

We were standing in my living room. Books had been thrown off their shelves. Pictures lay in broken frames, covered in shards of glass. Mort stood by the newly repaired front window, looking out onto the street.

"That's three times," he said, turning to Pa. "I've seen them three times."

Pa nodded, but didn't explain.

"Who, Pa?"

"Nothing," he muttered. "Don't worry about it. We'll talk later."

"Pa," I said. "What the hell is it? This is my house and my problem. Now what's going on?"

Mort turned away from the window and let the slat on the blinds drop back into place. His lips were pressed together in a thin line.

Pa threw up his hands. "You gotta be such a hothead," he said. "*Marone a mia!* All right, three times since we been here a black sedan comes by. We told the cops and then they come by. So far, ain't nobody run into nobody. In fact, it might not even be the same black car."

"Yeah," Mort added. "I swear to God, it looks like the same car but it don't look like the same guy driving it. Hey, I'm old. Maybe it's my mind playing tricks on me, a co-inky-dink maybe, you know?"

He was trying to play it off like he'd been hit, out of the blue, by an attack of senility, but Mort wasn't suddenly incapable of knowing what he saw and what it meant. He was playing Pa's game, protecting Pa's little girl from the dreaded truth, playing for time so Pa could protect his family the old-fashioned way, by himself.

"Go on upstairs," Pa said. "We moved the old bed up to the guest room. You and your sister need to sleep."

I felt a wave of emotion surge over me. My throat tightened. My cheeks flushed and all I could do was wipe away tears that streamed uncontrollably down my face.

This display was more than poor Mort was prepared to handle. He coughed and turned, busying himself by stooping down and picking up the broken shards of a vase. Pa walked over to me and wrapped a burly arm around my shoulders, pulling me to his chest. It was such a familiar gesture. It was what the men in my family did. When all else failed, they wrapped you in their arms as if to take you into themselves and give you the strength they had in abundance.

"I know you want to get these guys. But you can't be effective without any sleep," he said. "Rest for a little while. We'll keep watch." Pa walked me to the stairs, patted my shoulder and hugged me once more before giving me a gentle shove toward my room.

"Mark my words," he said gruffly, "your sister is already snoring in the guest room. You sleep. Things will look better after you rest."

I nodded, dragging my body up the stairs one step at a time, sniffling and hiccuping as I went. I collapsed onto my bed and buried my head under a pillow that still smelled faintly of Gray's cologne. The last image I held in my memory as I drifted off was that of Gray hovering above me, resting his weight on his strong arms and smiling down at me as he leaned closer to kiss me.

While my conscious brain thought only of Gray Evans, my unconscious sought out Nick Komassi and brought him to me in my dreams.

"You never do what I tell you," Nick said. He was sitting on the edge of my bed, looking very much alive except for one thing. He was wearing white long underwear, and he was smiling.

"Nick," I said, "what are you doing here? You're dead."

I sat up, pushing the pillows behind my back and staring over at him. I remember thinking, This is the strangest dream I've ever had.

Dead Nick could read minds, apparently, because he answered me.

"Sophie, this is not a dream. Listen to me. I can't go on until this is finished. I told you to go look for the video. You'd better get it before the others do."

Now I was awake, or at least in my dream I thought I was awake. The entire episode was so vivid, so real, that I wasn't sure that this was, in fact, a dream.

"Nick, I'm sleeping. You're dead. I'll get to it when I wake up."

Nick shook his head. When I stared hard at him, I could see that he shimmered a little bit, as if his edges were blurring.

"Sophie, this is important. Get out of bed and go get that tape."

"Nick," I said, "this is a dream. You are dead. Furthermore, the FBI, the Mafia and I have all searched this house. I haven't seen any videos other than the two or three movies I own. It's not here and neither are you!"

I closed my eyes and willed myself to have another dream, a non-Nick dream. It was a technique that worked when I was younger, but not now. Clearly I was too tired to direct my own dream life. Nick wasn't leaving. He leaned over and shook my shoulder.

"Sophie, I can't go on, you know? Go on, as in, to the afterlife? I can't go until you take care of my unfinished business."

That did it. That was so Nick, always getting me to run his little errands because obviously *my* life wasn't as important as his. *My* agenda could wait. Nick needed me to go downstairs, look in the armoire that held my limited movie collection, and retrieve a videotape of a murder.

"Damn it, Nick, I have a life here. I was up with you for over twenty-four hours. I sat by your bed and held your hand, and does that count for anything with you? Oh no. You can't let me sleep for even an hour. I've gotta run downstairs and prove to you there's no videotape of a murder. Well, you know what, buddy? You can just get it yourself if it's so damn important! Now go away! I'm dreaming you and I'm tired!"

With this, I scrunched back down under my covers, ignoring Nick and rolling over onto my stomach. Even with my pillow firmly clamped to my head, I could hear his sigh of frustration.

I ignored him. Nick Komassi wasn't going to irritate me

anymore. He was dead and I'd be damned if I was going to dream about him or be haunted by his ghost. Really, I thought, the guy had some nerve.

"Sophie," he said, "you have been sleeping for almost six hours. Get up and go find that tape."

"Six hours?" I lifted the pillow just far enough to look at the clock on my bedside table. Sure enough, it was almost noon.

I clamped the pillow back over my head and moaned. "Go away, Nick! Leave me alone."

"No can do, Sophie," he said, bending closer and lifting the pillow. "I've got places to go and people to see. I can't leave until I know you're going to be safe."

I glared up at him. "Buzz off, Nick," I said. "You never gave a damn before. Why start now? Nick, heaven is not like the Boy Scouts. You can't do a good deed and get your merit badge. You're already dead. You can't do it in retrospect. We covered all that already. Go on. Saint Peter's waiting."

Even unconscious I felt like an idiot. My ex-husband was still trying to micromanage my life, even after death, and even in my dreams. I shook myself and squeezed my eyes tighter.

Nick was not above using guilt and shame to manipulate from beyond the grave. He sighed. He moaned softly, as if he was in pain, and then he played the Roman Catholic trump card.

"Sophie," he said, his voice loaded with angst, "my mother is waiting for me. I see her. She's reaching out her arms and calling to me. Sophie, if you have a shred of human compassion left for my soul, you'll do this one last thing for me."

I was going to kill him. If he hadn't already been dead, I would have finished off the job. Nick Komassi didn't care about his mother. When she'd been alive, who was it who remembered her birthday, bought the cards and sent the flowers? It sure as hell wasn't Nick. And yet, I could see her, crying and stretching out her flabby arms to clasp her boy to her ample bosom. It was an image that prevented sleep as surely as amphetamines. Damn that Nick!

I sat up, or at least I dreamed I sat up and swung my legs over the side of the bed, then watched as they went right through Nick's translucent body. We both stared, not quite believing what we'd seen.

"Whoa!" Nick breathed. "I really am dead."

I rolled my eyes. "You think you'd be in my bed if you were still alive?"

Nick shrugged. "I guess you got a point there," he said. He gestured impatiently. "Well, get a move on. I don't have all day. Time's awasting."

I stood and turned to look at him. Was it my imagination, or was he blurring more? I had to shake myself to remind myself that this was, after all, just a dream and a total figment of my imagination. I was only going along with it because my brain wouldn't let me exchange the dream for something more realistic, like, say, winning the lottery.

"I'll be right back," I said. But Nick wasn't having any of that. He followed me soundlessly down the hallway. I didn't quite have the nerve to look back over my shoulder and note whether his feet were actually touching the floor. Hell, they never did while we were married, why would he start now?

"Wait!" he called as I started down the stairs. "Where are you going?"

I gave him The Look. "Downstairs to check the videos like you wanted."

Nick shook his head, and I watched as it seemed to leave trails of light in an arc of movement.

"Not there, idiot. Anybody could find it there! I put it in with your teaching supplies."

I stopped, frowning as I tried to remember where I'd put them.

"I don't have any movies…." And then I remembered. I had a copy of *Shrek* for rainy days when recess outside wasn't an option and my little students needed a reward. It was in an art supply box, buried under stacks of paints, crayons, paste and scissors, and had been put into a plastic storage tub.

"How did you…"

Nick shook his head. "It wasn't easy, I'll tell you. I had to sneak into your classroom and swap it out."

I shuddered. "What if I'd left it when I moved?" I said.

Nick smiled. "Not you, Sophie. You're a creature of habit. You boxed your stuff up and brought it home every summer. You added to it and reorganized it, but you never threw anything away. I just wasn't expecting you to move. That made it difficult. Now where is it?"

I stood at the top of the stairs, my eyes closed, trying to envision the unloading of the big rental truck with my worldly belongings packed tightly inside. I thought hard, trying to visualize my plastic tubs of teaching materials. With a sudden flash, I remembered. The storage boxes were at the top of the closet in the guest room. I turned away from the stairs and walked past my room, toward the end of the corridor.

"Don't wake up Darlene," Nick cautioned. We were just outside the door, my hand on the knob, when he said this. I looked back at him.

"How do you know she's still in there and sleeping?" I whispered.

Nick gave me a look, as if to say, *I'm dead. I know it all.*

I shuddered and turned the door handle. Darlene was sacked out across the guest bed, still wearing her broomstick skirt and sandals. She lay on her back, mouth open and snoring so loudly I no longer had to wonder how Nick knew she was sleeping.

We crept slowly across the floor toward the closet. I

pulled open the door, only to have it stick, then screech as I tugged at it.

Nick and I looked back toward the bed. Darlene had stopped snoring. I held my breath, watching my sister, praying that she wouldn't wake up and see us.

I carefully edged the door open and saw the big pink tubs sitting on the upper shelf. As I worked to slide them silently toward me and down onto the floor, Darlene snored on, now and then pausing to mutter something unintelligible.

Just as the second plastic bin slid forward and down into my arms, Darlene sat bolt upright in bed, opened her eyes and said, "Why, Nick, you're still here."

I froze, my heart pounding against my rib cage. Nick took a couple of steps toward the bed and answered her. "Yeah," he said, his voice as casual as if they were standing around at a family picnic. "I had a couple of things to take care of before I went over, you know?"

The bedsprings groaned as Darlene shifted her weight. "I know just what you mean," she said. Her eyes were focused on Nick and she seemed not to even notice me. "Don't worry, I'll watch out for Sophie. She's finding her destiny, Nick, and it wasn't you, after all. So if that's what's holding you back—"

"Nah, nothing like that," Nick interrupted. "I know she'll be just fine. Go on back to sleep. I didn't mean to disrupt you."

The bed groaned again as Darlene flopped back against the mattress and sighed agreeably. "I just love these kind of dreams, don't you?" she murmured.

"Yeah, kid," Nick said, "they're a real kick in the ass."

Darlene was soon snoring again. I straightened up and walked over to the bed, where Nick stood staring down at my sleeping sister.

"Come on, before she wakes up again," he said, turning to me. "You know how she is with the questions."

I gave him a sharp look, but said nothing. I had questions of my own. I turned around, grabbed the bin labeled Rainy Day Crafts and left the room with Nick right behind me. If he thought I was going to hand any video I found over to him, well, that just wasn't an option.

I closed the door to my room, placed the tub on the floor and pried the cover off. Construction paper, glue, glitter and various craft materials filled the box. It had obviously been searched, because things weren't as I'd left them, but the vandals hadn't been thorough, for deep down inside the crate, past magazine photos and miscellaneous doodads, was the art supply box, along with six identical boxes full of supplies. I reached for the box and pried up the lid.

At first pass, it seemed to be the *Shrek* videotape. But when I looked closer, I saw the original movie label had been carefully peeled off and placed over another cartridge.

Without waiting for Nick's instructions, I got up and stuck the tape in the bedroom VCR and turned the TV on. A woman and a man stood locked in an embrace, passionately kissing. They appeared to be in a hotel room. As I watched, at the far right edge of the shot I could make out something moving, someone hidden out of the lovers' view.

The movie was shot through a window because I could see the edge of a curtain framing the action. Nick's work, obviously. Another Peeping Tom video. Another innocent pair of lovers captured in their most intimate moments.

The woman was naked except for a pair of thong panties. Her hands were resting on her companion's shoulders. He pulled her into him, cradling her in his arms. I started to turn away but the camera suddenly zoomed in on their faces.

The woman, tall with black straight hair that fell neatly over her shoulders, broke the embrace and moved a step or two away from her lover. She was staring at something he couldn't see, a look of horror transforming her face into a masklike grimace.

The boyfriend, a head taller than his companion and dressed in jeans and a black T-shirt, was still smiling at her, unaware of the danger that lurked just behind him. A third figure had stepped out of what appeared to be a hotel room's bathroom. He was a short, squat man wearing a dark colored windbreaker and holding a black handgun with a long barrel. He held the weapon straight out in front of his body, aiming it at the woman's companion.

Before I could move, the man with the gun fired. The boyfriend fell forward, dropping to the floor, obviously dead, shot at close range in the back of the head. The woman screamed, her upper body covered in the blood spatter from her lover's violent death. She seemed to have forgotten her armed assailant as she dropped to her lover's side and began a high-pitched keening that chilled me to the core. The sound of a door slamming echoed in the background as the movie faded to black.

"Oh my God! Nick, who are these people? What happened?"

I looked up, ready to hear the rest of the story, needing to know what had happened. But Nick had vanished.

"Nick!" I screamed, not caring now who heard me. "Come back here, you bastard! What is this?"

But Nick still didn't answer me. It was Darlene who came running, panicked and still half-asleep.

"Sophie, Sophie," she said, moving to my side and wrapping her arms around my shaking shoulders. "Hey, shh, it's all right," she cooed. "You were having a bad dream. Shh. I'm here. It's all right now."

She hugged me tight against her warm body, sighing and rocking me gently back and forth. When the trembling stopped, she let me push away from her and reach over to grab a tissue from the nightstand.

"Are you okay?" she asked, her voice filled with concern and sympathy.

"I'm fine," I said, but my voice cracked, giving me away. "I had a nightmare about Nick. He was—"

"Hey," Darlene said, interrupting my explanation, "what is that?" She was pointing to the TV. The screen had somehow returned to the last image, freezing on the tableau of the woman leaning over her dead lover. "Oh, my God! That's terrible!"

I hit the power button on the remote control and the screen went black.

I sniffed, suddenly smelling something that I hadn't noticed before. Darlene stopped and inhaled, her forehead wrinkling into furrows of concentration.

"Do you smell that?" she asked. "What is that? I can almost think of it, but not quite."

It would come to her in a minute. It was unmistakable to me. Paco Rabanne cologne. I always said he wore too much of it, but Nick didn't care. "Gives 'em something to remember me by," he'd say, and laugh.

Chapter 15

"You have to call Gray," Joey said. "He needs to get that videotape to the FBI."

We were standing by the dining room doorway, overlooking the kitchen and a hastily assembled war council that included my entire family, half the retired population of Neuse Harbor and Durrell the dog. I had descended the stairs to a houseful of company, all drawn, as the Mazarattis are, by a death among us, even if it was an ex-member of the family and a man who in recent years had treated us all like dirt.

Ma was cooking, as usual. She stood with her back to us, stirring a huge stockpot of sauce and muttering to herself in Italian. Now and then she would look over her shoulder, shake her head grimly and return to her work.

Joey's wife and children milled about, helping Ma, carting bags and boxes in and out of the house. Angela had supervised the general cleanup of the downstairs devastation—I knew this much from Joey. She did it more in an effort to avoid Ma than anything else, but also because she was a born organizer. She had to be; she was married to my brother, the poet, the man of concepts but not details.

Mort, Pa, Frank and the other old guys, minus Pete, who was still recovering in the hospital, sat around the table mapping out strategy. They wore grim, determined expressions and wrote copious notes on small pads of paper that Mort provided.

"It's my years in the military," he stated, as if this explained everything. "You gotta write stuff down, especially at our age. Once it's here," he said, gesturing with a forefinger to the side of his head, "it's gotta go there." He gestured to the paper. "Or we're all sunk. Right guys?"

There was a chorus of gruff grunts followed by an immediate return to business.

"Like I was saying," Joey continued, his voice pitched low so Pa and the old guys wouldn't overhear us, "we've got to bring the police in on this, and I don't think we can sit around delaying any longer."

I hadn't shown the movie to anyone other than Darlene and Joey. I didn't want to involve the old guys.

Darlene turned around and looked over her shoulder, hearing something we hadn't. "Well, speak of the devil and up he jumps."

Gray Evans walked across the back porch, and she leaned forward to open the back door for him.

"There you are!" she cried. "We were just talking about you."

Gray was watching me. His expression was somber still, but lighter, as if the weight between us had lessened a little, only it hadn't. If anything, Nick's death was going to push us further apart, because I carried the burden of the videotape and having to explain how I'd suddenly "found" it after receiving an afterlife message from my ex-husband.

I motioned to Gray, letting him follow us from the back porch, past the old guys in the kitchen and on into the dining room before I spoke to him. "I found what everyone's been looking for," I said, and handed him the *Shrek* carton.

Gray seemed puzzled at first, but nodded and moved toward a window, where he could examine the tape in a better light.

"Wait!" Ma cried, startling us all by suddenly appearing in the doorway. "Don't move!"

Gray turned and looked at her, frowning as she crossed the room toward him. She reached deep inside the bosom of her dress and tugged to release something.

"There is evil here," Ma said to Gray, her eyes burning with intensity. "You can't fight the dead without protection."

Her voice was loud, carrying clearly to the men sitting at the kitchen table. At the mention of the word *dead,* every Italian in the house crossed themselves. In fact, every time Nick's name was mentioned we crossed ourselves. It didn't pay to take chances with evil vibes.

Ma pulled a thick gold chain with a small gold medallion attached out from the recesses of her dress and lifted it over her head. "Here," she said, offering it to Gray. "Wear this. It will protect your unborn children." Her eyes traveled from Gray to me, as if there were some significance to be made from her gesture.

Gray was clearly confused, but took the offering because Ma wouldn't have it any other way.

"Is *corno,*" Ma said, holding the golden horn-of-plenty medallion out to him. "It will keep you safe from the evil eye." She crossed herself again and looked almost fearfully around the room. "It was my father's. Now you wear it."

"Your father's? Oh, Mrs. Mazaratti, I can't accept this," Gray began. But the hand was quicker than the eye and Ma slapped him upside the head before he knew what was happening.

"You take or else!" she cried. "The children are all that matter!"

Gray rubbed the side of his head slowly and nodded. "Thank you, ma'am," he said. "The children. Yes." He carefully placed the chain around his neck and leaned down to kiss my mother on the cheek. "Thank you, ma'am," he said, his voice gentle and filled with warmth. "I won't let anything happen to it."

"Don't worry about that," Ma said gruffly. "Is for my grandchildren. You carry the future of my family." With that, Ma vanished back into the kitchen.

There was no way for Gray to understand without an explanation that the horn was worn by men to protect their fertility, and I for one wasn't about to tell him. The man radiated enough sexual energy to take care of himself in a battle against the evil eye. When and if we ever got to a place where a discussion of children and fertility ever came into play, I'd explain. But for now, that possibility seemed as faraway to me as space travel.

"The movie," Joey said. "Soph found it in her teaching supplies. Nick told her about it before he died."

"Well, actually afterward," Darlene began, but Joey silenced her with a warning glare.

Gray studied the cassette carefully. When he had finished, he looked up at me.

"I take it you just found this and were about to call?" There was no mistaking the tone, the barely suppressed anger that boiled just beneath the surface. His jaw was clenched and I knew he thought I'd been holding back.

I met his steady gaze and said, "Something like that, yes."

Gray didn't believe it for a minute, and as I'd had the tape for well over an hour and shown it to my brother before discussing our presentation to the authorities, I couldn't sell the lie any harder than I already had.

"Let's talk," he said, and when I motioned toward the living room he cut me off. "Upstairs, if you don't mind. I believe I saw a TV and VCR in your room?"

I felt my face flush under Joey and Darlene's knowing scrutiny. This was just great.

"Okay, come on. You can watch the tape. After that I think you'll understand that we were, of course, going to call you or the FBI right away."

And I would've called him, but he was obviously feeling that I'd known about the tape for longer than I'd said and had preferred to protect Nick over coming to him with the information. I followed Gray up the stairs, motioning Joey and Darlene back. It wouldn't do for them to take the heat, too. After all, Joey had wanted to call Gray as soon as I'd told him.

"I'm sorry for your loss, Sophie," I said sarcastically as we reached the second floor. "I know you must've been through an ordeal, even if he was your ex-husband and treated you like dirt. I know you were so sleep deprived that you didn't think right off the bat to call me...." I let my voice drift off as I turned and glared at him.

There was a barely perceptible softening of his features. "Listen, Sophie, I am sorry that you've been through such a hard time." He ran his hand through his closely cropped hair and seemed to be almost at a loss for words. Almost.

"Sophie, I want this over with for you. I want you safe. I want your family and friends to be safe, too. I apologize, but I was trying to do my job. It's all I know to do. It's not just my duty—it's personal. People I care about are in danger. I don't understand why you seem not to see that."

The agonized look on his face tore at my heart. Deep down inside, where the true Sophie Mazaratti doesn't deceive herself, I knew he was being completely honest. The trouble was, I didn't always trust my assessment of the truth, not in light of Nick or any of the events of the past few years. I wanted to let go and believe Gray, but the guard dog in me couldn't. Not yet.

"You left. You just weren't there anymore. I didn't deserve that," I said.

I heard the catch in my voice and saw his reaction to it. He looked pained. He started toward me and kept on coming even when I backed up a step.

"Sophie, I wouldn't do anything in the world to hurt you, not intentionally. I thought you were taking care of Nick and didn't want me around. I thought the best thing I could do would be to find the people who tried to attack you the other night. I thought I was helping you."

I couldn't stand it, couldn't stand to be inches away from his strong embrace and yet so far away emotionally. I went to him, walked right into his arms and felt him wrap himself around me.

"I don't know what you want from me, Sophie," he whispered. "But I would give you the universe if I thought it would make you happy."

I couldn't say a word. Instead I lifted my head and watched as he lowered his to meet my lips. We kissed like starving lovers, hungry for the feel of skin touching skin.

It was Gray's pager that brought us back to the present reality. It vibrated against his belt, rumbling through both our bodies insistently.

"I'm sorry," he whispered, pushing back enough to grab the offending device from its holster.

"I know. Duty calls and calls and calls," I said.

He was looking at the tiny screen, pushing the button to light up the display, and frowning.

"Sophie," he said, "I'm sorry. I'm going to have to leave in a minute, and I really need to know about the video. Can we switch gears, just for now? I promise—"

I raised the tips of my fingers to his lips and stopped the explanation. "Gray, I'm fine. Let me tell you everything Nick said and then you can take it from there."

He couldn't have known how transparent the relief was on his face. I almost wanted to laugh, but settled instead for a terse, comprehensive explanation of Nick's last words to me. I never mentioned the dream or whatever it was. I showed Gray the short clip and told him that Nick had hoped to make money on the film and that it had backfired on him. I told him everything Nick had said all over again, in detail, even the parts that didn't seem to have a meaning to me.

"He said they were after him," I said. "I don't think Tony Lombardo was the only one looking for this."

"Who? Did he give you any names?"

I thought hard. "No. Wait. There was one name he mentioned. In the hospital he said something about a woman named Kathy, remember? He said she brought him down here after Connie ran off."

Gray's brows furrowed and he shook his head. He ejected the tape from the VCR, then slipped it into the inside pocket of his suit jacket.

"Okay. I'll take this back with me and see if the feds can figure anything out. They'll send it up to Philly and see if this is what we think it is. Nick didn't travel outside of Philadelphia to make his tapes, did he?"

I shrugged. "I just don't know. I had no idea he was taking pictures, so I suppose he could've traveled to Alaska and I wouldn't have known about it. He was never gone overnight, that I can remember."

Gray nodded, then pulled me closer. "I hate to leave you," he said, "but I've got to follow up on this. Listen, I think the less said about the tape, the better. Okay?"

"What about the men you arrested? Do you think one of

them is the killer? None of the ones I've run into looked like that, but why else would they want the tape? Won't they think I still have it?"

Gray's eyes met mine. "It's a risk," he said. "I'll have plain-clothes people sitting on this place, just in case. You could stay with your parents for a few days, but I know you don't want to bring them into this, so count on my people watching this place during the day and me covering you at night."

My stomach turned cartwheels at his last words. I could just imagine how he'd cover me. I closed my eyes and tried to focus on the rest of his statement. To his credit, he didn't seem to think that he was the only person in the universe capable of protecting me. He knew he had good officers working with him. He had to know that Pa, Joey and the old guys were looking out for me, too.

"Hey, you guys done?" Joey asked, appearing in the doorway.

"Yeah," I said, attempting a smile that both Joey and Gray had to see for the sham it was. "You got food ready or what?"

I broke the hold Gray had on my shoulders and took his hand, pulling him along with me downstairs into the bright kitchen and away from dealing with any more issues. After he'd gone I stood on the front porch considering how the pieces of the puzzle fit together and thinking about what my next course of action should be. While Gray and the old guys had the best of intentions, they couldn't provide an iron-clad guarantee of protection. I needed to do my part to insure that no one else I cared for was hurt by the by-product of Nick's perverse activities.

The afternoon heat scorched New Bern, searing the narrow street in front of my house, shimmering off the metallic surfaces of cars and tin roofs, and layering a thick blanket of muggy, humid warmth over every surface. I wiped a sheen of perspiration from the back of my neck and watched Della labor in the garden.

She moved in slow motion, her rail thin body a mere stick inside the oversize clothing that hung on her frame. Durrell had retreated to the relative shelter of the magnolia tree, preferring to lie under a low hanging branch rather than following his mistress as she slowly cleared weeds and brush.

Darlene joined me, her eyes following my gaze and watching Della, with a tight, closed expression on her face.

"You're feeling sorry for her," my sister said in a hushed tone. "Don't. She's the one who picked this line of work."

I closed my eyes and tried to will Darlene's bad attitude away. "I am not feeling sorry for her," I lied. "It's just so damn miserable out there. I thought she might take a break soon or something."

Darlene sighed. "I'm sure you offered and she martyred herself and turned you down."

That was exactly what had happened, but Darlene probably watched the entire interaction from the living room window, so it wasn't as if she suddenly had clairvoyant insight.

"Give her a break, Darlene."

She looked at me. "Sophie, you are not open to messages from the other side. I am. I can read people because I have help. Others share their wisdom with me. That's how come I know Nick was really here and not a dream."

I shook my head. "Darlene, you weren't there. It was a dream. Nick is dead and that is that. My unconscious had been working on possible answers to what Nick could have hidden and where, and my dream merely helped me see that."

She smiled her irritating I-know-something-you-don't-know smile and stared past me, past Della and beyond the houses across the street. She probably wanted me to believe she was sharing a joke with the more enlightened ghosts and beings of the afterlife. Behind us, Ma, Joey and Angela came out into the driveway, laden down with bags. Joey's three kids followed them, each carrying plastic containers carefully balanced as they trailed after the adults.

"Put it in the back seat," Ma ordered. She turned and watched, directing the placement of her parcels and seeming to be impatient with the length of time it was taking to load her car.

"Dinner's at six," she barked. "I want everybody there. We got things to discuss."

Joey extricated himself from Ma's overloaded car and looked around. When he spotted Darlene and me watching the show from the porch, he made a face at us.

"Right, Ma," he said, quickly recovering as he felt her attention turn from the car's interior to him. "We'll be there."

Ma, the woman voted by us kids as being most likely to actually have eyes in the back of her head, spun around and looked at the two of us standing there.

"Dinner," she said. "Be there."

"Yes, Ma," Darlene cooed. "Wouldn't miss it."

I started to say something about how I couldn't be there but Ma stopped me short.

"Don't start, you," she said. "Bring my boy."

Darlene turned to me and sighed. "My car's parked behind hers," she said in a low voice. "She'll drive over it if I don't move it. Let's go somewhere. We need a break. Let's ride down Middle Street and get some ice cream."

She was off, without waiting for me to answer her. She expected me to fall in behind her. After all, in Darlene's world, who wouldn't want ice cream?

"Let me grab my purse," I called after her.

She waved one hand over her shoulder and kept on moving. Knowing Darlene, she probably didn't even have money to pay for the treat. I stepped back into the house, grabbed my pocketbook from the living room and flew back out onto the porch, shutting the front door firmly and waiting to hear the lock catch.

Darlene was sliding behind the wheel of her car while Ma gunned the engine of her Taurus and looked impatiently in the rearview mirror.

"Ma," I called, "she's waiting for me. Don't get yourself all hot and bothered. We're going!"

Ma wasn't listening. She had the windows rolled up. The air-conditioning was blasting and the radio booming Sinatra. Ma was oblivious. Joey was walking toward his car, followed by his family. It looked as if I was finally going to have some time to get ready for Gray's arrival without a riot of family members all wanting to know the details. If I was lucky, I'd return and find only Pa and the old guys on duty, but then luck hadn't been my long suit lately.

Darlene's car was a nightmare of New Age music and scents. Even with the windows rolled down, the patchouli smell was unbearable. I was sneezing before we left the driveway.

"Why don't you trade this tin can in on a real car?" I asked her. "You don't even have air in here."

Darlene ignored me and turned up the volume on her cassette player. She knew I hated her music. How can anyone listen to something that sounds like whales calling to each other? Or worse, choirboys singing just out of earshot, so you're forever straining, trying to figure out what the words are only to realize it's really just high-pitched wailing. It drives me right up the wall. Darlene says it's relaxing. I say it's probably some form of subliminal hypnosis and she's been given the suggestion to buy as much stupid music as she can find. In fact, the same people who made that tape probably sell the patchouli incense Darlene burns.

We drove down the road with me half hanging out of the passenger-side window and her humming along with the beached whales. By the time we reached the ice cream shop, I was a near basket case and Darlene was at peace with her universe. Neither one of us noticed the black car before then or knew how long it had been following us. I didn't become aware of it until it pulled out around us and had almost passed from sight.

"Darlene," I said. "Look!"

She was busy executing her fanatically perfect parallel parking job. By the time she turned her head, the taillights were winking out of sight.

"What?"

"That car, it looks like the one that hit me last night. The same one that's been driving by the house, the one from the restaurant."

"What restaurant?"

It was hopeless. Darlene's head was up on her astral plane and there was no reclaiming her brain.

It was pointless to try and bring Darlene down to earth, so instead I went on high alert. Black cars were common, but lately, black cars had signalled impending disaster. If it came back, I'd need to be ready.

I let Darlene lead me into the ice cream shop, but my attention remained focused on the street outside.

When I ordered a scoop of chocolate chip, Darlene almost curled her lip in disgust. "That is so pedestrian," she said, her tone haughty with distaste.

"Darlene, it's not vanilla. Give me a break."

Darlene looked at me. "Yeah," she said, "chocolate chip is what vanilla lovers order when they feel self-conscious about ordering vanilla. You wanted vanilla, admit it. I know you. All your life you've ordered vanilla. You're just trying to be something you're not…different."

I pulled back, stung by Darlene's sudden attack. Her

face registered shock, as if she were hearing the words from a stranger instead of hearing them come out of her own mouth.

"I'm sorry, Sophie," she said. "I don't know where that came from." She stood in front of the ice cream counter, her rainbow sundae dripping down the side of her hand. Tears welled up in her eyes and began spilling over onto her cheeks.

How had this happened? I wondered.

I threw a five dollar bill onto the counter and led Darlene to a corner table. The tiny shop was almost deserted. It was midafternoon, midweek, and the tourists and business people were too sensible to be out in the midsummer heat.

Miserable, Darlene sat watching her ice cream melt and run down her hand. When she finally looked up at me, her eyes were bright with tears.

"Sophie, it's not easy being the oddball," she said. "Don't you think sometimes I'd like to be just plain old vanilla?"

She seemed to realize how this sounded, because she brought her free hand up quickly to cover her mouth, and tried to rectify the matter with more words. "I didn't mean you were plain, or even old, it's just that—"

"I get what you're saying," I interrupted.

Darlene sighed and dug out a spoonful of her multicolored ice cream. "I'm not like anybody else I know," she said. "I don't think like you and Joey. I think about other things, and most of the time that's fine with me. I like my life. It's just that, sometimes I wish I could be normal. You know—vanilla."

This was not Darlene, not my sister, not the in-your-face, New Age, come-as-you-are believer in the cosmos. Something was wrong. I waited, knowing that with Darlene, no secret could remain hidden for long. I tried to divide my attention between my sister and watching the road outside.

"Wendell's daughter is just out of rookie school," she said, and stuffed her mouth full of ice cream, sprinkles and whipped topping.

I wasn't sure where we were headed with this, so I smiled inanely and said, "That's nice. So, she's following in her dad's footsteps."

Darlene nodded glumly. "And her mom's. Her mom was a sheriff's deputy before she got sick."

"Really?" I murmured, still puzzled.

Darlene shrugged. A flash of black caught my eye and my attention strayed to the view from the plate glass window. The black sedan, tinted windows and all, was driving slowly past the front of the shop. For one horrified minute, I imagined the car window rolling down and a hand sticking out, aiming a gun at us as we sat, exposed in the ice cream shop. I shifted slightly in my seat, preparing to lunge across the table and throw Darlene to the ground should the situation warrant action. But the sedan passed the storefront window.

"I wouldn't know if it's nice for her or not," Darlene was saying. "Wendell won't let me meet her."

"What?" My attention shot back to my sister's miserable face. "What do you mean, he won't let you meet her?"

Darlene spooned more ice cream into her mouth, swallowed and went on, oblivious to the outside world and the passing of the black car.

"Oh, it's not like he right out says it or anything. He just changes the subject."

I looked at Darlene and frowned. "Well, honey, maybe it doesn't have anything to do with you. Maybe he and his daughter don't get along. Maybe he's afraid to introduce her to anyone because she might feel he was trying to replace her mother."

Darlene rolled her eyes. "No, no, no. That's not it. The woman died five years ago. His daughter sounds like a practical person, not possessive or emotional. I bet she's just like her father. No, I don't think that's the problem. I think Wendell's afraid because I'm so different from his wife and daughter."

"What do you mean?"

My sister looked at me, giving me her best eye roll paired with a headshake of disgust. "Please," she said. "I'm thirteen years younger than Wendell. I look like a hippy because, hell, I am one. I talk about feelings. I am—" here it comes, I thought "—a professional therapist."

"So?"

Darlene had disposed of her rainbow sundae and now had a blue-and-red tongue and purple lips. She wiped the lower half of her face with a tiny square of napkin and sighed.

"I'm just not your Southern conservative," she said. "I'm not even close. Now, don't get me wrong, I think that's one of the reasons Wendell likes me so much, but now he's faced with introducing me to his family and all of a sudden he doesn't know what to do." Her eyes welled up again. "I think he's ashamed of me," she whispered.

My heart broke right in half. How dare that Wendell hurt my sister with his own insecurity? I wanted to march right down to the police department and whip his tail for even hesitating. How could anyone love Darlene the way he seemed to and be ashamed of her at the same time?

I reached for Darlene's hand, but she was already moving back from the table and rising to her feet.

"Let's blow this pop stand," she said. She had pulled the emotion back in, tucking her hurt away inside herself and trying to act like good old Darlene, the unaffected Queen of Karma.

"I'm with you," I said, pushing my chair back.

"Besides," she added, "that black car has been by three

times, or haven't you noticed? We're just a little bit exposed, don't you think?"

Darlene sailed out of the shop and onto the sidewalk. I stared after her for a moment. If Wendell Arrow was too insecure to claim his diamond in the rough, then Darlene didn't need him.

"Like a fish needs a bicycle," I muttered under my breath, and hurried to catch up.

Darlene was scanning the street when I joined her. "No sign of them," she said. "Let's get while the getting's good."

We climbed back into Darlene's tin can and took off down Middle Street, past gift and antique shops, past the tinted windows of businesses, and around the corner toward my house. There was no black car hot on our trail.

"I'm going to swing by the library," Darlene said. "I need to drop off a book."

I nodded, about to jump out of my skin with impatience but aware it would do no good to rush her. As Darlene approached the book drop, my cell phone rang.

Gray didn't waste time on pleasantries. His voice, deep and familiar, was tight with energy and he sounded completely focused on the task at hand. This was Gray the Cop calling, and he was all business.

"Just thought I'd let you know the tape's in Philadelphia," he said.

"Good. What's the story?"

Darlene, barely curious, reached between us for the book that was buried somewhere in her back seat.

"I couriered the tape to the FBI field office in Philadelphia and they confirmed Nick's story. It seems Nick accidentally took pictures of a mob hit on an undercover FBI agent. The murder happened over two years ago, and while the feds pretty much knew who was responsible, they didn't have any proof until now."

I felt my pulse quicken and my hands grow icy cold despite the heat. "So Nick was right—it was a mob hit?"

Darlene drew back from the book drop and whipped around to stare, openmouthed, at me.

"Oh, that's not the worst of it," he added. "Apparently Nick thought he could blackmail the guy the cops think is responsible for the hit."

"So the two goons who rammed me wanted the pictures. They killed the FBI agent? Who were the guys in the other car?"

Darlene's eyes were huge. She had turned sideways in her seat and was mouthing the question, "What? What?"

I shook my head at her and strained to listen as Gray went on. "No, the agents in Philadelphia think a crime boss named Tony Lombardo ordered the hit after he found out that the victim had infiltrated his 'family.' Lombardo sent his top enforcer, a guy named Benny Deal, or Benny the Nose, to do the job."

I sighed. "So was it Benny in the picture?"

An impatient soccer mom driving a vanful of little boys honked at Darlene, wanting her to move away from her spot in front of the book drop. Darlene waved a hand out the window and pulled forward on the street. I looked at my surroundings as Darlene settled us into a shady spot under the spreading arms of a huge pin oak. It was all too surreal.

I was sitting in historic New Bern, surrounded by freshly painted old homes and flowering gardens, with brick sidewalks and smiling people, but I was discussing a mob hit that had put my life in danger.

"It was Benny Deal in the picture," Gray said. "But Benny's dead. His remains were found about a month ago in a landfill near the airport."

I had the instant vision of seagulls swooping over mountains of trash and sludge dredged up from the marshlands that surrounded the airport. I could smell the brackish air and the ever-present odor of jet fuel and exhaust. I imagined Benny in a green Hefty bag, adding to the overall fragrance of the dump, fertilizing what would one day become a new runway.

"So if the killer's dead, why come after the video?"

Darlene was about to squirm out of her seat with the agony of not hearing the other side of my conversation.

Gray's voice continued, tinny through my cell phone. "Because now there's a link back to Lombardo. They can at least grab him on accessory or even conspiracy to commit murder. It's circumstantial evidence, but now they can nail Benny, and Benny was Lombardo's right-hand guy. It creates a chain leading back to Lombardo. The investigation can pick up again. The Feds will get a search warrant and who knows, maybe something'll turn up."

I sighed. "So what will you do now?"

Gray's voice sounded stronger than it had since I'd met him, confident and certain. "No problem. We pick up those two guys again and send them back up to Philly. Once the others hear that the authorities have the evidence, they'll lose interest in you and go away. It'll all be over."

"So you think Lombardo's men killed Connie, too?"

Darlene punched my thigh. "What? What's he saying?"

"Yeah, at least that's what makes the most sense. It's possible that a rival family or someone else with an interest is behind this, but the only people we've found so far lead us back to Lombardo. Nick must've come down here to get the pictures, and Lombardo's men followed him. They were probably trying to break into your house the night Connie got killed."

"Did something go wrong? Why didn't Nick find the tape? Why didn't Lombardo's guys break in and get it? Why did Connie get killed?"

Gray said, "I don't know what went wrong, but I think they

were all trying. I think Nick tried to scare you away from the house by burning your car and leaving nasty messages. Then Lombardo's guys figured Nick knew where the tape was and were following him, waiting for him to do their work for them. When that took too long, they started coming after you. Don't worry, I've put out an alert. We'll pick them up and that should be the end of it."

Darlene moaned, slipped the car into Drive and pulled out into the street. From her general direction, I figured we were headed home.

"Darlene and I were eating ice cream on Middle Street a little while ago," I said. "We think they circled the block a couple of times, watching us."

Gray's voice tightened. "What? I thought I told you to stay put. What were you doing out?"

Darlene picked up speed, zooming toward home. She was muttering to herself, something that sounded like a commentary on my failure to communicate with her while also talking to Gray. The woman had no patience even if she was a trained therapist.

"It was just ice cream," I protested. "We had to move the car so Ma could get out. We were just around the corner from the house." Well, almost.

"Yeah, and in that time they followed you. That surprises me, but then, they're pretty desperate. At least you made it home safe."

Okay, I lied. "Yeah. See? Nothing to it." It wasn't exactly a lie. Darlene was about to make the turn onto my street.

"Well, stay inside. It shouldn't take long before they're back in custody." Gray put his hand over the receiver and I heard muffled voices, then he was back. "I've gotta go. I'll call you when it's clear." He was gone, the line dead; whatever it was had to be urgent.

"Tell me, tell me, tell me!" Darlene demanded. "What did he say?"

She rounded the corner, gasped and hit the brakes. Ahead of us was total chaos.

Chapter 16

In the midst of chaos was one black sedan boxed in by a car, a pickup truck, a crowd of onlookers and the Old Guy Militia.

"Oh my heavenly Goddess!" cried Darlene. "What now?"

I peered ahead and tried to figure out the scene. Mort, bandy-legged in his khaki shorts, leaned against the open door of his elderly four-door Chevy. He had the black sedan blocked from proceeding farther down the street. Resting on his shoulder and across the open doorway of the car was a shotgun. Mort was sighting down the barrel, a determined look on his craggy face.

The sedan was cut off from making a rear getaway by a battered and rusted out old Ford pickup, vintage 1944. Pa stood on the running board, a megaphone in hand, saying something.

I figured the megaphone was responsible for the crowd of neighbors and tourists. We'd drawn the Tryon Palace visitors, the ones who'd wandered off to view local gardens and now thought they'd become extras in a movie.

"They're going to die!" Darlene screamed. She threw the car into Park and jumped out, leaving it running and sitting in the middle of the street behind the turned-sideways pickup truck.

"Darlene, wait!" I yelled, hopping out to run after her.

But the old guys were in strict command of the perimeter. Frank whirled around, his bald head covered by a World War II helmet, and stuck out an arresting hand. Belts of ancient ammo were strapped diagonally across his chest and he was holding a huge, but elderly pistol in his other hand.

"Halt!" he said firmly. "Stay where you are. We've got it under control."

Darlene stopped in her tracks, wide-eyed, and said, "But what about your rotator cuff? Frank, that gun's too heavy for you to hold like that."

Frank blinked but held fast. He didn't answer Darlene, choosing instead to turn his attention back to the scene.

Pa wielded the megaphone like a seasoned professional.

"The men in this car are armed and dangerous," he was saying. "Take cover."

A few old ladies in floral polyester giggled and clapped enthusiastically, clearly charmed with my father. My neighbors, on the other hand, given the events of the past few days, knew better and ran like startled rabbits, with the exception of my closest neighbors, Bill and his partner. Bill stepped to the edge of his walkway, a small black gun in his hand.

"Mr. Mazaratti," he called to Pa, "I got you covered from this side."

His partner, dressed today in a brightly colored Hawaiian shirt and sporting fuchsia-pink, flower-topped flip-flops, stepped out from behind his brave companion and flashed a huge orange Super Soaker water gun.

"I got game!" he called. "Don't underestimate the power of my weapon. It's loaded with Russian vodka and only a whisper of vermouth!"

Bill shot out a cautionary arm and shoved the man back behind him. He raised the pistol and pointed it straight at the driver of the car.

"Gentlemen, you are surrounded," announced Pa. "Step out of your vehicle or we will blow you straight to hell!"

Mort grinned, as if he would like nothing better, and inched his rifle up a bit to bring it level with the middle of the black car's windshield.

"Slowly," Pa called to the vehicle. "Very slowly open the doors. Throw your weapons out and then exit the car with your hands up over your heads."

The street, minus the tourists who were still clueless, held its collective breath. After ten seconds the driver's door opened, then the two back doors. Three handguns were tossed out onto the street.

"Throw the rest of them out here, too," Pa called.

An Uzi submachine gun followed, then a thin black rifle, two additional handguns and three knives.

Pa turned to look at Frank. "That's most of it," he said, "but I don't buy it's all. Be careful."

Slowly, very slowly, three men emerged from the vehicle. I recognized two of them as being the men who'd hit my car, but the third man was a complete stranger. He was tall and thin, balding with wisps of black hair combed across his scalp in an attempt to fool himself into thinking all was not lost in the hair department. The men wore dark dress slacks and golf shirts, gold bracelets and necklaces. It looked like a business outing instead of the sinister stalking of innocent victims.

"Is there some kind of problem here?" the thin man asked.

He attempted a grim smile, but stopped at the sight of the Super Soaker. "You're kidding, right?" he asked Bill's partner.

The young man shot him right in the heart with 180-proof liquor. "Gotcha, sweetie pie," he called. "I ain't no joke."

"Call the police," one of the mobsters begged, obviously more afraid of Pa and his cronies than the cops.

"Maybe," Mort answered. "And maybe we'll just take care of this ourselves. Maybe we don't think the police are doing such a hot job and we'd like to police the neighborhood."

The three men huddled together in the middle of the street, trying to look tough and failing miserably.

"Did you kill that girl?" Mort asked.

Silence.

I reached Pa, dialing 9-1-1 as I walked. "These guys work for the Lombardo family," I said, loudly enough to be heard by the gangsters and Mort. "Nick made a video of one of their guys killing an FBI agent who was working undercover within the Lombardo organization. That's why they won't go away."

Pa's face tightened. "Wiseguys, eh?"

"Now that the police have the tape, all they'll need to do is pick up this garbage and take it back up North."

"Damn Yankees!" Bill's partner cried. "Let's lynch 'em, boys!"

"Trey, shut up!" Bill snapped. "This is serious."

Trey stuck out his lip. "Well, who's kidding?" he answered.

I heard the communicator's voice saying, "Police emergency, can I help you? Hello? Hello?"

Once again I gave the address, but before I could finish I heard the sound of sirens racing toward us. Someone sensible had already called.

Mort looked disappointed when the cruisers swung onto the street from both directions. Within seconds the three Lombardo family employees were lying across the hood and trunk of their car, handcuffed and in custody. Pa and Frank wandered around the edge of the scene to join their disappointed buddy, commiserating about the kind handling their captives were now receiving, and discussing how they would've gotten the men to confess given enough time.

"Well," Darlene said softly, "that's that." She was staring at the men and frowning. "Which one do you think actually did it?" she asked.

I stared back at them. Each one looked completely capable of killing without remorse, and yet who could judge an actual killer by appearance alone? I could envision the trio following Connie, aka, "Connie Bono," down to New Bern. Connie and Nick. They were naive and stupid, and now they were both dead. What did it matter who actually did the killing?

I sighed, suddenly tired of everything and everybody. I wanted to sleep, for days or weeks, or maybe even months. I wanted to wake up later, when I didn't feel hurt and defeated and, above all else, so terribly sad.

Gray arrived as the three suspects were packed into separate squad cars. He listened as Pa detailed the trap they'd laid for the sedan, and smiled to himself when no one was looking, his eyes taking in the ancient artillery and the rusty vehicles.

"We wasn't going to use our good cars," Frank said. "Guys like us can't afford to have our insurance rates go up."

Gray nodded, all business, saw to the wrapping up of the details, and gave his okay when the old guys requested permission to go home.

"There's a Phillies game on," Pa groused, but I knew he was headed home for a nap in the recliner.

"Yeah, and I got chores to do," Mort added.

Darlene hadn't said a word. When Gray's unmarked car had pulled up onto the scene and it had been him and not Wendell, she'd disappeared. I remembered the hurt in her eyes and knew that unless something changed, and quickly, Wendell would be losing the best thing to ever happen to him. Stupid man.

Gray walked over to me and touched my arm, smiled when I looked at him, and lowered his head to talk to me.

"I'll be in charge of getting them processed," he said. "It might take awhile. I have a couple of other things to handle, too, before I can take off and relax."

I looked at my watch. It was already after four. "Ma wants us for dinner," I said. "I'll tell her…"

"Tell her I got tied up," he said, "and go on without me. If I get away at a decent hour, I'll stop by your place later."

The way he said that last, with the emphasis, made me look up at him, reading the intent and knowing he meant more than for just a quick nightcap. My stomach flipped over and my heart started its familiar banging away at my chest.

"Okay." It was the only word I could manage, because in addition to feeling excited, I was aware of a new emotion that seemed to spread through me like a flame touching dry tinder. Panic. I was absolutely terrified. Nothing stood in our way now—no ex-husband, no threatening killers, no emergencies, nothing.

If Gray noticed the way I felt he didn't point it out. He kissed me quickly on the top of the head and turned to follow his three charges back to the police department. His mind was on business, not pleasure. Clearly Gray didn't see relationships as terrifying catastrophes the way I did.

I stood on the sidewalk, watching everyone go, and felt an overwhelming relief at finally having some time to myself. Behind me, Trey's voice called, "Champagne cocktails, anyone? Hors d'oeuvres?"

I turned around and realized the boy wasn't kidding. He held a tray at shoulder height and was handing out plastic flutes of bubbly liquid and offering what appeared to be meatballs to anyone and everyone who still remained in front of our two houses.

When he reached me, the food was gone, but I grabbed a glass and let myself feel caught up in the air of celebration for a moment. Barry Manilow sang through Bill's outdoor speakers "Her name was Lola…." and the three elderly tourists were quickly becoming Trey's surrogate mothers.

Bill edged up to me and smiled shyly. "He's such a nutcase," he said, "but I love him."

I looked over at Trey and saw him begin to dance with one of the women. He was bright-eyed and laughing, carefree and oblivious to anything but the spirit of the party.

"What's not to love?" I asked.

Bill gazed after his boyfriend and smiled. "We're so different. I guess that's why it works."

"Who knows why things work out?" I said, and felt a fresh wave of panic wash over me. I grabbed another champagne cocktail from the tray Bill held and downed half of it without thinking.

Bill's eyes met mine and I knew he read me. "Nothing like a fresh start to shake things up, huh?" he said. "Go crash for a while. Things always look better when you're bright-eyed and bushy-tailed."

I smiled and hugged him, a tentative first hug of many hugs, and watched him walk away. He was right. I was tired and overwhelmed and flooded with too much emotion happening too quickly. There would be time to think about what it all meant later, much later.

The champagne had gone to my head. I left the impromptu party, thinking the entire situation would look better after a snack and a nap. I stood in the kitchen for a minute, staring into the refrigerator and waiting for something appetizing to leap out at me, but nothing did.

Every time I thought about food, I thought about Ma, then Ma feeding Gray, then Gray looking deep into my eyes. Food lost its appeal as butterflies swarmed through my stomach and my heart raced in my chest. Who could eat at a time like this?

I gave up on food, turned off my cell phone, unplugged the downstairs phones and drifted upstairs to bed, my head as fizzy as the champagne. I pulled down the covers and slipped between the cool sheets, still fully dressed and once again too tired to care. It was only going to be a short nap, I promised myself; then I'd get up and figure out what to do with Detective Gray Evans.

I fell asleep thinking about him, but dreamed about Nick. I remember thinking to myself, *This is so stupid. Why am I dreaming about you when I want to dream about Gray?*

In my dream, Nick was fishing, hooking something that bowed his rod, something that he struggled to pull from the water. He tugged and tugged, reeling the line in, and sweating with the exertion. Finally, with a mighty heave, he brought it up. It was a rusted, red bicycle.

We were sitting on the edge of the dock, and when the bicycle surfaced Nick turned to me and smiled. "How about that?" he said. "Fish do need bicycles!"

We looked back at his catch, but it was no longer there. In its place floated the horribly bloated body of Connie Bono. I screamed over and over again until Nick dropped his rod and grabbed my shoulders.

"Wake up!" he said. "Wake up! They're here." He looked over his shoulder then back out at the water. I heard the sound of wood shattering. "Quick," Nick said, "wake up!"

I did. I sat up in bed, gasping, drenched in sweat, with tears running down my cheeks. My heart was banging against my chest wall and I felt absolutely terrified.

"It's only a dream," I whispered to myself. "A bad, bad dream."

I peered out beyond the bed into the darkened room, and then looked at the clock on the bedside table. It was after eight. I'd slept through dinner at Ma's. I hadn't even called.

"Great," I swore under my breath. "Now Ma will be mad. I need that like a hole in the head!"

I swung my legs over the side of the bed and hopped down onto the floor. Bleary-eyed, I changed into fresh jeans, a T-shirt and sneakers. I began to make my way out of the room and down the stairs. I had to call home before home decided to call on me.

I wandered into the kitchen, got distracted by the refrigerator and realized that I was starving.

"Burgers," I muttered to myself. "Junk food." I grabbed my purse and the keys to Ma's car from the counter, scribbled a hasty note to Gray saying I'd be back in a few minutes if he came by, and headed for the car. Durrell was waiting for me in the backyard, his look too pitiful to resist.

"Where is your mom?" I asked him.

Durrell didn't answer. Instead he whined, the same sound I would've made had I been a dog and my stomach was growling.

"You like burgers?" I asked him. His smile grew wider. "All right. Come on. We'll pig out. At least my mom loaned me a car to drive," I said. "Looks like yours didn't care if you ate."

Durrell ran to the car, barely waiting for me to open the door before he jumped inside and stood on the front seat, waiting. I looked over at Durrell. He was resting his furry chin on the window ledge, sniffing the night air for all he was worth, clearly in doggy ecstasy.

I drove across town, purchased a fast-food feast suitable for four hungry adults, and kept on driving, wandering around town, then out into the county for what must've been close to an hour. Durrell was in doggy heaven, eating people food and smelling new smells. I was in my own form of heaven, wolfing down thick burgers and crisp fries and contemplating the eventual return of one Detective Gray Evans. Somehow, the food bolstered my confidence and the thought of spending a large quantity of time with the man no longer frightened me. Eventually, I gave in to the inevitable. I had to go home, call my mother and apologize for doing the unthinkable, missing one of her meals.

I pulled up into the driveway, cut the engine and sat there until Durrell moaned.

"Sorry, buddy," I said, opening the car door. "It's called procrastination." But I was thinking that while I had one painful chore to take care of, I was almost assured of a pleasant reward at some point later in the evening. After all, hadn't Gray said he'd be stopping by after he'd processed his three mobsters?

I climbed the back steps and let myself into the darkened house. I was halfway across the kitchen before I heard the voices. At first I thought I was hearing things, then wondered if I'd left a TV on somewhere. Almost immediately I came to my senses and realized people were talking and I didn't recognize any of their voices. The sounds were coming from the basement.

I tiptoed, silent in my bare feet, to the edge of the basement door and stood listening.

"My father's dead because of you," a vaguely familiar female voice suddenly said.

"Your father is dead because he did a foolish thing and got caught," a cool woman's voice answered. "I had nothing to do with it."

The younger woman interrupted, but as she did, I recognized her. It was Della, but without her deep Southern drawl. "You set him up. Your husband had my dad killed because of you."

The other female voice spoke, softer, kinder in tone, as if

she was trying to soothe Della, but I couldn't make out the words. Without thinking, I edged down the steps, sticking close to the far wall and holding my breath in an attempt to hear what was being said.

"Don't make it worse," I heard the woman say. "I loved your father and he loved me. He would want you to help me. If I don't find the video, my husband will. He'll kill me."

Della laughed, but it was a harsh sound, and cruel in its anger. "Me help you? Who helped my dad? You could have stopped it. I know you could have stopped it."

She sounded like a child, lost and overcome with grief.

"Kathy," the woman said, "I didn't know. Tony never discussed family business with me. I didn't know who your father was until two weeks before he died. By then it made no difference who he was—I loved him."

Kathy... Wasn't that the name of the person Nick had said was coming for him? I looked at Della and felt the remaining pieces click into place. Della was Kathy.

I moved soundlessly down two more steps until I stood in the darkened shadows of the landing. Three figures, two women and a man, stood below me, two of them holding guns. Della—Kathy—held her gun straight out in front of her, aimed at the woman whose back was to the landing. The male figure stood off to the side, holding his weapon in front of his body, aiming it at Della. Behind them the door to the backyard swung on one hinge, broken into two splintered pieces.

"Mom told me Dad was having an affair, but I didn't believe her. She wouldn't leave me alone until I followed him." Della's face darkened. "I lied to her. I told her she was wrong. It would have killed her, knowing about you."

The gun in Della's hand wavered, then steadied as she supported it with her free hand, training it tighter on the woman across from her.

"Don't do it, Kathy," the woman said. "He'll kill you before you can pull the trigger."

Della never took her eyes from the other woman's face, never lost sight of her target. "Tell him go ahead—shoot. Do you really think I wouldn't squeeze one off in time?"

It was like a bad movie. I stood there, trying to piece it together, waiting for them to tell me more. Kathy/Della's dad was the FBI agent? That hardly seemed possible. The woman across from her was Tony Lombardo's wife? What in the hell was going on?

"I have no choice, Kathy," Mrs. Lombardo said. "Tony'll kill me if he finds out. I can't let the police have that video."

"Then they won't be able to put your husband in jail," Della said. "If they arrest Tony, he won't be able to kill you."

Mrs. Lombardo laughed. "You don't know the Lombardo family. He won't spend one hour in jail."

They don't know, I thought. They don't know the police already have the tape.

"How did you find out about the tape?"

Mrs. Lombardo laughed softly. "That stupid girl tried to get me to buy them from her."

"Connie?" Della asked.

"She wanted to beat her incompetent boyfriend to it. She was greedy. She wanted money from me *and* from Tony. I just got to her first, that's all."

As my eyes adjusted to the light I could see the scene below me more clearly. Tony Lombardo's wife stood just beneath the landing. She was as tall as Della, but with long, jet-black hair, just like in the film.

Della was crying silently, tears running down her cheeks. The gun trembled slightly in her hands, the only other sign of her thin edge of control.

I held my breath, waiting to see what would happen next.

I looked at the three below me and didn't like the odds. I'd been lucky to get this far without them seeing me.

"Sophie?"

Above me I heard the front door open and the sound of my brother's voice. I sank back against the wall, watching the others.

Mrs. Lombardo's accomplice swore. "I thought you said nobody was home."

"Shut up!" Della ordered. "Maybe they won't come down here."

"Hey, Sophie!" Darlene was with him. My heart began to beat faster and my throat went dry.

Their footsteps were moving right toward the open basement door. I knew the only light in the house came from the cellar below me. Before I could react, Joey stood at the top of the stairs, and then he was moving.

"Joey! No!" I screamed, and lunged forward.

"Shoot!" Mrs. Lombardo cried.

Joey saw me but didn't listen. He glimpsed my face and reacted, moving quickly forward. I glanced down, saw the man below us raise his gun, saw Della lunge forward, and jumped to push Joey back.

I was too late. As I reached for him there was a deafening roar, a flash, and the acrid scent of gunpowder filled the air. Joey was blown back away from me, hitting the wall as his shoulder exploded into a red splotch that quickly grew bigger.

There was another gunshot. The basement was plunged into darkness and below me I heard the sounds of running footsteps, grunting, and then silence.

"Darlene! Call 9-1-1!" I yelled, not knowing where she was or even if she was nearby.

"I tried," she whispered. She was beside me in the darkness, the scent of patchouli filling the air as she felt Joey's chest with her fingers, moving surely toward the site of his wound. "The phone lines are dead. I didn't bring my cell phone."

I heard scurrying below us, the sound of scraping feet and rapid movement. I heard a woman cry out, as if in pain.

"Darlene," I murmured urgently, "we have to get help. My cell phone's out in the car. I'll stay here with Joey. Go get the phone and call the police."

"Sophie, I can't."

"Darlene, do it!"

"No, it's not that. Sophie, they hit an artery. If I let go, he'll die. I can't switch with you. You have to go."

I ran back up the few steps to the kitchen, hoping I could call the police and get back to Joey and Darlene before anyone else got to them. I ran out of the house, into the backyard, and toward the car.

A movement to my left caught my attention. She ran almost silently, rounding the back of the garage and dashing across the yard toward the alley and freedom. Without thinking, I threw myself into her path. We collided with a painful crunch of bone on bone, and fell to the ground.

The woman beneath me yelled out in fury and pushed me, struggling to escape. It was Tony Lombardo's wife, fighting like an animal to get away from me.

I don't remember having any conscious thought, but rather I saw my brother, covered in blood, shock registering on his face as the lights went out and we were plunged into darkness. It was that vision of Joey that I was fighting for, that urge to keep this woman from getting away with hurting my brother that propelled me into action. I grabbed her long black hair, wrapped it around my hand and pulled as hard as I could.

She screamed and brought both hands up, wrapping them around my neck and squeezing with a surprisingly strong grip. She had six inches and at least forty pounds on me, but I was trained to take her. It required almost no effort to flip her over onto the hard ground and pin her beneath me. I felt the air whoosh out of her lungs, felt her fingers loosen from my throat, and was rewarded with a squeal of pain as I kneed her in the stomach.

She wasn't finished. I started to move back, ready to bring her up off the ground when she took me off guard, spitting in my face, unleashing a maelstrom of kicks and wrenching one hand free to grip my own hair, jerking my head back painfully.

I dug my fingers into her face and pushed her backward, breaking her grip with my forearm. I heard her scream as we fell to the ground, but something inside me had snapped and I no longer mistook her pain for capitulation. Suddenly she was gone, lifted off my body and flung aside like a rag doll. I gasped, taking in cool air and seeing the world slowly stop spinning as my eyes focused on Gray's concerned face.

People were running around us and past us. I choked, trying to find words, but unable to do more than gag and cough.

"Don't talk," Gray said. "You're okay. The neighbors called 9-1-1."

"Get the others," I gasped.

I struggled to sit up and found I couldn't move. Gray's arms were pinning me to the ground.

"Get off me, you idiot! Joey's inside. He's hurt. There's a guy with a gun…"

Gray nodded and started to move, but as he did I saw Tony Lombardo's wife move her hand. A tiny silver handgun gleamed in the reflection of the light over the garage.

I shoved the unwitting Gray, hard, and launched myself with a strength I didn't know I had. The gun flashed as I made contact with her body. She flew backward once more, the shot going wild as she was thrown.

This time I wasn't taking chances. I drew back my fist and slammed it into her face with everything I had, trying to punch through her. The force lifted her back and then she was down, unconscious, on the ground in front of me.

"Inside!" Gray directed someone.

Sirens again wailed to a halt in front of my house, as the welcome help continued to arrive. A drop hit my arm, then another hit my leg as the first few splashes of a summer shower began to move across the neighborhood.

As Mrs. Lombardo began to move and moan, Gray pulled her arms behind her back and handcuffed her. Her face was swollen and dirt-streaked and she seemed disoriented. She stared past us, out into the darkness, shoulders slumped in the posture of defeat.

"Joey!" I struggled to my feet, dizzy with the effort, and tried to run toward the house. I managed a fast limping pace, wincing as I climbed the back steps and entered the house. Someone had turned on the lights and the glare blinded me momentarily.

When I found my brother he was unconscious, tended to by Darlene and a tall, raw-boned female officer. The two of them leaned over Joey as the officer opened a portable first-aid kit and began pulling on gloves.

"I can take care of him until the ambulance gets here," Darlene said quickly. "I'm a professional therapist."

The young officer looked up at her, continued to pull on her gloves and gave her a quick smile. "I'm sure you can," she said, "but I'm a professional EMT. I need to get him prepped for an IV. Why don't you to keep the pressure on the wound site. Can you do that?"

Darlene nodded, her face almost as pale as Joey's. One tear escaped from the corner of her eye, but she didn't seem to notice. Her entire attention was on our brother.

"Goddess," I heard her whisper, "please help us. Please?"

The redhead glanced up sharply. "Goddess?" she echoed softly. She continued to work, rolling up Joey's sleeve and swabbing the crook of his arm with an alcohol soaked piece of gauze.

"Yeah," Darlene said. "God is a woman."

"God is every woman," the young officer said.

I looked over the edge of the banister at the scene in the basement. Mrs. Lombardo's accomplice lay sprawled on the floor, a pool of dark red blood surrounding his inert body. No one seemed to be paying any attention to him; instead two officers were stooped over Kathy/Della, talking in low tones. I saw her legs move as she struggled to sit up, helped by the two policemen.

"Oh, man," she murmured, seeing the dead guy in front of her. "I guess I killed him, huh?"

Her gun lay on the floor a few feet away and I saw her glance at it, then turn away. Behind me at the top of the stairs, I heard the sound of more people arriving, EMTs with a gurney.

I moved, wanting to get out of the way. Detective Wendell Arrow was just arriving, stepping through the broken pieces of the cellar door and reaching the spot where Della stood, staring at her victim.

She looked up at Wendell, her eyes huge in her pale face and said, "I did it. He was gonna shoot Sophie if I didn't."

Wendell looked up toward the steps, saw me and moved on to where Darlene was trying to help the medics load our brother onto the stretcher.

Darlene turned, as if she felt his presence, her face crumpling with grief as she began to cry. Wendell looked stricken. He moved, taking the steps two at a time and passing me in his haste to reach my sister.

The young redheaded officer beside Darlene turned, saw

Wendell and began to speak. "He'll be all right. He got hit in the shoulder."

Darlene and Wendell came together and he took her in his arms. He looked over Darlene's shoulder at the woman in uniform.

"I didn't know you were back on active duty."

From my vantage point on the stairs just below them I could see the girl smile. "I've been out of the hospital for a week," she said. "I was going crazy just sitting around."

Darlene raised her head from Wendell's shoulder and looked at the redhead. The stairs were well lit now and it was easy to read the young officer's name tag. R. Arrow, it said.

"Darlene, this is Becky, my daughter."

Darlene wiped at her eyes, rubbing them as if not quite believing what she was seeing.

"Hey," she said weakly.

"Pleased to meet you," Becky said. "Dad's told me a lot about you."

Darlene stood there for a moment, frowning. "He did?"

The EMTs had Joey at the top of the stairs and I moved, edging my way past the trio and following Joey's stretcher.

"I'll ride with him," I murmured to Darlene as I passed her. "Meet me over there."

Darlene seemed to snap back, sealing her tearful emotions away and becoming stronger. "I've got to go," she said to the father and daughter. "It was nice meeting you."

She turned to me. "Let's go."

Wendell and his daughter, Kathy/Della and the Lombardos were all forgotten as we climbed into the back of Joey's ambulance and made the quick trip to Craven County Medical Center. Halfway there, Joey regained consciousness and moaned.

"Marone a mia," he whispered. "The fun never ends with you two." He gasped.

"Shh," I whispered.

Joey swore in Italian. Darlene looked down at him. "That's physically impossible," she said mildly.

Joey groaned again and gave up, closing his eyes and drifting off as we pulled into the hospital driveway.

Chapter 17

Joey was on his way to surgery when Gray arrived with Kathy/Della. He beckoned to me from the curtained entrance of her cubicle.

"The doctor's checking her over before I take her to the station," he said, reaching to touch my arm. "How're *you* holding up?"

"Awful," I said. I felt globally miserable. My brother was on his way to surgery and even though everyone hastened to reassure me that it wasn't my fault, I still felt responsible.

Gray didn't try to say all the words I'd already heard. Instead he gestured toward the cubicle. "She wants to talk to you," he said. "She said she'd only talk to you. Do you mind?"

"Kathy?"

Gray nodded and said, "Her real name is Kathy Moon Garrison. You know who she is, right?"

The bits of overheard conversation flooded back into my

head and I nodded. "Is she really the undercover agent's daughter?"

Gray sighed. "Yes. She was a freshman at Temple when her father died, a drama major. She dropped out and the word was she was planning on entering the police academy in the fall."

"How old is she, Gray?"

He shrugged. "Near as I can figure, she's about twenty, but she won't give me anything until she sees you."

I looked at the curtained wall a few feet behind us and nodded. "All right. Might as well. Joey'll be in surgery for a good two hours."

Gray let go of my arm and led the way, pulling the curtain back and letting me enter the tiny space where Della— Kathy—sat on the edge of a narrow examining table.

"How're you doing?" I asked.

She looked worse than usual, pale, unkempt, her clothes dirty and ripped in places from her fight in the basement. Most of all, she looked young, much younger than Gray's guess of twenty.

"Okay," the girl muttered. "You were the only one good enough to trust me, and I don't want you thinking the worst."

I nodded. "Thanks."

"I'm a fuckup," she said. "I guess that's why I got into all this mess. When my dad got killed it was like, time to grow up, you know? I felt like it was my fault. Maybe if I'd done something or said something it would've helped. When he died I had to find out what happened, you know?" She didn't wait for me to agree with her. "I didn't even know him. He was hardly ever home. The therapist they made me go see in high school said I got in with a rough crowd just to show him I didn't care."

She shrugged, one tear snaking its way down the side of her dirty face. "When Mom said he was running around, I told her she was nuts, but after a while I started thinking maybe he was. I mean, he always said he was working on something, but I heard him talking to that woman one time on his cell phone and I got to thinking maybe Mom was right."

Outside the curtained cubicle, I could hear the sounds of the emergency room springing to life as someone new arrived. The back bay doors hissed open, calm efficient voices could be heard issuing orders, and another life-and-death situation took precedence over the less severe patients who waited for attention.

"After he died, I started trying to find out what happened. I guess I did pretty good, 'cause I got one of Dad's friends to tell me everything they'd found out. That's how I heard about Nick's tape. A snitch told somebody Nick was talking about a tape, but when they went to interview him, he clammed on them."

Della shook her head. "It was easy," she said. "I was a girl and Nick loves girls." She blushed. "Sorry. That was stupid."

"Stupid?" I echoed, clueless. I was aware of Gray in the background, quietly listening and almost certainly remembering every word.

"Saying that, I mean. He was your husband."

"Don't worry about that," I said. "Tell me what happened."

Della shrugged. "It was pretty easy. I hooked up with Connie's band and started visiting Nick in jail. At first Connie took me, but then I went on my own. When it got time for him to get out, I told him Connie was two-timing him with another guy, a mobster named Tony. Nick went crazy. It was pretty easy from there."

I felt myself getting anxious and impatient. "So how did you get to New Bern? Did you come down with Nick?"

Della nodded. "It was all I could think of to do. My dad's partner said they knew who killed him, or had him killed— they just couldn't prove it. I thought if I got the tape it would make the case. Then, a day before Nick was due to get out of prison, Connie took Nick's car and disappeared."

"And?"

Della smiled softly. "I figured that left Nick needing help. So I was waiting for him at the gate when he got out. He knew right away when Connie Bono wasn't there that she'd ripped him off. I told him I felt bad for him on account of his girlfriend doing him dirty. I told him I'd help him. So that's how we got to New Bern. Connie Bono knew the video was with Nick's stuff. She just didn't know where."

"Did Nick kill Connie?" My throat went dry as I asked the question.

Della frowned. "Hell, no. She was dead when we got here. Tony's wife did that."

Gray cleared his throat. "How do you know that?" he asked.

"She told me. She said Connie was trying to sell the pictures to the highest bidder, her or Tony, and so she followed Connie down here." Della shrugged. "It's just her stupidity that made her off Connie before she had the video. I guess she thought finding it in the house would be the easy part."

Della looked up at me, her eyes pleading. "I didn't want to hurt you. Nick came up with the idea of me working for you. Then Tony's people showed up and it was just a big mess. Nick and I got separated and I was on my own."

The curtain rustled and a male voice called out, "Knock, knock!" and entered without waiting for an answer. A young doctor with brown-rimmed glasses stood inside the curtain, chart in hand, and smiling. "Well," he said, "looks like you've been on the receiving end of some cuts and bruises, huh?"

That was the very least of it, I thought. I stood up to leave, then turned back to Della.

"I'll take care of Durrell until you can come get him," I said. "Where is he?"

Della shrugged. "I don't know. He's not my dog. You can have him if you want."

"What?"

She smiled wryly. "Nick got him from the pound. He said you were a sucker for ugly dogs and you might take me in easier if I had him, sort of like insurance."

The look on my face must have registered because in an instant she changed, becoming apologetic. "Honest, Sophie, at that point I really thought we were doing the best thing for you and my dad. I didn't know it would turn out so bad. Really."

I nodded and walked out into the hallway. "Honest, Sophie..." Della's voice echoed over and over again in my head.

Chapter 18

It was a command performance. Ma commanded and we performed. Three days after it all came to a head, Ma made dinner and this time no one was excused. It was like the Resurrection; on the third day Jesus comes back and explains all to the disciples. Ma had that sort of Catholic sensibility about her. She wanted the pieces put in place, the ends tied up and the Last Supper served, even if it came after the fact.

She spared no effort to capture our attention. She cooked all day, producing veal Spiedini, stuffed squid with tomato sauce, lemon and garlic chicken, pasta with spinach and potatoes, and a host of other dishes that flowed from the kitchen in an endless stream of smells and textures.

The dining room wasn't large enough to accommodate us all. So Pa and the old guys fashioned an L-shaped extension to our large wooden dining table, hastily manufactured with sawhorses and sheets of plywood, then draped in white sheets.

The chairs were borrowed and the silverware was a combination of family heirlooms and everyday stainless. The china came from the attic, the kitchen and Darlene's apartment.

We were all there. Joey, released from the hospital and surrounded by his family, laughed and cut up like always, his heavily bandaged arm and a blue sling the only indication of his brush with death. Pa's friend Pete sported crutches and seemed just as even-tempered as he'd always been. Wendell Arrow and Rebecca came, along with my neighbors Bill and Trey, the police officers Ma now claimed as her own, and all of Pa's cronies and their wives. The women from Ma's water aerobics class even made a showing. Everyone was here, all except for one. Gray Evans had yet to make his appearance.

I stood in the living room, trying not to look through the sheers that veiled the bay window, trying not to act as if I'd even noticed his absence, but not fooling anyone. Joey finally came over to stand beside me, nudging me softly with his sling and acting wounded when I bumped his back.

"Oh, great, hit a crippled man, Soph! That's how it is around here, no respect for the hero in his own country."

I raised an eyebrow. "You, a hero? As I recall, I'm the one who attempted to push you out of harm's way when you blundered onto the scene of a crime in progress."

Joey slapped his good hand up to his forehead in mock horror. "Oh, sweet Mother of God, is that how it is? You can't even deal with reality. Blunder? So now I blundered? Oh, I think not. I had a carefully calculated plan. If you'd just stayed where you were, I could've handled the entire situation."

A car turned onto the street and I glanced out at it, hopeful, then disappointed when it made the circle and disappeared from view.

"What?" Joey said, his voice dropping so only the two of us could hear what he said. "Where is he? He is coming, right?"

I looked at my brother and saw my every thought, doubt and feeling mirrored in his eyes. He always knew, that Joey.

"So, what's with you two?" he asked.

"I don't know," I said. "I haven't talked to him since it happened."

"What?" Joey's voice rose and I saw Pa glance over at us and frown.

"I told him I needed some time to think, that's all," I said. "So I—"

Joey looked horrified. "So you've been ducking the man! Soph, how could you do that to him? *Marone!* What's with you? After all he's done, you're blowing the guy off? Aw, Sophia!"

Joey shook his head and looked at me, squinting as if this would help him see past my face and into my brain.

"Wait," he said, his voice taking on an "aha" quality. "You're not ducking him because you have to think about it. You're ducking him 'cause you're scared. You're chicken!"

"I am not! I needed a little time to think about it, that's all. There's been a lot going on, Joey. It's not like I've had any time to examine this and be sure."

The wrinkles on Joey's brow relaxed as he listened. He seemed a little less worried about my sanity and more like he understood.

"Soph, you know what?"

"What?"

"You think too much, that's what! You're all grown up now, so act like it. Talk to the man." He was looking over my shoulder, watching Gray's beige Tahoe pull up in front of the house. When he was certain that I'd noticed, as well, he looked back behind him into the rooms filled with friends and family, all talking and laughing together.

"Before you say it, yeah, I called him. Now, go take care of this," he said, nodding toward Gray.

He left, turning away and leaving me to answer the door. I walked slowly to the front door and had my hand on the knob, turning it, as Gray reached the porch. I opened it before he could ring the doorbell.

"Hey," I said, smiling, but aware that my hands were icy cold and my stomach was lurching as if I'd suddenly landed on top of a runaway train.

"Hey yourself, stranger," he said. The smile was there, but his eyes were full of questions and uncertainty. "Long time no see."

I glanced behind me at the houseful of people and stepped out onto the front porch, closing the door softly behind me.

"We need to talk," I said.

Gray nodded, his eyes searching my face and taking inventory. "I figured."

The door swung open behind us and Ma stood there, her hands on her hips, managing somehow to smile and look impatient all at once.

"So," she said to Gray, "you are here. *Bene!* Now we eat. Come on!"

She grabbed us, propelling us into the house ahead of her and bringing up the rear. There was no escaping Ma.

"Everybody!" she called. "Let's eat!"

Pa stepped up to Gray, shook his hand and led the two of us into the dining room, motioning and directing the others to their places while Ma coordinated the delivery of the food. Pa walked to the top of the long table and took his place as the head of the family, the silent cue for us all to bow our heads.

"Heavenly Father," he began. The room was pin-drop silent. "We're here today to honor and thank you for the lives you have spared and the many gifts you have bestowed upon us."

Pa, breaking with tradition, spoke in English instead of Italian.

"I look around this room and I see my family and friends. I feel the love that grows here between us all, and I feel grateful." Pa's voice cracked. I winked one eye open and lifted my head ever so slightly, just in time to see him pull out an oversize white handkerchief. He blew his nose loudly, and there were several muffled giggles from Joey's kids.

Without so much as lifting her head or opening her eyes, Ma reached out and slapped Joey soundly.

"Hey!" he cried. "What's that for?"

Pa, seemingly oblivious, went on with his blessing. "I just want to say thank you for the food, my family's safety and the gift of so many good friendships." There was another pause, then another loud honking sound as Pa blew his nose again and continued, but this time with the traditional blessing in Italian.

At the sound of "Amen," we all lifted our heads, and I was surprised to see tears in the eyes of most of the guests sitting around Pa's table.

"I love youse guys," Pa said, his voice gruff with thinly veiled emotion. He raised his glass of Chianti and held it out toward the assembled gathering. "Now eat!"

Everyone laughed and the party continued. The food kept emerging from the kitchen, platter after platter and course after course. I sat next to Gray and realized that eating was impossible. I couldn't bring myself to look at him, but his presence was everywhere. I felt him; felt the heat that seemed to radiate from his body and the current of energy that ran between the two of us like electricity. I was aware of everything he did and said; even the slightest movement from him brought an automatic heightening of awareness in me. It was driving me crazy.

Darlene sat next to me, with Wendell next to her and his daughter on his other side. The three of them laughed and carried on while I sat like a frozen marble statue.

Darlene leaned toward me. "She was depressed," she whispered.

"Huh?"

"Sophie! What's wrong with you? Keep your voice down! Becky—she was depressed. Every year around this time she gets really depressed. It's called an anniversary reaction."

I looked at Darlene and frowned, feeling stupid.

"This is the time of year her mother died," Darlene said, her voice almost too low to understand. "That's why Wendell didn't let me meet her. She was in the hospital and he didn't feel he could tell me."

I nodded. "Why not?" I asked.

Darlene sighed. "Because he was protecting her," she said, shaking her head slowly. "He didn't think she'd want people knowing she was in a psych ward." Darlene smiled indulgently. "Poor baby. He just doesn't get biochemical imbalances. Nowadays, they get you on the right medication and you're fine."

She reached out and patted his knee without even turning her head to look at him. He was talking to his daughter, but as I watched, I saw his hand slip down to clasp hers. I witnessed this, feeling as if everyone else had an understanding that continued to elude me. Darlene and Wendell made love look simple.

I thought about it for a moment, about how it felt to watch her and Wendell, how out of place I'd felt as the bystander. Then I thought of Nick and how much pain he'd caused me. Did I really want to feel like that again?

The voice in my head said, *Do you really think Gray is like Nick?*

"Don't be ridiculous," I muttered under my breath.

"I can't help it," Gray's voice answered. "You bring it out in me."

I nodded and reached over to take his hand. "Gray, I'm not the same woman I was when I married Nick, and I don't ever want to be like her again. But I couldn't just walk off and let Nick die alone, either. I needed to be able to say goodbye. I needed to let go of that phase of my life."

Gray nodded. "I know that now. I'm just sorry I couldn't see it when you needed me. I'm sorry, Sophie."

I squeezed his fingers and smiled. "I guess things were a little hectic, huh? You were trying to take care of me and you didn't think I was listening."

Gray looked into my eyes. "You know, I haven't met the other Sophie," he said. "It's the one I know now who stole my heart."

I squeezed his hand tighter and started to speak, but the firm pressure of a hand clamping down on my shoulder stopped me. Ma had snuck up on us and now stood just behind our chairs with her strong hands resting on our shoulders.

"Hey," she said, smacking me lightly on the side of my head. "What? My food is no good for you?"

"Ma, no, I…"

To my surprise, Ma broke into a huge grin. "Aha!" she cried, turning to beam at Gray. "So it's your fault my daughter, she no eat!"

Gray smiled right back at Ma, but didn't say anything. Ma took this for an affirmative answer and nodded. She started to turn away, then, lightning quick, turned back. *Smack!* Her hand landed upside Gray's head and he yowled in mock pain.

"Hey!" he cried. "What did I do?"

Ma beamed down at him. "Nothing," she said, bending over to kiss him gently on the cheek. "Nothing at all. Now eat!" With one final mock swipe, Ma left us, wandering down the table, talking to her guests and laughing, lapsing into Italian every now and then as she dispensed some particular piece of wisdom.

Gray watched her for a moment, then turned back to catch me watching him.

"What?" he asked.

"Nothing," I said. "Nothing at all!" I leaned over, clear in my intent, and kissed him. I felt his arms close around me and heard the giggles of Joey's children as they turned to look at Aunt Sophie kissing her handsome detective.

"Marone a mia!" my brother cried. "Have a little respect here, will ya!"

The room dissolved into laughter and I could hear my sister's voice rising above the others.

"I knew it all along," she was saying. "I told her. You can't mess with destiny. I should know because, after all, I am a professional therapist!"

* * * * *

Framed by the murderous claws of the *allosaurus,* the man stood. Looking at her.

Whoa. The hairs stirred at the nape of Raine Ashaway's neck. Here was something…different. His impeccable black dinner suit fit in with this glitzy Manhattan crowd, but his utter stillness… *Where have I seen you before?* She'd never forget a face like that, no woman would, and yet…

"See somebody you know?" inquired Joel, whose last name Raine had forgotten. An assistant fund-raiser for the American Museum of Natural History, Joel had been assigned to smooth her path through the evening's gala. It was his job to see she met the right people and stroked the right egos.

"No… But who is that guy? He sure seems to know *me.*"

Joel scanned the drifting guests on the far side of the museum's most famous dinosaur exhibit. "Which one, that oh-so-distinguished blond to the left of that *fabulous* diamond choker?"

"No, no. Mr. Tall, Dark and Forgot-how-to-smile. See the woman with the ruby earrings? Just to her— Arr, he's turned away."

Which was just as well. They were neglecting their current prospect. Raine smothered a sigh. God, did she hate fund-raising! But the deal she'd cut with the museum included her coming to New York to help make this event a success.

Judging by the sapphire necklace that draped Mrs. Lowell's bosom and matched her blue hair, the old girl could afford to bid in the benefit auction tonight. Minimum opening bid was a million dollars.

"Now, Raine," said Mrs. Lowell, "you're the expert, so I want you to tell me." She waved a plump little hand at the rearing dinosaur skeleton beneath which they stood. "Could a brontosaurus really stand up on her hind legs like that?"

The AMNH's most spectacular exhibit featured a five-story-tall mother barosaurus rearing to defend her baby from the attack of an allosaurus. The tableau was poignant, terrifying, heart-stoppingly dramatic. It was the first thing a museum-goer saw when he pushed through the big bronze revolving entrance doors and into the echoing rotunda. The fossil castings stood on a knee-high dais that filled the middle of a hall the size of a basketball court. Raine adored the display.

Joel's toe tapped her heel, a signal perhaps to make it short. It was time to move on. More likely he meant, *Now, don't correct her and tell her that's a barosaurus.* Joel had learned already tonight that Raine was a stickler for facts when it came to dinosaurs. All the Ashaways were.

"Well," Raine said diplomatically, "if a circus elephant

can stand on its hind legs with only a rope of a tail for balance, then why couldn't she, with a forty-foot caboose for a cantilever?"

"And who do you think won the fight?" Mrs. Lowell asked worriedly.

Knowing what she did about Tyrannosaurus rex's older, nimbler cousin, Raine hadn't a doubt who'd triumphed. She shrugged. "Hard to say. She'd outweigh him four to one. If she lands a punch…"

"And what are you going to name our new dino, Mrs. Lowell, if you win the bidding tonight?" Joel broke in with a twinkle as he squeezed Raine's elbow.

Mrs. Lowell chuckled. "I'll name him Erwin Elwood, of course, after my dear papa. He was the fossil hunter in our family. My sister and I collected ostrich eggs, and my late brother…"

As she half listened to the conversation, Raine found her gaze snagged by the same dark watcher. Now they contemplated each other from reversed sides of the battling dinosaurs. Where *had* she seen him before?

She gave him a slow smile. *So here I am. What's your intention?*

He didn't respond. A hand tipped in long red nails landed on his sleeve. With their eyes locked, Raine couldn't see more of the woman. But he glanced down at those fingers, smiled wryly to himself—then turned aside.

Raine drew a breath, her first in a minute. *What was that about?*

So that…was Raine Ashaway.

Kincade supposed he'd seen photos before. The Ashaway All Web site contained expedition shots featuring various members of the family, as well as pictures of the dinosaur specimens they offered for sale. But he'd never seen this Ashaway without a wide-brimmed hat shading her vivid face. He hadn't expected a huntress, with hair like moonbeams rippling on troubled water.

"Did you hear one word I said, Cade?" Amanda whatever-her-name-was fingered his lapel as she pouted prettily.

"Nope." Not that he'd have missed much. She'd latched on to him as soon as he'd arrived. He'd tolerated her prattling, because she made good cover. She let him appear to be mingling, while he studied his quarry.

"You're almost…scary when you look like that. What on earth are you thinking?" she teased.

He was thinking that vengeance might turn out to be more than a sworn duty. Taking Raine Ashaway down? That might also be a pleasure.

If you enjoyed what you just read,
then we've got an offer you can't resist!

Take 2 bestselling
love stories FREE!
Plus get a FREE surprise gift!

BOMBSHELL

COMING NEXT MONTH

#45 DOUBLE VISION—Vicki Hinze
War Games

U.S. Air Force captain Katherine Kane had been sent to the Middle East to look for a suspected terrorist weapons cache, but stumbled upon much more than she had bargained for—American hostages, biological weapons and the most feared terrorist in the world, a man Kate could have sworn was locked away for good. But seeing was believing, and Kate suspected the criminal mastermind was no double vision after all....

#46 CHECKMATE—Doranna Durgin
Athena Force

Her marriage on the rocks, FBI legal attaché Serena Jones took refuge in an assignment to a foreign land only to be caught when rebels took over the capitol. Trapped in the building but free to move inside, Serena would take on the crafty rebel leader and lay a trap using the weapons at hand—her dying cell phone, her wits and an unexpected ally, her estranged husband....

#47 TRIGGER EFFECT—Maggie Price
Line of Duty

Hours after arriving in Oklahoma City, Paige Carmichael had clashed with a tough homicide detective, had her briefcase stolen and wound up in the E.R. And when she was asked to consult on a murder case, things didn't get any better. Because the killer knew Paige held the key to solving the mystery, and was determined to keep her from revealing the truth—by any means necessary.

#48 AN ANGEL IN STONE—Peggy Nicholson
The Bone Hunters

Archaeologist Raine Ashaway was determined to beat her rival, Kincade, and buy a precious rare fossil. But when the fossil's owner was murdered, Raine was plunged into a mystery that led her to the other side of the world. She had to join forces with Kincade. And with a killer on their heels, they'd have to learn to get along....

SBCNM0505